Lady Ashby's Major Scandal

BY

Myretta Robens

www.lachesispublishing.com

Published Internationally by Lachesis Publishing Inc.
Rockland, Ontario, Canada

A catalogue record for the print format of this title
is available from the National Library of Canada

ISBN 978-1-77359-019-6

A catalogue record for the Ebook is available
from the National Library of Canada
Ebooks are available for purchase from
www.lachesispublishing.com

ISBN 978-1-77359-018-9

Copy Editor: Joanna D'Angelo

DEDICATION

To Captain Sneed, who always thought I could do it.
And to Sandy Tabor who showed me that Isabel wanted
to be a heroine.

ACKNOWLEDGMENTS

To my writing friends, particularly Megan Frampton, my darling critique partner and Joanna D'Angelo, my excellent editor.

Lady Ashby's
Major Scandal

CHAPTER 1

Lincolnshire, May 1814

A single candle illuminated the library. Isabel could barely distinguish the outline of the massive desk at the far end of the room and the bookshelves lining three of the walls. But she had been here before and knew what she had to do. By the end of this night she would be betrothed to the Earl of Caenby.

Isabel stood in the middle of the library with her hands on her hips and squinted into the darkness. The dim light was romantic, but the room smelled a bit too much like leather and ink. She wished she had brought her perfume. No room would be the worse for a hint of jasmine.

The weak light of a waning moon picked out the low settee in the corner. Isabel smiled. There was her destination and, she hoped, her destiny. This damask-covered piece of furniture would help her accomplish what countless dropped hints and whispered enticements had failed to do. There, the Earl of Caenby would finally realize that she was meant to be his countess.

Isabel crossed the room, her slippers silent against the deep pile of the carpet. Taking care not to wrinkle the skirts of her elegant silk gown, she bent to position some cushions against the back of the settee. If there was one thing her ten long years with the late Baron Ashby had taught her, it was to take care of the details before setting a plan in motion.

When everything was arranged to her satisfaction, Isabel settled herself on the upholstered seat, removed the pins from her hair and leaned back. After a moment, she sat up again, loosened her tapes and shrugged her gown off one shoulder. Then she waited.

And waited. She had sent a note that should have brought the earl to the library ten minutes since. As the clock on the Adam mantelpiece ticked away the minutes, Isabel wondered, not for the first time, if a planned compromise might be an inauspicious way to begin a marriage.

But it was too late to wonder now. The door to the library eased open and Isabel could see the silhouette of a man's head against the dim light of the hall sconces. "Come in." Her voice was a low, intimate murmur.

The door swung inward and Isabel wriggled her gown a little lower around her shoulders. "Over here."

The dark figure hesitated at the threshold, shrugged, closed the door with a soft click and crossed the room.

The cushions sank as he lowered himself onto the settee. She leaned forward, seeking him in the dark. Her hands met a solid wall of chest. She hesitated only a moment before sliding them over his broad shoulders and wrapping her arms around his neck.

Isabel inhaled deeply, imbibing the fascinating scent of clean linen, sandalwood and masculine flesh. She pressed herself against the hard chest and moved sinuously.

At last.

Strong arms came around her and hauled her close. A mouth came down on hers and demanded a response. Lips like velvet caressed her own and a tongue of tantalizing sweetness sought entrance to her mouth.

Isabel parted her lips and met the invading tongue, inviting it to continue the incursion, offering the access it demanded and that she suddenly could not wait to provide. Warmth flooded her body and left her lightheaded. Had she known Edward kissed like this, she would have cornered him months ago.

His mouth was an unending source of delight. No sooner had Isabel adjusted her rhythm to the fierce duel of tongues than his retreated and the kiss became a field of pleasure. The pressure of his lips shifted from level to level, from demanding to coaxing, from ravenous to tender.

And just as Isabel was lulled into a voluptuous haze, he nipped at her lips and, drawing the lower one into his mouth, sucked like a boy with his first lemon drop.

The kiss went on forever. Floating in the warm stream of desire, Isabel forgot why she was there, forgot everything but the pressure of smooth lips, the wine-scented breath, the texture of his tongue, the comfort of his arms.

Gradually, Edward's embrace eased and his hands drifted to her shoulders and lingered there, the palms making soft circles against her skin. He skimmed his hands down her arms and her loosened bodice fell away from her body. He hesitated only briefly before sliding his hands into the gaping front of her gown.

Isabel gasped as confident hands closed on her breasts, stroking deftly over the sheer lawn of her chemise until she ached. She emitted a low gurgle of surprised pleasure and arched her back, pressing her breasts upward, begging, inarticulately, for more.

Thumbs circled her nipples and then grazed the tips. With a soft moan, Isabel fell back against the cushions, breathing heavily. She had never imagined that Edward's hands would be so hard and masterful, that they could bring such pleasure.

Burning, Isabel reached up and drew her dark lover down with her. Her lips parted and the library door opened.

Not now!

Isabel came to her senses. This was what she had

planned, was it not? There would be time enough for pleasure once she and Edward were wed. She sat up, making a show of covering herself, and looked toward the door. Her aunt appeared, holding a large branch of candles and with her, just as Isabel had hoped, stood the entire party.

Straightening her clothes, Isabel surveyed the group. Her aunt and her maid, the Broadribbs, Lady Augusta, Sir Henry and Maria Kendrick crowded the doorway. And, right behind Lady Louisa, Edward Burnet, Earl of Caenby.

Wait!

Isabel whirled around to find Major Sidney Chamberlayne standing at attention beside the settee: half-pay officer newly returned from the Peninsula, younger son without a feather to fly with. No title, no fortune, no prospects. Her heart sank.

"But, you were…"

The major stood ramrod straight in stricken silence, his face drained of all color.

Isabel grabbed at her clothes and lurched to her feet, struggling to pull up her bodice in earnest. She faced the group who had by now crowded into the room. "It is not what you think." She turned a pleading look toward the earl.

"Edward…"

The earl examined the disheveled couple standing before him, an astonished smile stealing over his face. "I take it I am to wish you happy."

As Isabel stammered, searching for a response, Sidney Chamberlayne stepped forward and stood beside her, his face a grim mask. "I thank you, Lord Caenby. We thank you. We hope, of course, to be married as soon as possible."

Isabel fainted.

* * *

Sidney watched the earl usher his guests out of the room and Lady Louisa close the door firmly behind him. Then he returned his attention to the insensate woman sprawled on the sofa. His head spun. How had this happened? One moment he had been thoroughly enjoying the favors of a willing lady and the next moment he was betrothed. Had she meant to entrap him? That hardly seemed likely.

Without doubt, she was lovely. Sidney had been fascinated by her creamy skin and generous figure the moment he laid eyes on her. And, although she had greeted him graciously and possibly even given him a second glance, it was obvious that Lady Ashby was not interested in a half-pay officer even if his brother was an earl.

When he looked up again, he found Lady Louisa examining him with a critical eye. He remembered her vaguely. He had met her once or twice when he was a boy and he knew his mother spoke highly of Louisa Colton.

Sidney read the question in Lady Louisa's keen gaze and straightened from his contemplation of her somnolent niece. "I will marry her."

"Indeed you will, young man." Despite her age, Lady Louisa could have faced down Sidney's entire regiment. "Be at Bruton Place by the end of the week and bring a special license." When Sidney remained mute, she continued, "I know your mother and brother, young man, and most likely your commanding officer. I will see you ruined in society and in the army if you do not make this right."

Sidney could feel his jaw tighten. "Madam, if you think I will not do my duty by Lady Ashby, you do not know me very well."

"I do not know you at all, sir. But I believe that is about to change. I will see you in London." Opening the door to admit Isabel's maid, Lady Louisa turned on her heel and stalked out.

* * *

On a gasp, Isabel regained consciousness. "Get away from me." She jerked herself upright and flung out an arm, knocking the vinaigrette out of her maid's hand. "What?"

Why was she in her bedchamber at Caenby Castle? The maid offered the vinaigrette that must have brought her to consciousness. Isabel grimaced at her. "Where did you find that vile stuff?

When the maid abruptly drew back her hand, Isabel shook her head. "Pay no attention to me, Willington. I think you had better just go away."

As the maid closed the door behind her, Isabel threw herself back on the bed and inspected the hangings. They were expensive and elegant like everything else in Caenby Castle, damn it all, and they were meant to be hers. How had someone other than the earl found his way into the library at just the wrong moment?

Isabel had given Willington explicit instructions about how to get the earl into the library and then the rest of the guests. Her ploy had failed miserably. Isabel could feel tears of frustration threatening to spill over. She groaned and buried her face in her pillow. It was a foolish idea to begin with. She probably deserved her comeuppance.

Isabel slammed her fist into the mattress and gritted her teeth, vowing to find a way out of this mess. She rolled back over and pulled herself up against the headboard to review her options just as her chamber door opened to admit Lady Louisa.

"What do you want?" Isabel was in no mood to face her Aunt Louisa's acerbic tongue.

"I came to see if you were well, my dear. Why else would I come?" Louisa Colton approached Isabel's bedside.

"I imagine you came to read me a lecture."

"Do you believe you deserve a lecture?" Lady Louisa assumed an expression that Isabel knew all too well.

Cringing, Isabel hoisted herself up higher on the bed. "I was remarkably stupid."

"Indeed you were, young lady." Louisa plumped herself onto the nearest armchair. "What were you doing in the library in the dark?"

"Oh!" Isabel slid off the bed and began to pace the room, taking care not to step off the cream-colored Aubusson carpet, lest she damage her delicate stockings. "Oh, it is a disaster. It was to be Edward. Why was he not the one to come to me? I gave Willington explicit directions. What was that... that... *major* doing in the library?" Isabel stopped suddenly, aware that, in her agitation, she had spoken too plainly.

When Lady Louisa responded with a single raised eyebrow, Isabel decided she had nothing to lose.

"I must see Edward right away." Isabel turned and sat at her dressing table, trying to tuck her hair back into its pins. After several unsuccessful attempts, she dropped her brush onto the table. "Where is Willington? She's never around when she's needed."

"If I am not mistaken," Lady Louisa said, "you sent her out just before I arrived at your door." She gave Isabel a trenchant look.

"Well!" Isabel shrugged eloquently and turned back to her mirror. "Nevertheless..."

"Nevertheless, my dear, I would suggest you refrain from chasing after the earl."

Isabel regarded her reflection as she spoke, leaning forward to search for a sign of wrinkles. Finding none, she sat back. She may have turned thirty in the past week, but she had retained her youthful appearance. Hadn't she?

She glanced at her aunt. "Chasing? Have I been chasing?"

"If you haven't then I would like to know what you might call that little scene in the library?" Lady Louisa's gaze narrowed as Isabel straightened in her chair.

"Very well. If you insist on discussing this. I just thought to give Edward a little nudge. It's obvious we are meant to be together and he has been dragging his feet for months. And I'm not growing any younger." In truth, she had thought to be married to the earl before she turned thirty. Now it was too late for that.

Thirty and unwed. As the date had approached, Isabel had conceived an overwhelming desire for the security of a ton marriage. The round of gaiety on which she had embarked when her mourning ended did not promise much in the way of certainty. The thought of spending the rest of her life as a merry widow, with no children or husband, loomed cold and lonely.

"It is obvious to me that the Earl of Caenby is smitten with Maria Kendrick and has not turned an eye on any other woman since he met her." Lady Louisa leaned back and ran a smoothing hand over her violet skirts. "But that is neither here nor there. You are now betrothed to Mr. Chamberlayne."

"What nonsense!" Isabel whirled around to face her aunt. "Mr. Chamberlayne no more wants to marry me than I want to marry him. It is absurd to think that we should marry simply because of a minor indiscretion and I will not hear of it. Not another word."

"He seems a perfectly nice young man and you obviously want to marry again or you would not have played out this evening's little farce." Louisa's expression plainly said she would brook no argument.

"I want to marry the Earl of Caenby." Isabel could hear her own voice rising and strove to calm herself. She would not permit herself to sound like a petulant child. "Lord I was such a fool." Good. Her voice sounded under control.

"You have acted foolishly, my dear, but you are not

a fool. However, I think you have failed to see that Lord Caenby doesn't wish to marry you."

"Well, you may be right." Isabel sighed gustily and rose from her chair. "But that has nothing to say to my marrying a penniless nobody who happened to..." Isabel's speech faltered at the memory of what Mr. Chamberlayne had happened to do. "...happened to enter the library at the wrong time."

Lady Louisa's face set in a determined expression. "You have been compromised – and by your own hand. You will have to pay the piper."

"Compromised? Nonsense." Her temper returning, Isabel stalked to the dressing room door and flung it open. "I am a widow, not some milk and water miss." She peered into the darkened room with no notion of what she was seeking.

"And yet," Lady Louisa said, "you intended to trap the earl with just such a compromise, did you not?"

"Oh, honestly. Must you be so reasonable?" Isabel gave her aunt a frustrated glance. "This is a matter of the heart."

"I think not." Lady Louisa rose from her chair and moved toward the chamber door. "I think this is a matter of the will and you have had yours thwarted. Get accustomed to it, my dear. I do not believe Sidney Chamberlayne will be easily led. Sweet dreams."

As Lady Louisa closed the door behind her, Isabel threw herself on the bed and grabbed a pillow. Burying her face in the soft cushion, she groaned. She was as annoyed with herself as she was with the outcome of this night's adventure. Furious, really, that she had allowed her fear of growing old alone to drive her into an alliance she had never contemplated and certainly did not desire.

* * *

Sidney Chamberlayne was packing when his host tracked him to his room.

The Earl of Caenby strode into Sidney's room and made himself comfortable before the banked fire. "Where do you think you're going?"

"I am to London to procure a license, as I am sure you must be aware." Sidney did not look up from his trunk.

"This is not necessary, you know." The earl shifted anxiously in his chair.

"Oh, I'm afraid it is," Sidney said.

"Don't tell me it's because of that stupid remark I made about wishing you happy. Isabel Ashby has been trying to haul me before a vicar ever since I inherited the earldom. I didn't mean anything by it. And she will survive a jilting."

Sidney snapped to attention and whirled to face the earl. "This is my betrothed you are speaking of, Edward, regardless of the circumstance. And I will thank you not to drag her name or her reputation through the mud."

"You mean to marry her?" The earl's tone was incredulous.

"I do. I compromised the lady and I intend to meet my obligations."

"Your obligations?" The earl stood and walked to the other side of the trunk, facing Sidney. "She is a widow, man. She can take care of herself."

Sidney straightened from his task and glared at his friend. "She is a lady who has been found in dishabille in my arms. Do you intend to marry her?"

"Me?" The earl's voice broke on the word. "No. No, I mean to marry Miss Kendrick. I mean to marry for love."

"Most commendable," Sidney said, dryly. "I mean to marry for honor."

"Oh lord, Sidney, return to your regiment. It is where you belong."

"My regiment is not presently engaged, as I am sure you read in the papers, Edward. I am slated for a glorified clerk and have very little taste for it." Sidney peered into his trunk. Had he forgotten anything?

"Are you marrying the little widow for her estate, then? It is not a bad match in that respect." The earl seemed truly puzzled.

Sidney looked up, striving to keep his expression empty. "Not for the money, no. Nor for the widow, although I will admit that kissing her was a delectable experience. I am marrying her because it is what I should do." He hesitated and then went on. "What I *will* do."

The earl shook his head despairingly. "I got you into this mess, Chamberlayne. What can I do?"

"You have already done it, Edward. Wish me happy." Sidney bent to fasten the straps around his trunk.

CHAPTER 2

London, May 1814

Isabel stepped across the threshold of her townhouse and tossed her bonnet to the butler who caught it with an ease born of long practice.

"Welcome home, your ladyship." Wharton set the bonnet on a sideboard and turned to catch the pelisse, flying in his direction.

Isabel had been tossing her cloaks and bonnets to her butler ever since she first arrived at Bruton Place as a new bride. Baron Ashby had been a stickler for everything that was proper. Isabel, a wife at eighteen years, fresh out of the schoolroom, and not ready to accept that she was a baroness, rebelled in this one small way. Her husband corrected her every time, but Wharton never batted an eyelash. Even after her husband's death, she persisted in the habit, a private joke and an acceptable way to say "thank you for your unspoken support' across uncrossable class lines. She still enjoyed this little game and thought her butler did as well.

"Hello Walton. Tea, as soon as possible."

"Right away, your ladyship." Wharton passed her pelisse to the waiting footman and turned to greet Lady Louisa who had trailed her niece into the house.

"Did you have a pleasant journey, my lady?"

Louisa waved a dismissive hand at the butler. "It was at least quiet, Wharton. I am simply glad to be home. Where is she?"

"Lady Ashby is on her way to the morning room. I am about to order tea."

Louisa sighed as she peered down the sunny hallway toward the morning room. "Make sure there is brandy on the tray as well. I need a restorative."

Isabel was staring out the window onto Bruton Place. "Are you here to read me another lecture?" she asked softly, recognizing the violet scent that always preceded her aunt.

"Whatever were you thinking to kiss the Earl of Caenby in his drive before his servants and everyone?" Louisa took her accustomed chair.

Isabel joined her aunt, gracefully arranging her skirts around her as she settled on the settee. "I thought I had nothing to lose." She looked candidly at the older woman. "As you so acutely observed, Caenby is probably going to marry Miss Kendrick. Think of it as my farewell salute."

"You play with fire, my dear. You have already jeopardized your reputation by being caught in the library with the major. It is indeed fortunate that he is a gentleman and will protect your character."

"Oh, pooh." Isabel's forehead creased in an irritated frown. "Did you see the major lurking about to protect my character before we left? And why should he? That little incident will remain buried in Lincolnshire."

"You forget, Isabel, Lady Broadribb was on my heels in the library. The scandal could be—Oh good."

Isabel looked up, startled by Louisa's exclamation, then saw the butler bearing a tray. She sighed, relieved her aunt was making a comment on the tea and not her shriveled reputation. Her world had been upset enough without finding her stalwart aunt suddenly addled.

Wharton set the tea tray in front of Isabel, then poured a generous glass of brandy and handed it to Lady Louisa with an extra flourish. Isabel filled a delicate Sevres cup with the golden brew, inhaling the fragrant steam, while her aunt indulged in her own restorative. Conversation was suspended until Wharton closed the door behind him.

As the door latch clicked, Louisa took one more sip as though to brace herself. "What do you plan to do?"

"Nothing." Isabel set her cup on the tray and rose from her chair. Stretching, she strolled to the window overlooking the street. The sun of an early summer afternoon streamed through the ivory damask draperies, casting a muted glow over the room.

"I will do nothing," she repeated, her face raised to the warmth of the sun. "I will wait to see if Lady Broadribb might not find a more interesting on dit. We can always flee to Hampshire until it blows over."

"If indeed it does." Lady Louisa contemplated the remains of her brandy for a moment before getting to her feet, glass in hand. "I will take this to my chamber and leave you to consider our conversation."

By the time Isabel turned away from the window, she was alone. "There is nothing to consider," she said to the closed door. But she was wondering, a bit uneasily, if perhaps there might be.

Isabel threw herself onto a low chaise set before the window, sending a fine swirl of dust motes up into the low angle of the afternoon sun.

She lay on the chaise, one arm thrown over her eyes, and thought about what had happened at Caenby Castle. She'd left London in a hurry, anxious to be with the earl and anxious to demonstrate both her affection and her worth as a countess. She had not expected to find the earl making sheep's eyes at a local, young woman.

Pushing that fact to the back of her mind, and overwhelmed by the prospect of turning thirty and finding herself without a husband or children, Isabel had sparked a plan to encourage the earl into matrimony. But all had gone dreadfully wrong when Sidney Chamberlayne had stolen into the library in the dark.

Isabel swung around and sat up, burying her face in her hands. It was a disaster. And yet, she could not erase the memory of Sidney Chamberlayne's kiss—the sensuous slide of his lips as she opened to him, the powerful way he'd taken possession of her mouth and the bold way his tongue had claimed it.

And his hands. Isabel's heart pounded as she recalled the moment his hands had closed around her breasts. She felt anew the startling stab of longing that shot through her when his thumbs caressed her nipples, like a flash of lightening from the tips of her breasts to her very core. Isabel fumbled for her handkerchief.

Nothing in her marriage had prepared Isabel for the physical sensations the major had elicited. Oh, her husband had been all that was kind, but he was old and not very much interested in physical pleasure and had never even intimated that she should expect any. He seemed to enjoy the activity well enough as he tried valiantly to father an heir. But he never touched her except for what she had come to think of as the "weekly ritual" and that touching had been of a rather perfunctory nature.

Isabel stood and began to pace. The sun was dipping toward the horizon and the room was transformed from the golden glow of late afternoon, to a darker, sadder umber. Isabel did not send for candles. Somehow, the color suited her mood.

The piercing memory of Sidney Chamberlayne's touch faded and Isabel regained her senses. She was not stupid. She knew full well that physical pleasure was just that. She had been at school with girls who had mistaken pleasure for love, married for it and lived to rue their mistake. She would never be so foolish. Her next marriage, like her last, would be a marriage of advantage. She would marry for wealth and position and the respect of society. She would never marry because a man's touch sent shivers down to her toes.

Isabel shrugged off the feeling of disappointment that accompanied this acknowledgement and rang for candles.

*   *   *

Sidney had been back in London for nearly a week, long enough to visit Doctors' Commons and return with a special license in his pocket, long enough to have taken up his clerical post at Whitehall, long enough to have established himself in the Spartan room he had claimed in his brother's town house.

Sidney had intended to move into bachelor quarters when Wellington's army had spat him back up onto the heaving mass of London. But his mother convinced him that his presence would be of consequence to his sister who was just making her curtsey to society. Of all the people in his family—and there were only five now that his father had died and passed the earldom on to Harold—his mother and Julia were the two to whom he could deny nothing.

Sidney sat on the edge of the unadorned walnut bed and looked around the little room that had probably been meant for the governess. He had not been able to bring himself to move into family quarters. The luxury was too oppressive after so many years on a camp bed. He'd outfaced his mother's disapproval to move into an austere room next to the empty nursery.

He closed his eyes and inhaled deeply, mentally preparing himself for the day ahead. Much as he loved his mother and sister, he had told no one that he would be married before the month was out. Sidney pulled at the hem of his waistcoat and left his room. His family must be told and the sooner the better.

*   *   *

"Come." The Countess of Haddon turned from her writing table to see who was knocking at her door. "Sidney!" His mother's face lit up. Although she had never said as much, Sidney had always suspected he was the favorite of her three sons.

"Come and have tea with me, dearest. I hoped you would stop by before you left the house today." The countess extended her hands.

Sidney leaned over his mother and kissed each hand and then her cheek before taking the seat she had indicated. "No tea, thank you, ma'am."

"You have been so somber since you returned from Caenby's. Is something amiss?" The countess replaced the proffered cup on the tea tray.

Sidney sat in silence for what seemed like several minutes, trying to decide how to approach the subject on his mind. He looked at his mother's face, softened by age from great beauty into warm loveliness. He loved her dearly and feared that his news would give her pain.

"Mother, I am to be married."

"What?" The countess's eyebrows shot up and her teacup clattered onto her saucer. "I beg your pardon, Sidney. I must have misheard."

"No, Mother. You heard quite well," Sidney hesitated, compressing his lips into a hard line. "I shall marry Lady Ashby within the se'enight." He delivered his news in a quiet monotone.

"Lady Ashby? Surely not. Have you been coerced?" The countess's face coalesced into a mask of disapproval.

Sidney could feel his face heat. He should have known that the countess would come so close to deducing the truth. And yet, Isabel Ashby would be her daughter and he would not have them begin in distrust. "No," he said quickly.

"Do not tell me you compromised her." The countess looked scandalized.

Sidney sighed. "I would prefer not to discuss this with anyone." He gazed earnestly at the countess, unwilling to sacrifice either his future wife's reputation or his mother's good opinion. "Even you, mother. I simply wished you to hear it from my lips."

The Countess of Haddon rose from her seat and stalked across the floor and back. She came to a halt directly in front of Sidney. Looking imperiously down from her full five foot two inch height, she said, "I forbid it."

Sidney smiled affectionately up at the glowering countess. "You know you cannot forbid it. I may be your youngest son, but I am eight and twenty."

With a grunt of exasperation, the countess flung herself back into her chair. "That... that... woman is not acceptable. She has run with a fast crowd ever since she was out of mourning. I cannot bear to think of you wedding her."

Sidney leaned forward in his seat and took his mother's hands gently in his own. "What is known all over town is simply the gossip that follows any beautiful widow. I do not condemn Lady Ashby for whatever the tabbies are serving with their tea. I beg you do the same."

The countess's forehead creased in consternation. "You'll say no more?"

Sidney shook his head, his heart heavy at his mother's distress. "I will not."

Taking his face between her hands, Lady Haddon scrutinized her son's countenance as if trying to read his thoughts. "I want you to be happy, Sidney," she said softly. "I have always wanted that for all my children."

"You must trust me, mother." Sidney regained his mother's hands, kissed them once more and placed them back in her lap, silently hoping that her misgivings were misplaced, silently hoping she wasn't right.

"We shall see." The countess settled implacably

back into her chair. "I do not give you my blessing, Sidney, but I'll not otherwise stand in your way. Now go. I feel suddenly very fatigued."

* * *

The corridors of Whitehall were quiet the following morning as Sidney strode toward the little closet into which he had been tucked. He was not used to town hours and found himself nearly alone in the halls of power. No one had precisely explained what function a cavalry officer might successfully perform behind a desk and no one seemed to be available to ask.

Sidney opened the door to his office and surveyed the battered mahogany desk that took up most of the room. Crossing the worn carpet, he dropped into a chair and pulled out the book he had the foresight to bring. Cracking it open, he settled in to wait for someone with information to arrive.

Sidney couldn't concentrate. He let the book drop into his lap and leaned back, looking around the room. The freshly painted walls underlined the otherwise shabby appointments, making the small room look like an afterthought, something thrown together so that the army would have some place to put Sidney Chamberlayne.

It seemed a piece with the rest of his life. He had never been in such turmoil. Sidney smiled wryly at the thought. He had been in battle so many times he had lost count. He had fought when it seemed unlikely he would be alive in the morning. He had watched friends die. Yet, this—this strange confluence of an unexplained occupation and a marriage he had not intended—seemed more foreign than any territory he had ever trod.

Sidney imagined someone would eventually explain his position at Whitehall. But he was fairly certain there would be no easy explanation of Lady Ashby—Isabel—

the woman he was to marry. He had no doubt that the marriage was the proper and honorable thing to do, but the lady herself was a mystery.

Sidney smiled again, this time a smile of remembered pleasure. His betrothed had been a delightful armful. He shook his head. He should never have responded as he did to her invitation, never have taken a woman into his arms without knowing who she was. He was hard pressed to account for such uncharacteristic behavior. But, did he regret it? He thought perhaps not.

CHAPTER 3

"What is it, Waldo?" Isabel was deeply engrossed in her novel and annoyed by the interruption.

"There is a Major Chamberlayne to see your ladyship."

"What?" Isabel catapulted from her seat, nearly trampling Wharton who pulled back the gentleman's card he had been about to present and retreated to the door.

"Tell him I am not at home... No! Wait. Put him in the garden room." Isabel closed her eyes and took a deep breath. She might as well see him and dispatch the problem right away.

"Yes," she said to her butler, who was hovering by the door. "Yes, put him in the garden room.

"And do not," she added as Wharton turned to leave, "under any circumstances, tell Lady Louisa that he is here."

Isabel remained motionless in the middle of the floor, staring at the pattern in the red carpet. Her mind whirled. Did she truly want to see Sidney Chamberlayne? It was not too late to send a footman to say she wasn't there.

And if she did see him, what did she mean to accomplish? Of course. She meant to release him from any obligation he might feel. Why then did the mention of his name leave her head whirling and her body thrumming with the memory of his touch?

Isabel shook her head, dislodging several honey gold curls along with the memory of Sidney's kiss. No. Any thought of that incident in the Caenby library must be obliterated. It meant nothing and Major Sidney Chamberlayne was definitely not the kind of man she wished to marry. Yes, Lord Ashby had left her a town house, a country estate, and sufficient income to support her comfortably. But marrying a half-pay soldier—a younger son with few prospects and little likelihood of a title—would make it difficult to ensure good matches for any children they might have. Besides companionship, there were many things to consider in a potential marriage. No. Major Sidney Chamberlayne would not do.

Isabel crossed to the pier glass and tucked her curls back into place. Turning before the mirror, she looked over her shoulder and tugged the cherry red sprigged muslin into order, smoothing the bodice and shaking the wrinkles out of her skirt. She leaned forward, ran a finger over her eyebrows and, just before turning away, pinched her cheeks.

* * *

Sidney surveyed the long room. It was simply decorated and the creamy yellow walls were mostly obscured by pots of exuberant vegetation. The far end of the room boasted fine French windows giving out onto the back garden of the town house. In fact, the room looked very much like Isabel Ashby, lush and golden with a promise of fecundity and a carefully applied veneer.

The furniture was obviously created for comfort, but pristine for all that. Four years on the Peninsula left him unsuited to such an environment. He perched uncomfortably on the edge of a settee, fearful that the delicate piece of furniture would collapse under his heavy frame.

Finally driven to his feet by his unease, Sidney began quartering the room, his situation roiling in his mind. Isabel Ashby had trapped him into marriage. He should not find her so compelling. Yet he did. He found himself at the back of the room, contemplating the wisdom of slinking out the French window into the garden before Lady Ashby appeared.

Following his conversation with his mother, Sidney had elected to walk from Haddon House to Bruton Place, each step accompanied by the memory of the countess's objections and his own doubts. Offering for Lady Ashby was the proper thing to do. But his mother made it plain that it would be difficult for his family, and worried that it would be painful for him. He regretted the necessity, but did not, for a single footstep, think that he had another choice. The last footstep had brought him to Lady Ashby's door and thence to this room where he waited, with a license in his pocket and determination in his heart.

Nevertheless, Sidney was still examining the brass door latch when he heard footsteps behind him. He dropped his hand from the door frame and turned smartly back toward the room.

"Major Chamberlayne." Lady Louisa's face plainly expressed her surprise at finding him there.

"My lady." Sidney bowed. "It is a pleasure to see you again."

"And I am gratified to see you, Major." Lady Louisa took her accustomed seat and waved Sidney toward a facing chair. "Were you planning an escape when I entered?"

Sidney could feel himself color to the roots of his hair. "I…"

Lady Louisa smiled slyly. "Never mind. I know you find yourself in a less than comfortable position and I am grateful you are here. Has Isabel been informed?"

"I believe I have been placed here at her direction, Lady Louisa, but I have not yet seen her."

"It is of no moment. I dare say she will join us

directly. Will you be so good as to ring for a footman?" Lady Louisa gestured toward the bell-pull. "Let us have tea."

Sidney stopped in the middle of the floor. "Tea? Is that...? That is..." He bit off his stuttered question and crossed the floor to yank the bell-pull before returning to his seat.

"You do not feel that this is a social call, do you?" Lady Louisa asked.

Sidney winced. "I hope you will pardon me, Lady Louisa. I am particularly unused to making afternoon calls in town."

"Nonsense. I was with you at Caenby. You behave very prettily in company." Lady Louisa cocked an enquiring eyebrow at Sidney. "You are here to conduct business."

Sidney looked up in surprise. He was not accustomed to having his motives questioned. Nor was he accustomed to being judged so accurately on short acquaintance. He was beginning to realize, however, that it was unlikely he could evade Lady Louisa's perceptive eye.

The door swung open and Sidney turned his head, expecting the tea. Instead, he found the arresting figure of Isabel Ashby. He rose to his feet drinking in the rich beauty of the young widow.

Standing in a swath of sunlight, Isabel was luminous. The afternoon light, filtering through her muslin dress, created a creamy aura around the faint outline of her graceful body and burnished her hair to the color of old gold. Sidney's gaze traveled to Isabel's face and found the only counterpoint to the warm apparition before him. Her countenance was parchment white and her expression stricken.

"Lady Ashby..." Sidney started toward the door.

"What are you doing here?"

"I beg your pardon?" Sidney halted in confusion and

then realized that Isabel was not even looking at him.

"What you doing here, Aunt?" Isabel glared at Lady Louisa.

"I am entertaining your guest, Isabel. I have sent for tea." Lady Louisa showed no sign of remorse. "Would you have me do otherwise?"

"Did Wheaton tell you he was here?" Isabel's eyes had not left her aunt's face.

"No, my dear, if by that you mean your butler. I stumbled upon Major Chamberlayne on my own. Had I known he was here, of course I would have come sooner." Lady Louisa looked up at her niece and then at Sidney who was still at attention in the middle of the floor. "Will you be sitting, dearest, or will you require the good major to drink his tea standing?"

Isabel's pale face pinkened, but she quickly took a seat by the table.

Sidney shook himself out of the trance into which he had fallen and returned to his own seat. As the tea tray was delivered to the room, he contemplated Isabel. Away from the wash of sunlight, she was still a beautiful creature. Even drawn up in a pout, her full lips invited kissing.

He hadn't intended to marry. After so many years in the army, Sidney felt most at ease among his comrades in arms. But he could not deny that Isabel Ashby was an intriguing woman. The honeymoon would not be a hardship and he expected he would return to his regiment before he had to deal with the daily exigencies of marriage.

As Lady Louisa blithely poured the tea and passed the cakes, Sidney leaned forward to look directly at Isabel. "I would have a private word with you, my lady."

Isabel narrowed her eyes and examined her guest. Glancing quickly toward her aunt, still busy with the tea things, she nodded.

"Aunt." After a short interval, Isabel cleared her

throat and tried again. "Aunt!" When Louisa looked up, Isabel assumed a bright smile. "You won't mind if I show Major Chamberlayne the garden, will you? We'll take tea when we return," she added, looking unconvinced of this likelihood.

Beaming, Lady Louisa gestured Isabel and her beau toward the French windows.

Sidney rose and stood beside Isabel's chair.

"Stop doing that," she snapped.

"My lady?" Sidney was truly confused.

"Stop appearing at my elbow. It is unnerving."

As Sidney made to move away, Isabel reached out and drew him back. Slipping her hand into the crook of his arm, she said, "As long as you're at my elbow, you may lend me yours. Please escort me to the garden." She cocked her head at him, but her expression remained prim.

*   *   *

The summer roses in the small back garden of the Bruton Place house were in full bloom. The blossoms on a dense thicket of French roses surrounding a small fountain were so dark they were almost purple. The high stone walls supported a cordon pear and the paths were bordered with pinks and candytuft. All else was cool and green.

Sidney hesitated on the flagged terrace to absorb the quintessential Englishness of the landscape. The dense green, punctuated by the soft color that only an English summer can produce, was balm to his parched soul. Greedily, he inhaled the scent of luxurious growth and damp earth and imbibed the delicious moisture through sun-hardened skin. Lord, but he had missed England. He wondered how far his next posting would take him.

Sidney felt the woman at his side stir and looked down, studying Isabel's expression for a clue as to what she was thinking. Her beautiful face was set in a mask of impassivity. Her gaze, like his, had been roaming the garden, but now she turned her face up to look at him.

Her eyes were beautiful: a brown so light that they nearly matched her hair—amber, even to the dark flecks so commonly found in that precious substance.

Lightly, Sidney touched her hand and nodded toward the far end of the garden where a white bench was installed beneath a trellis. "That seat looks inviting."

Isabel nodded and stepped onto the path leading to the trellis. She had not uttered a word since they'd left the house.

She sat on the bench beneath the cool shade of the honeysuckle and spread her skirts neatly around her. She looked up at Sidney with a question in her eyes.

The major hesitated a moment, contemplating the wisdom of going down on one knee. He discarded the notion as absurdly sentimental and took the seat beside her.

Sidney stared at the back of Lady Ashby's townhouse searching for the proper words. Isabel, immobile beside him, gave no indication of interest. He wondered, once again, how she felt about this unfortunate situation.

Sidney turned toward Isabel and took her hand. She did not withdraw it, but it lay in his like a lifeless thing.

"Lady Ashby?" Sidney's voice was low and determined.

Isabel raised her head and met his eyes. "Major Chamberlayne?"

Bloody hell. This was harder than he anticipated. For a moment, Sidney contemplated kissing her senseless and then jumping the high wall at the back of the garden. Instead, he tightened his grip and said, "Will you do me the honor of becoming my wife?"

* * *

That was it? Isabel stared, dumbfounded at the sun-burnished face of the gentleman opposite her. Well, yes, she had expected a proposal. Lord knew that Aunt Louisa had been on about it since they got in the carriage to return to London. And when the major had arrived at her door this afternoon there was only one thing it could have been. But, good heavens, could he have been any less animated? Was it possible that this half-hearted proposal came from the man who had kissed her 'til she couldn't think?

Isabel gave herself a mental shake. What difference did it make? She had no intention of marrying him anyway and this half-hearted proposal only made it easier to refuse him.

She came out of her reverie to find Major Chamberlayne gazing at her with a perplexed expression.

"My lady? Is there... something amiss? Is there someone to whom I should apply?"

Aunt Louisa! Isabel's thoughts skittered back to the woman waiting in the drawing room. If she returned without a betrothal, Aunt Louisa would never let her hear the end of it. Isabel closed her eyes wearily. This small misadventure had become so... complicated.

Opening her eyes, Isabel gazed evenly at her reluctant suitor. "I thank you, Major. That is a kind offer." Isabel drew a deep breath. "But I... I..."

Her gaze slid from the major's face and desperately roved the garden but found no alternative there. Fixing her eyes on a pear tree in the far corner, Isabel steadied herself and said, "I would be honored to be your wife."

Suddenly exhausted, Isabel leaned back against the side of the arbor. She had done it. She had bought herself a month in which to effect a graceful escape from this disgraceful situation. It would take almost that long to call the banns.

"No, my lady." Sidney retrieved Isabel's hand and saluted it with a soft kiss. "It is I who am honored."

Isabel blinked. *Good heavens, so formal and all for nothing.*

Standing, Sidney reached down and helped Isabel to her feet. "Shall we share our good news with your aunt?" His voice was even and his expression closed.

He would have to do better than that if he wanted to convince Aunt Louisa this was good news. Well, it was neither here nor there, was it? It was only until she could think of a way to escape this farce.

Sidney placed Isabel's hand into the crook of his arm and they began what felt like a three-mile stroll across the garden. Approaching the terrace, Isabel saw her Aunt Louisa's face peering through one of the panes in the French windows. As they set foot on the flagstones, the face disappeared. Isabel glanced up at Sidney. For the first time since he had arrived, he was smiling.

*   *   *

She had accepted. Sidney suppressed a sigh as he realized that the woman at his side would soon be his wife. He knew nothing about her, really, except that she was a widow with a sizable fortune left to her by her husband, a baron many years her senior. There was some talk about her in the *ton,* but that was not unexpected when it came to beautiful widows. She was known to run with a fast set, but had not been linked with anyone in particular since her husband's death.

Well, no one but the new Earl of Caenby. Gossip had it that she had set her cap for the earl. Sidney suspected that he had been caught in that web. He looked down at her out of the corner of his eye and saw only a petite woman with creamy skin, honey hair and a bemused expression on her face.

It occurred to Sidney that he had not really expected Lady Ashby to accept his proposal. Her response at

Caenby made it quite clear that she was not interested in anyone but the earl. But her aunt had made it equally clear that she expected him to make the proper amends for the ridiculous situation in which they had been discovered.

Without thought, Sidney clicked his tongue against his teeth. This was a sorry mess. He did not want to marry and likely could have escaped the entanglement and left Lady Ashby to face down any gossip on her own. He inhaled deeply and looked down at her again. She was extraordinarily beautiful. And here, away from her usual court of admirers, her brittle façade faded into an air of vulnerability that surprised and touched him. What was done was done. They entered the drawing room.

Lady Louisa arose and assumed an attitude of surprise. Sidney suppressed a chuckle. He would like being related to this doughty lady.

"Oh, my dears. You are back so soon." Louisa bent an enquiring glance on her niece, but it was Sidney who spoke.

"We have returned to ask you to wish us happy, my lady. Your lovely niece has agreed to be my wife."

"She has? Oh. Yes, of course she has. How truly wonderful, major. When is the wedding to be?"

"Friday."

"August."

CHAPTER 4

"Friday?" Isabel whirled to face Sidney. "We cannot be married on Friday. We must decide—uh—when we will be married, where we will live, buy wedding clothes. We will need at least two months."

"Friday," Sidney said, his voice firm.

"This Friday?" Isabel's voice rose to a dangerous pitch. "We... we... the banns must be posted." *There. Let us see him get around that little obstacle.*

Isabel watched, wide-eyed, as Sidney reached into his jacket pocket and extracted a folded document.

"Well?" she said.

Sidney bowed and held the paper toward Isabel. "A special license, my dear Lady Ashby."

Isabel reached for the paper and Sidney pulled it back, replacing it from whence it had come and giving his pocket a pat.

"We will marry on Friday," he said.

"No." With effort, Isabel restrained herself from stamping her foot. "It will be a scandal."

"It will be a romance," Sidney countered. "I met you at Caenby and could not keep my eyes—or my ring—off you. We will be the love match of the season. You have agreed to relieve my suffering by consenting to be my wife."

"Oh!" Isabel spun back toward her aunt. Holding out her hands in entreaty, she said, "You must see that we cannot rush into this marriage."

"I see no such thing," Lady Louisa replied. "I think Major Chamberlayne is acting exactly as he ought."

As Isabel had suspected, she would find no refuge in that quarter.

Returning to her newly betrothed, she attempted a more reasonable argument.

"But, really, Major. Why must we hurry? Should we not be seen to be... er... courting? Would that not be best?"

"Lady Ashby, we were seen doing more than courting not two weeks ago. We cannot prolong this. Moreover, my sister is in her first season and I will not have it overshadowed by either speculation or preparations for my marriage. We will marry on Friday. With your permission, my mother will call on you tomorrow to discuss arrangements."

"Your sister? Your mother? Wait." Isabel's head was spinning. She really knew very little about this man with a special license in his pocket.

"Wait," she repeated. "You have not had your tea. Aunt Louisa will be so disappointed if you do not stay for tea."

"Oh, indeed." Louisa agreed, giving her niece a perplexed frown. "I have sent for a fresh pot and Cook will be annoyed if we send back another and do not eat her lemon biscuits."

After the three were seated and Louisa had poured the steaming tea and inquired if the major took sugar, and Isabel had piled the major's plate with several delectable sweets, including the promised lemon biscuits, the party lapsed into an uncomfortable silence.

To keep from squirming in her chair, Isabel finally spoke. "So, major, do tell us about your mother and sister and... the rest of your family?"

Lady Louisa looked sharply at Isabel. "My dear, you have met the major's family."

Isabel shook her head. "I do not believe there are Chamberlaynes among my acquaintance." she hesitated and glanced toward Sidney. "Until now, that is."

"Surely, my dear, you remember meeting the Countess of Haddon at Lady Grealey's musicale. And I am almost sure you danced with the earl at Almack's last season."

Isabel blanched. "The Earl of Haddon?" Major Sidney Chamberlayne was the Earl of Haddon's brother? Had she known that? Of course, he was a gentleman or he would not have been among the party at Caenby. But... Haddon's brother?

"Why yes, of course," Isabel said, quickly regaining her poise. "You must forgive me, Major. I quite forgot that the countess was your mother."

"Naturally." Sidney took a sip of his tea. "Never having met me before, there is no reason you should make the connection. I have spent far more of my adult life in Spain than in London."

"And you do not very much resemble..." Isabel stopped and bit her lips. This was perhaps too personal.

Sidney continued for her. "No. I do not resemble either my mother or my eldest brother. I assure you however, I do look very much like the late earl."

Isabel blushed. Did the major think she was impugning his legitimacy?

"Fortunately," Sidney continued, seemingly unperturbed by the observation, "my sister, Julia, also has my mother's fine looks."

"And will Lady Julia join us for tea tomorrow as well as your mother?" Lady Louisa asked, ignoring her niece's dark look.

"I'll extend the invitation, if I may." Sidney focused on Isabel. "I know she will be anxious to make your acquaintance."

"Will be?" Isabel straightened in her chair. "Does she not know? Have you not told your family?"

"I have not told my sister," Sidney said. "But, of course, I informed the countess before I came here."

"Oh." Isabel subsided into a dejected posture. Every

avenue of escape seemed blocked. But, she was far from resigned to this marriage.

Sidney placed his cup on the table beside him and rose. "If you will excuse me, ladies, I must be on my way."

Lady Louisa cleared her throat and gave her niece a speaking look before extending her hand. "I cannot tell you how your call has delighted us, Major," she said.

Isabel had jumped to her feet at Louisa's look and remained waiting for Major Chamberlayne to take his leave of her aunt. She took the opportunity to appraise her betrothed. *Her betrothed!* She suppressed a small shiver. He was not the husband she had imagined. Certainly, he was the brother of an earl, but he was not an earl and he was not Caenby, whom she had convinced herself was the husband she desired.

Although Major Sidney Chamberlayne did not have the Earl of Caenby's fair countenance and polished appearance, he was not ill-looking. He was tall and well-muscled and, like many of the returning soldiers, heavily tanned, emphasizing his already craggy features and his proud ridge of a nose. The burnished skin made for an appealing contrast with his coal black hair and made his dark brown eyes look almost black.

Isabel pulled herself back from the edge of admiration with the reminder that, his fine clothes notwithstanding, he looked more like a soldier than a gentleman.

Sidney made a final bow to Lady Louisa and turned to offer his arm to Isabel. "Will you walk with me to the door, my lady?"

With a backward glance at her aunt who was making shooing motions with her hand, Isabel gingerly placed her hand on Sidney's arm and let him lead her out of the room.

Once they had gained the hall, Isabel snatched her hand back and stopped dead. When Sidney stopped beside her, she wheeled to face him. "Why are you doing this?"

"I am expected at Haddon House," Sidney said, his expression unreadable.

"That is not what I mean, and you very well know it." Isabel gritted her teeth against her growing frustration. "Why do you insist on marrying me?"

"Why should I not, madam? Do you not believe you are worth marrying?"

"Oh, for heaven's sake!" This time Isabel did stamp her foot. "Must you be so obtuse? I know you do not wish to marry me and yet you are making it impossible for me to cry off. I want to know why."

Sidney said nothing, looking down the long hallway, its shiny woodwork and Persian carpets warmly lit by the fading sun.

Isabel followed his gaze and, for a moment, allowed the beauty of her home to soften her heart. The spacious townhouse on Bruton Place had been her London home since she wed the baron and she had gradually put her unique stamp on it. She always felt safe here. This was home.

The major shifted and Isabel snapped out of her reverie to repeat her question. "Why? Why are you so determined to marry me when you know full well I do not want it?"

Sidney's gaze shifted to Isabel. "I heard you, Lady Ashby. I have an answer to that question, but I suspect it is not one you would like to hear."

"I would like to hear the truth," Isabel said. "And I would like to hear it now before it is too late to do something about it."

"Oh, I assure you, my dear." Sidney's voice was smooth and certain. "It became too late when you accepted me in the garden. If you meant to refuse me, that was the moment. And yet, you did not. The event has been set in train and we will see it through to the end."

Isabel took another tack. "Does your mother approve of this havey cavey proposal?"

Sidney placed his hands on Isabel's shoulders and turned her to face him. "She will call tomorrow afternoon. I suggest you ask her that question."

Isabel's eyes widened at the sensation of Sidney's calloused palms through the fine muslin of her sleeves. "You think I would not dare." She said, surprised to hear her own voice issue forth as a breathless whisper.

"I do not yet know what you will dare, Isabel." Drawing her closer to him, Sidney put his lips to Isabel's and delivered a slow, simmering kiss that Isabel felt right to the tips of her toes. "But I must admit that it is one of the first things I hope to learn."

Sidney executed a smart about-face and strode down the hall.

Isabel retreated to the garden room and threw herself into a deeply upholstered chair partially concealed by a low hanging fern.

Lady Louisa, still sitting by the tea table, looked enquiringly at her niece. "So you accepted him. I must admit, I thought I would have a fight on my hands to see this done."

Isabel's pensive expression turned to a petulant scowl. "Why do you think I accepted him? I knew you would give me no peace until I had."

"And now...?" Lady Louisa asked.

"And now, I am to be wed on Friday... apparently." Isabel slouched back in the chair and wrapped her arms across her chest, placing her hands where Major Chamberlayne's had been. Why had he kissed her in the hallway? Why must he kiss her at all? She wished he would not. Things were confusing enough without the memory of his mouth muddling her thoughts.

"You seem rather sanguine about the event." Lady Louisa's voice roused her from her abstraction.

Isabel rose from her chair and went to kneel before her

aunt. Taking Lady Louisa's hands in hers, she looked up into her Aunt's soft blue eyes. "Oh, Aunt. You know it is not what I want. And I thought I was so clever in accepting. I thought to give myself time to find an acceptable way out. Now, there seems no exit."

Emitting a deep sigh, she laid her head on Lady Louisa's lap and felt the older woman's hand begin to stroke her hair. She stayed motionless for a time, enjoying the tenderness of her aunt's touch. "What am I to do?" she finally asked.

Without ceasing her ministrations, Lady Louisa answered. "You are to marry, my dear. And you are not to fret. This will not be as bad as you believe."

"Why?" Isabel asked in a small voice. "Why are you so anxious for this match?"

"My dearest girl, I want you to be happy."

Isabel jerked upright. "And you think marriage to a stranger will accomplish that?"

"I hope that marriage to a good man will accomplish that." Lady Louisa leaned back and closed her eyes for a moment, sighing wearily. "You have been at loose ends since Edgar died."

Isabel started to speak and Louisa held up her hand. "I know you were married young and it was not a love match. But you are not meant to be a widow. You are yet young and it's time for you to marry again."

"To marry someone I don't know?" Isabel lifted her head but remained on the floor before her aunt's chair and reached out lightly to touch Louisa's hand. "How can that make me happy?"

Louisa took Isabel's hand and gazed intently at her. "You must trust me, my dear. Marriages have flourished after less auspicious beginnings than this."

"Do I have a choice?" Isabel asked in a defeated voice. "I might have brazened out Lady Broadribb's gossip, but I do not see how I can avoid the expectations of the Countess of Haddon." She shook her head. "I am well and truly in a box."

Isabel gazed vacantly toward the garden in which her life had recently taken so desperate a turn. Did she really have no choice? So it seemed at the moment and she wondered how she felt about it and what she should do.

She would wait. Perhaps the countess would not appear tomorrow. Sidney was so... proper, he would certainly not marry without his mother's blessing. Would he require the earl's blessing as well? These might be fruitful avenues to explore.

* * *

Isabel's unease lasted through dinner and into the long summer twilight. Dinner was long over and Lady Louisa had retired to her bed, but, despite the emotional rigors of the day, Isabel could not sleep. She wandered out into her garden, aromatic and comforting. She spent a long time wandering among the roses, watching the sun go down and savoring the delicious scent of early summer.

The roses always reminded Isabel of her childhood home. Her mother had a trellis laden with the fragrant blossoms near the front gate. She was suddenly assailed by an unexpected longing for Hampshire and for her childhood. It had been a sweet time, if too short, before her father had contracted her advantageous marriage to Baron Ashby.

Isabel dropped onto the arbor bench where she had received her more recent proposal of marriage. Or rather, she corrected herself, her only proposal of marriage. Her father had coolly informed her of her marriage to the aging baron and had left it to her mother to dry her tears and explain the facts of life for the daughter of an impoverished squire.

And now, she was promised by her own hand to another man she had not chosen. Isabel rested her head against the trellis and fell into a brown study.

Sidney Chamberlayne was different from the baron in almost every way she could imagine. He was young and strong. He was not unattractive. She couldn't deny that his kiss had been enjoyable—no, something more. His kiss had been tantalizing, as if something even more pleasurable was just beyond her grasp. But this wasn't a love match. He had no title to bring to the marriage. Nothing but himself.

Isabel shook her head. This was useless maundering. Her time would be better spent preparing for tomorrow and the countess's visit. And whatever might come after that.

CHAPTER 5

"I will do no such thing, Sidney." The Countess of Haddon's voice was as cold as a winter midnight. "What are you thinking to ask me to do such a thing?"

"Mother…" Sidney frowned at the stubborn glare on his mother's face. He read her well enough to know this would not be an easy argument.

"Mother," he repeated. "I have asked Lady Ashby to marry me and she has accepted."

"Of course she accepted, you fool. Who would not accept you?"

Sidney's lips quirked as he tried to suppress a smile. "Many women would not accept me, Mother."

"Hmph!" The countess raised a hand as if to dismiss such a ridiculous thought.

Impulsively, Sidney bent over and kissed his mother's cheek. "I am not a prize, my dear, as you would realize were you not looking at me through a mother's eyes."

Lady Haddon lifted a hand and placed her palm along her son's sharp jaw line. "You're too much of a prize to throw yourself away on a scheming widow."

"Scheming, Mother?" Sidney straightened and looked down at his mother with a puzzled frown. "I think not and I'll thank you not to speak so about my future wife."

"Oh Sidney!" Lady Haddon rose and, shaking out her skirts, paced to the writing table and back. "How could you have come to this? And how could you have promised my attendance without speaking to me?"

"You are my mother," Sidney said quietly, his dark

gaze softening. "And you are the Countess of Haddon. I trusted that you would act in a manner that was both appropriate and... affectionate. This should not come as a surprise to you. I told you that I was to be wed to Lady Ashby."

"Oh!" The countess's voice was tight with frustration. "I really thought you would come to your senses."

"I was never out of my senses and I did not do this frivolously." Sidney moved his gaze from his mother's perturbed countenance and glanced around her morning room. It was nearly dark, but the room was well lit with candles, as was his mother's custom.

A window was open and the perfume of the damp grass mingled with the warm beeswax, a scent that evoked a feeling of serenity from early childhood. He drew the fragrance deep into his lungs and returned to his mother, pulling up a hard-backed chair beside her more comfortable seat.

Leaning forward, Sidney took his mother's hand in both of his. "I believe you have always trusted me," he said.

The countess nodded and Sidney continued, "Please trust me now. Please believe that I'm doing the right thing. Please give me your support."

Lady Haddon looked sharply at her son. "Do you need my support?"

"No, I don't," Sidney said wearily, "but I think you know how much I would like to have it."

"Oh, my boy." The countess withdrew her hand from her son's but immediately placed it against his cheek. "My dearest Sidney."

Raising her other hand, she cupped Sidney's face. "You know how difficult it is for me to deny you anything, especially after so many years without seeing your dear face. Yes, I will take tea with Lady Ashby."

"Tea?" The bright voice of Lady Julia sounded from the doorway. "Is there to be a tea party?"

Sidney, after taking his mother's hands and kissing them, stood to face his sister with an affectionate smile. "Indeed there is and you have been invited as well."

"I have?" Julia looked to her mother for confirmation.

Lady Haddon nodded and Julia asked, "Will there be anyone interesting there?"

"I hope you find it so," Sidney said. "You are to meet the lady I am to marry."

"Marry!" Julia flew across the room and threw herself into her brother's arms. "Sidney! You never said. Oh, a wedding and yours, you sly devil." She took her arms from around his neck and laughed delightedly.

"Who is she?" Julia's sparkling eyes looked up at her big brother. "Are you in love?" She tore herself away and whirled about the room. "A wedding," she caroled, hugging herself as she danced to her mother.

"Calm yourself, Julia." Lady Haddon put a quieting hand on her daughter's shoulder. "We will meet the lady soon enough. Sidney will tell you all about it."

The countess cocked a warning eye at Sidney and turned back to her daughter. "But don't pester him and do not pester me. In fact, why don't you take a turn about the garden before it is too dark to enjoy it?"

"Oh, excellent notion." Julia, who had been about to sit down, sprang back to her feet and reached for Sidney's arm. "Do take me out to the garden and tell me of your courtship."

Sidney rolled his eyes at his mother and allowed his sister to lead him away.

"So…" Sidney and his sister were only a few steps from their mother's door when she pounced on him. "Who is she? Do I know her? Is she beautiful? Will I like her? When did this all happen?"

Taking a deep breath, Sidney decided that this was as good a time as any to begin telling the tale that would be told to the rest of London. "I met her at Caenby

Castle. You remember my friend Edward Burnet, do you not?"

"Of course I remember Edward. I thought he was going to marry me."

"What?" Sidney stopped short, his expression clouded and his fists clenched. "Did Edward offer for you? I'll..."

"Oh Sidney. You are still so easy to tease." Julia gave him a saucy smile. "I was thirteen years old and I asked him to wait for me. I take it he has not."

"No," Sidney said, dryly, "I don't believe he has."

"Oh." Julia's shoulders sagged for a moment, but she came right about and turned her sunny smile on her brother. "But, this conversation was not meant to be about me, was it? You were telling me the story of your betrothal."

"Er... yes." Sidney took his sister's arm and continued toward the back of the house.

"Well, I was at Caenby visiting Edward. I met Lady Ashby on my first evening there. She is quite stunning, Julia, and dresses with great elegance."

"So are many women in London. It is not like you to be smitten by a pretty face, Sidney." Julia's brow furrowed.

Sidney dropped his sister's arm and strode a few feet farther before returning to her, a frown marring his broad forehead. "What do you know of me, Julie? You were a child when I left England."

Julia laid the tips of her fingers against Sidney's arm. The touch felt as if a butterfly had landed on his sleeve and Sidney's tension eased.

"I know," Julia said, "that you are man of deep feeling and not given to superficialities. I know that any woman you marry must possess more than a beautiful countenance and graceful form."

Sidney rubbed his eyes with the thumb and forefinger of one hand. "Of course, little one, there is much more to Lady Ashby than that. She is lively and opinionated and extremely stubborn." He smiled slyly at his sister. "I think you will find much in common with her."

"Isabel Ashby?" The Earl of Haddon stepped through the front door before Sidney and Julia reached the passage to the back garden.

Sidney pivoted to face the door. "Harold, how nice to see you."

"Have you taken up with the Widow Ashby, Sidney? Not very good *ton*." The earl's expression was a curious combination of boredom and distaste.

"Taken up?" Sidney returned his brother's disdainful gaze.

"Oh Harold, Sidney is to be married!" Julia's cheerful exclamation cut through Sidney's cold query.

The earl cocked his head at his siblings. "Not to Isabel Ashby."

"Yes, Harold. To *Lady* Ashby." Sidney's expression hardened into an obdurate mask.

"That was not a question, brother," Harold said in the voice that frequently brought debate in the House of Lords to a halt.

Sidney's dark eyes scanned his brother's face. "Wasn't it? Well, mine was quite definitely an answer. Lady Ashby and I are to be wed."

"Without the sanction of the head of your family?"

"If I must," Sidney's expression had not altered since the earl's first word.

The earl bent a cold look upon his younger brother. "And you are determined to drag the Haddon family into a misalliance just when your sister is entering society?"

"Really, Harold!" Julia inserted herself between her two brothers. "Do not be absurd. Sidney would never form a misalliance."

Julia turned to Sidney, a mischievous glint animating her clear eyes. "Is she truly scandalous?"

"No. She is no more scandalous than I am. You will see for yourself tomorrow."

"You are not introducing Julia to Isabel Ashby," the earl declared.

"No, I'm not," Sidney replied. "Mother is."

* * *

Sidney had lost count of the number of times he had rolled over in his little "governess" bed. Comfort was nowhere to be found. For a moment, he considered moving to one of the family rooms. It had been years since he had slept on a thick featherbed. Perhaps that was all he needed.

He swung his legs around and sat on the edge of the low bed, his bare feet flat on the floor, and rested his elbows on his knees. He stared out the window at the fluttering leaves in the light summer breeze and knew that the problem was not the bed or the heat or even the tension that currently swirled through Haddon House.

The problem was that he could not halt the constant tumble of images, thoughts, emotions invading his dreams.

Sidney left the room, pulling on his dressing gown as he padded down the third floor corridor in his bare feet. There would be no sleep until he sorted out his feelings.

The night air was cool against Sidney's skin and the grass damp under his feet. He and Julia had never made it to the garden that afternoon. After the contretemps with Harold, Julia had given them each a kiss and hurried off to dress for dinner. Sidney, in no mood for more conversation with his eldest brother, had left the house to dine with friends at The Guards' Club on St. James Street. He had returned before midnight and tried to sleep. But now, having failed in that endeavor, he was out enjoying the garden in the dead of night.

The countess preferred a garden in ordered disarray, cultivating the unruly growth of a country garden even here in the confines of Mayfair. The only thing the least bit civilized about the Haddon House back garden was the carefully tended paths leading the way among the dense and fragrant growth.

Sidney wandered through the pathways for a bit and, when he located the stone bench set in a hidden nook in the back wall, he lowered himself upon it and let his eyes grow accustomed to the dark.

He remembered a letter from Julia describing the uproar that had overtaken Haddon House after Harold tried to hire an improver to turn the garden into a series of formal parterres interspersed with what had apparently been all manner of statuary. Sidney grinned into the darkness. He would have liked to have seen his mother take on that fight.

His mother. Tomorrow, she would meet Isabel. And Sidney knew that, regardless of how the countess felt, she would be everything that was kind to his betrothed and that because she loved him.

Sidney leaned back against the rough stone and drew in the fragrance of the honeysuckle. His mind still whirled. He would be married by the end of the week. And, even now, after insisting on it at every opportunity, after persevering against Isabel's refusals, after entreating his mother and defying his brother, in the dark hours of the night, he still wondered why.

He did not doubt that, having been discovered in Lady Ashby's arms, an offer was the only proper response. Yes, the lady had not intended it to be him, but he had not spurned her attentions. In fact, he had reveled in them until the moment the door opened.

But his sleep was disturbed by the question of why he had not let her cry off when that was clearly what she desired.

Sidney shivered in the cooling air and drew his

dressing gown more tightly around him. He had no answer. He only knew that when it came to the point, he was determined to marry Isabel Ashby regardless of what that might mean for the future. He also knew he was abetted in this by Isabel's aunt and, somehow, the knowledge that Lady Louisa desired this union made him more sanguine.

* * *

Isabel stood in front of her bed glaring down at the four gowns laid out in a row. Each was more outrageous than the last and she wondered how she had come to own them.

She was quite sure she had never worn the crimson gauze over the flesh colored underdress, nor had she even removed from its wrapping the barely opaque gown with a bodice cut so low her nipples would no doubt peek over the trim. She could not imagine what errant impulse had ever caused her to purchase them.

Her gaze fastened on the last gown. She had worn that one, but only to bed. She intended to put on one of these curious choices in order to convince Lady Haddon that she was not the appropriate bride for her son. Surely the countess would forbid her son to marry a woman who would take tea with her future husband's mother dressed like a harlot.

This tea could be her last hope of ending the betrothal that had been arrived at so precipitously just a day ago. No, she admitted to herself. It was put in train two weeks ago in the library of Caenby Castle and she had only her foolish self to blame for that.

But, the major was so… insistent. What could he mean by it? Any other man would have grasped at the chance she had offered to escape the parson's mousetrap. Surely he wasn't in love with her. He barely knew her. Was it her fortune? Well, he was a younger son. She supposed she could not blame him for fixing on a wealthy widow when one was thrown in his path.

Isabel paced the length of the bed, examining each garment. Perhaps she could not blame him, but she wouldn't countenance it. She tilted her head and examined her reflection in the window pane. She was still pleasing at thirty and shouldn't require her fortune to attract a husband.

Chamberlayne didn't seem like a fortune hunter, though, did he? He was a military man and, if anything, seemed like a man who belonged in the army.

Inexplicably, Isabel's eyes filled. What had she got herself into? This hasty wedding was not at all what she had in mind that night at Caenby. Not this quickly, not this groom, not this confusion.

"Bother!" She dashed the tears from her eyes and leaned forward to examine herself more closely. At least her nose wasn't red. She whirled back to the bed, took one last glance at the assortment of gowns and then threw the door open, leaving her room dressed in the pale green muslin she had donned after breakfast.

"Have my guests arrived, Wharton?" she asked as soon as she entered the drawing room. She nervously pleated the fabric of her skirt. Having abandoned the ridiculous gowns, she had no plan and felt all at sea.

"Lady Haddon and Lady Julia are here. Shall I show them in?"

"Please do." Giving her skirt one last twitch, Isabel faced the butler. "And please tell Cook we will have tea right away."

"Very good, my lady." Wharton gently closed the door.

Isabel stood in the center of the room, wringing her hands and waiting for her butler to return with her guests. She had hoped to have a plan to discourage the ladies from supporting the major's suit. She supposed she could still act in a manner so vulgar that they would take her in disgust, but now she thought she could no more do that than she could have received them in her night rail.

The door re-opened to admit two ladies and Wharton, who stopped at the doorway to intone, "The Countess of Haddon and Lady Julia Chamberlayne." He bowed deeply and backed out, almost running down Lady Louisa.

"Wharton!" Lady Louisa saved herself by ducking under the butler's arm and entering the drawing room with rather more speed and eccentricity than she or her niece could have wished.

Lady Louisa, however, retained enough of her self-possession to greet her visitors with enthusiasm.

"Harriet!" she exclaimed, advancing on the countess. "And can this be little Julia? My dear, you have become a beauty."

While Julia blushed and the countess beamed, Louisa turned a pleased smile upon her niece.

"Lady Haddon, Lady Julia, please allow me to present my niece, Isabel, Lady Ashby."

The countess shook her head doubtfully at Lady Louisa. "Lady Ashby and I have met. But, did I know she was your niece, Louisa? I declare, my memory gets worse with each passing year. I am pleased to see you again," she continued, smoothly turning to Isabel.

Isabel dropped a curtsey of precisely the correct depth. "The pleasure is mine. Please have a seat—both of you. Tea will be up shortly."

The next few seconds were fraught with a tense silence, finally broken by Lady Louisa.

"Major Chamberlayne is a charming young man," she said. "We are quite delighted with him."

"Sidney is very dear to me," the countess said, shooting a sidelong glance at Isabel. "I wish to see him happy."

Isabel stiffened and turned her attention to Julia. "I understand this is your first season, Lady Julia."

"Oh, please call me Julia." Julia turned the full force of her smile on Isabel. "We are to be sisters, after all."

Isabel could not help but return the smile. Sidney's sister was very appealing.

"Then you must call me Isabel. Are you enjoying the season?"

"It has been wonderful. And it will be even better now that Sidney is home. I hope you won't mind sharing my brother with me occasionally. I have heard how newly married couples are." Julia blushed lightly but never took her eyes off Isabel's face.

Isabel could feel herself coloring in response. Lady Julia Chamberlayne thought her brother had made a love match. What could she say to that? What did she want to say to that? The idea of disenchanting Julia Chamberlayne seemed like the worst sort of transgression.

As she and Julia continued to canvas the delights of a season in London, Isabel could feel Lady Haddon's eyes upon her. When the murmur of discussion between her aunt and the countess died away, she directed her attention to the woman who might be her mother-in-law.

"Lady Haddon," she began, wondering what she could say that would suit her purpose. "I do not know what your son has told you of our... er... surprising betrothal."

"Sidney has told me nothing," the countess said sharply. "But he is his own man and I require only a mother's prerogative: to know he will be happy." She paused. "Will he?" Her gaze was direct and her eyes, piercing.

Here was her chance. Isabel squared her shoulders and met the countess's gaze. "I do not know, your ladyship. I can promise nothing. Surely you know," Isabel rushed to add in response to the countess's raised eyebrow, "my acquaintance with Major Chamberlayne is only recently formed. That is, we met at Caenby for the first time."

"Naturally," the countess said. "Sidney is only just returned from the peninsula."

"Yes... indeed... well..." Isabel paused, unsure how to go on.

"Well?" the countess prompted, her expression softening a bit.

"Well." Isabel inhaled deeply. "That is to say, I am not certain I am the proper wife for Major Chamberlayne. Surely he deserves better." There. It was out.

CHAPTER 6

Friday morning. Isabel sat at her dressing table while her abigail finished brushing her hair. She usually luxuriated in the sensation of the brush gently tugging through her curls and her maid's soft hands coaxing her thick hair into obedience. But today she was too anxious to enjoy it. Downstairs, she could hear the indecipherable murmur of strange voices. She knew that the Vicar of St. George's was with her Aunt and, she suspected, Major Chamberlayne.

When the maid put down the brush and began fashioning Isabel's curls into an elaborate coil, Isabel waved her away. "Something simple, today, Willington. Something that will not make me look like a bride."

"I beg your pardon, m'lady." Willington retrieved the brush and began fashioning a simple topknot, trying valiantly to restrain her mistress's unruly curls. "But, if I may say so, should you not look like a bride on this particular day?" She applied the last hairpin and stood back, checking her work.

"Go away, Willington. I am sure you are needed somewhere downstairs." Isabel shooed her maid out of her room and returned to her mirror.

The face that stared back at Isabel looked paler than usual and seemed to have faint circles under its light brown eyes. She had certainly looked better. A soft knock interrupted her inspection.

Lady Louisa opened the door and peered in. "Are you ready, my dear?"

Isabel moved to the center of the room and held her arms slightly away from her body, palms outward. "As you see."

"You look beautiful, Isabel." Lady Louisa walked around her niece, stopping to straighten the bow that fell from the raised waist down the back of the simple silk dress.

"I look dreadful, Aunt." Isabel's voice was hoarse with unshed tears.

Louisa took Isabel's hand and squeezed it tightly. "You could not look dreadful on your worst day, my child. And you must trust me that today is far from your worst day."

"I feel dreadful, then," Isabel said, clinging to her aunt's hand like a lifeline. "Tell me I do not have to do this."

"Don't talk nonsense, girl. I have never known you to be missish and I must say it is not very becoming. You have never backed down from a challenge, Isabel. Don't start now."

"Oh, Aunt, don't try to manage me." Isabel withdrew her hand and whirled away, coming to rest with her back to Louisa and her chin in the air. She remained in that posture for several seconds, contemplating what was to come next.

"Very well." Isabel returned to Lady Louisa's side and took her arm. "Let's do what must be done."

Isabel half expected Sidney to be waiting for her at the foot of the stairs. She didn't know why she harbored that expectation, but she was disappointed to find the lower hallway empty. She supposed the muddy streaks on the marble tiles meant that he had recently been there. She gave a little shrug. With a wry smile on her pale face, Isabel descended to meet her destiny.

It was still raining. The day had dawned under the cover of thick gray clouds and it had only got worse. Lady Louisa ruled out Isabel's beloved garden room for the wedding and Isabel acknowledged that the room was really too dreary in rainy weather. Instead, once they reached the first floor, the two turned right.

The double doors were open and the light of a welcoming fire and a score of candles warmed the cool green of the drawing room and picked out the white woodwork and creamy plaster on the ornate mantelpiece and ceiling medallions.

Lady Louisa hurried into the room, but Isabel stood in the doorway for several long seconds examining the people standing around the fire. The vicar, chubby and red-cheeked, looked like a small, cheerful magpie in clerical black. Across from the vicar stood Major Chamberlayne and those of his family who had accompanied him.

Isabel, unable to take her eyes off the man she was soon to marry, barely noted the group around him. My, but he looked fine. She had been afraid he would wear his uniform, a thought that alarmed her for some unknown reason. However, the bridegroom had chosen a dark blue coat and gray knee breeches. His snowy linen was decorated with a simple, silver stud. His deeply tanned face looked stark and elegant against the white of his cravat.

Isabel tore her gaze from Sidney long enough to scan the room. The Countess and Lady Julia were here, but the Earl of Haddon did not attend. And who was that speaking with Sidney's sister? The man turned so that she could see his profile and the room tilted. What was the Earl of Caenby doing here? Blindly, she put out one hand and grasped the door frame.

*   *   *

A flash of color in the doorway caught Sidney's eye. He handed the license to the Rev. Hodgson and glanced toward the movement. Isabel, her eyes huge and her full lips as pale as her face, clung to the door frame as if she was about to faint. In two strides, Sidney was by her side.

Gently, Sidney pried her fingers from the door and placed them on his arm. His grave, dark eyes peered down at her. "Are you well, Isabel? May I get you something?"

Isabel's fingers dug into his arm. "What is he doing here?" she whispered.

"He?" Sidney's gaze swung to the focus of Isabel's attention.

"Oh, Caenby," he said. "He was in town and..." Sidney stopped dead, his lips forming a rigid line, heat creeping up his neck.

"Damn. This was stupid of me. Caenby is my friend. I actually forgot that he was..." Sidney's tone was hard and he left unsaid the words ringing in Isabel's mind: *the one you thought to compromise.*

Isabel clutched Sidney's arm and sagged toward him. He was left with the choice of supporting her or letting her drop to the floor. Removing her hand from his sleeve, he slid an arm around her waist and drew her up against him. "Steady," he whispered. "Let's not have a scene, all right?"

Isabel nodded, taking a deep breath and pulling herself up and away from Sidney's support. "No. By no means a scene, Major." She stepped into the room. "Shall we?" she asked over her shoulder.

Sidney moved to her side and took her arm. "You still mean to marry me?"

Isabel cocked her head at Sidney in a poor imitation of a coquettish glance. "Naturally. Unless, of course, Lord Caenby is here to carry me away."

Sidney grimaced at Isabel's sudden retreat into sardonic humor. "He is here at my invitation," he said firmly.

"Of course. Very well then..." Isabel threw a cool glance at Sidney and glided toward her aunt.

"There you are my dear, you look..." Louisa glanced at her niece's face and her words died away. "You look lovely," she continued brightly. "Just as you ought."

Sidney watched for only a minute before joining Isabel and her aunt.

"The vicar is ready." He offered his arm to Isabel, but looked at Lady Louisa.

Isabel drew a deep breath and put her hand on Sidney's sleeve, allowing him to lead her toward the far end of the room where the vicar stood, prayer book in hand.

Once Lady Louisa had shepherded the guests into place, the vicar opened his book. "Dearly beloved..."

Sidney watched the woman at his side out of the corner of his eye. She was lovely. There was no doubt about that. There was also no doubt that she was unhappy.

He had not expected her to accord this day any undue import by dressing extravagantly and she had not disappointed him in that. The silk dress was unadorned and the only jewels she wore were a single strand of pearls. Were it not for her admirable figure, the dress would be quite severe.

The gown was a glacial blue and Sidney thought it particularly appropriate. She stood by his side, her back straight as an arrow and her chin in the air. For all her bravado, she seemed fragile as an ice sculpture. The wrong word, the wrong touch and she would shatter.

"First, it was ordained for the procreation of children."

The vicar's words penetrated Sidney's thoughts. Ah yes, the procreation of children. Perhaps at the right touch his ice maiden would melt. It was a thought that kept him engaged through much of the rest of the ceremony.

"...if either of you know any impediment, why ye

may not be lawfully joined together in Matrimony, ye do now confess it."

For the first time since the vicar opened his prayer book, Sidney and Isabel looked at each other. Both knew there was no legal impediment. Sidney wondered what other impediments they would meet along the way.

"Who giveth this Woman to be married to this Man?"

Sidney jerked to attention. Who would give this woman? Why had he not thought of this? Lady Louisa was her only relative here, her only living relative as far as he knew.

"My father is dead, sir." Isabel's voice issued forth, cool and quiet.

"Then a friend must stand in his stead."

The room was utterly quiet save for the crackle of the fire and the sound of carriage wheels on the street.

Then Lord Caenby stepped forward. "I will."

"Take Lady Ashby's left hand," the vicar instructed.

Sidney closed his eyes and searched for calm. It wanted only this: to receive her hand from the man she hoped to marry. Could this marriage begin in a worse way?

"For as much as Sidney and Isabel have consented together in holy Wedlock, and have witnessed the same before God and this company, and thereto have given and pledged their troth either to each other, and have declared the same by giving and receiving of a Ring, and by joining of hands; I pronounce that they be Man and Wife together..."

It was over and Sidney remembered less than half of it. Apparently, both he and Isabel had consented to marriage in front of this company.

The moment the vicar closed his prayer book, Julia was at his side, fervently kissing his cheek. "I am so happy for you, Sidney," she whispered and then turned to Isabel.

As Sidney watched his sister embrace his wife—*his*

wife—the countess moved softly into place beside him and took his hand.

"I wish you only joy, son. I hope this marriage brings it to you."

Sidney glanced back at Isabel who was embracing Julia as if she were her own sister. As Isabel smiled warmly at Julia's youthful excitement, Sidney hardly recognized her as the cool, brittle beauty who had stood by his side not moments ago.

He squeezed his mother's hand and placed it in the crook of his arm. "I know you do, Mother and I have hope as well. Now, let us go see what Lady—er—Mrs. Chamberlayne's excellent cook has prepared for us."

"No, Sidney." The countess removed her hand from her son's arm and gave it a little pat. "You belong with your bride. Go to her now."

Sidney and the Earl of Caenby reached Isabel at the same moment. Sidney hung back and watched as Caenby took his wife's hand and bowed low over it. "May I wish you happy, Isabel? I do, you know."

Isabel raised her head and met the earl's kind eyes. She flushed slightly and her mouth settled into a wry grimace. "I know you do, my lord and I… I thank you."

The earl turned his attention to Julia who blushed and giggled. Sidney, feeling inexplicably relieved at Isabel's mild reception of the earl's good wishes, moved in to claim his wife.

The wedding breakfast was ample, quiet and interminable. Sidney sat at the head of the table and felt completely out of place. Lady Louisa, ensconced on his left did her best to keep the conversation lively. But Sidney could not keep from watching his wife at the other end of the table.

Isabel sat perfectly erect, a correct smile in place and no expression in her eyes. She ignored her plate to converse with all the guests within her reach, turning a polite expression on each in turn.

Sidney realized he barely knew his bride, but, at that very moment, he could not help but feel as though his insistence on marriage had marred some essential part of her. His heart clenched and he sent up a silent prayer.

* * *

Sidney and Isabel stood side by side in the entry hall at Bruton Place. The Earl of Caenby had gone and Sidney's mother and sister were waiting for their carriage and fussing over the newlyweds.

"It was a lovely wedding, my dears." Lady Haddon reached out and straightened Sidney's cravat in an unconscious gesture.

Obviously uncomfortable with his mother's proprietary action, Sidney took her hand between his own and moved it away from his shirt. "Thank you for coming, Mother." He leaned down and kissed her cheek.

"Yes." Isabel, who had been standing in remote silence at Sidney's side since bidding farewell to Caenby, suddenly spoke.

"Oh, yes. Thank you, my lady. It was good of you to come I know that... I know that this was not the wedding you wished for your son."

Isabel knew a brief moment of satisfaction at the look of astonishment on her husband's face at her plain speaking.

The countess, however, smiled. "Well, that is of no moment, my dear. I have great hope that it will be the marriage I wish for him." Lady Haddon drew her hand out of Sidney's and placed it against Isabel's cheek. "Take care of him, Isabel. He is very dear to me."

Isabel flushed and nodded, looking toward her new husband and then quickly away.

All exuberance, Julia flitted from Sidney to Isabel, hugging and exclaiming. "You must come to tea right away," she said to Isabel, holding onto her hand and beaming.

The countess intervened. "Julia. We will invite Isabel to tea next week. She needs some time to herself first."

Julia blushed becomingly. "Of course. Forgive me, both of you. I am just so pleased to have a sister."

"Ah." Lady Haddon looked toward the staircase. "Here is Louisa."

Lady Louisa, dressed for travel, descended the stairs followed by a footman carrying a portmanteau.

"Aunt!" Isabel hurried to the foot of the stairs. "What is this?"

Louisa nodded to the footman who moved past her to set the portmanteau by the door. "Harriet has invited me to spend the week at Haddon House."

Isabel stared at her aunt in perplexity.

"You are just married, my dear," Louisa said. "Lady Haddon and I thought you might like a week of privacy. We can discuss whether I should find a new home later."

"Find a new home?" Isabel looked stunned. "This is all too much. Your home is here. I do not think you need to go even for a week."

"Be that as it may, I have accepted Lady Haddon's invitation," Louisa said, pulling on her gloves. "I believe this is for the best and will see you next week."

As Lady Louisa leaned up to embrace her niece, Isabel threw her arms around her aunt. "Oh," she breathed against Louisa's cheek. "Oh, I do not want you to go."

Louisa took Isabel's hand and led her away from the group gathered in front of the door. "What is it, Isabel?"

"I don't know. This is all too sudden." Isabel shook her head and looked back toward her husband.

"You are no schoolroom miss, dearest. Do not underestimate yourself or the major. Now, walk me to the door."

* * *

As day slid into evening, the continual rain made the seam between the two invisible. Isabel disappeared into her room not long after the guests departed and was still behind closed doors. As darkness fell, Sidney found himself in Isabel's library looking for something interesting to read. The irony of the situation was not lost on him.

He found a surprising number of books on history and warfare, which he passed over in favor of Donne. He was in no mood for war in any form.

Sidney pulled a comfortable chair before the glowing grate and sat. Before opening the book, he looked around the room. It was small but well appointed. The highly polished mahogany bookshelves reflected the red damask of the walls. The intricate design of a Persian carpet warmed the tile floor beneath it. He felt surprisingly at home in Isabel's townhouse.

Sidney looked down at the book in his hands. John Donne's love poems. What fey impulse had prompted him to choose that? He let the book fall open where it would and shifted toward the light to read.

I bid me send my heart, when I was gone;
But I alas could there find none,
When I had ripped me, and searched where hearts
didlie;
It killed me again, that I who still was true
In life, in my last will should cozen you.

Yet I found something like a heart,
But colours it, and corners had,
It was not good, it was not bad,
It was entire to none, and few had part.
As good as could be made by art
It seemed; and therefore for our losses sad,
I meant to send this heart instead of mine,
But oh, no man could hold it, for 'twas thine.

Sidney let the book slide out of his fingers. What had caused the book to open at this poignant poem? Was it one that Isabel read or was it a favorite of her late husband? Either possibility contained echoes of an empty marriage.

Wharton slipped into the library and deposited a tray on the table by the fire. Although he longed to ask if his wife had eaten, Sidney refused to amuse the help by admitting he did not know. He nodded to the butler and examined the food, a collation of cold meat, cheese, bread and what proved to be an excellent claret.

"Oh, good." Isabel stood in the library door. "I see that Wharton brought you food."

Sidney set down his glass and rose from his chair. "Isabel..." He did not ask the myriad questions that came unbidden to his mind, beginning with *where have you been?*

"May I offer you some food... wine?" Sidney gestured toward the companion chair.

"No. Well, yes. I would have some wine." Isabel took a seat and waited for Sidney to serve her.

The couple sat in silence for several minutes, sipping wine and gazing into the fire.

"Your boxes are in the Baron's room." Isabel's flat statement was clearly an accusation.

Sidney shifted in his chair to look directly at her. "My boxes are in *your husband's* room. Where did you think they would be?" She had not moved and Sidney addressed her profile.

"I had not thought..." Isabel turned her head slightly and regarded Sidney from the corner of her eye.

"What had you not thought, Isabel? That I would live here? Did you think I would stay at Haddon House? Or did you think I would take you there with me?"

"No. No." Isabel faced her husband. "That is not what I meant. I had no expectation of living anywhere else."

"But you did not think I would live with you." Sidney's voice was flat.

"Yes. No. Oh!" Isabel flounced in her chair. "I don't know what I thought. You have barely given me a chance to think in the past week."

Sidney levered himself from his chair and went to stand before the fire. He looked down at Isabel, his gaze intent.

"And now that we are married?"

Isabel raised her head and met Sidney's eyes. "You are my husband as of this day, and this is your house. You should, of course, sleep in my husband's bed."

"Isabel." Sidney's voice was gentle and his expression bemused. "This house is settled on you."

Isabel dropped her gaze to the fire. "I am your wife; it is yours."

"Didn't your solicitor explain the settlement, Isabel?" Sidney asked. "This house is yours regardless of your marital state."

Isabel's head jerked up in surprise.

"I did not marry you for your fortune, Isabel." Sidney laid his arm along the mantel and looked intently at his bride.

"Did you not?" Isabel met his gaze. "I wonder why you did, then."

Sidney left his position against the mantelpiece and moved toward her. "I don't know if I can explain," he said. "It's something I am still discovering."

Isabel shrugged. As Sidney moved closer, she held up one hand. "Be clear about this. Regardless of whose house this is, there is one bed in which you may not sleep and that is mine."

Sidney stopped directly in front of Isabel and, reaching down, took her by the shoulders and raised her to her feet.

Isabel froze, staring wide-eyed at the man before her. Sidney allowed himself a brief smile. He raised his right hand to her shoulder and gently laid one finger of his left hand against her lips.

"It shall be as you wish, wife."

Isabel sighed, her relief obvious.

"But," Sidney added, "I retain the prerogative to try to change your mind."

Lowering his head, Sidney replaced his finger with his lips and kissed her.

CHAPTER 7

It had rained for five days. The unpleasant mizzle that had graced the Chamberlaynes' wedding day developed into a deluge and then slackened into a steady shower.

Isabel stood in her garden room, staring out the window. Sidney stepped quietly over the threshold and examined the elegant line of his wife's back, the soft sheen of her hair and the restless rustling of the sheet of vellum she held in her hand.

She remained a mystery to him. He supposed he had not expected to know all about his wife in six days, but he had expected to learn something.

Sidney exhaled slowly, considering what he *had* learned: Isabel favored strawberries and was a voracious reader. She loved her garden and chafed under the restrictions forced upon her by the weather. She was by turns prickly and flirtatious. Surprisingly, she had a sense of humor that came bubbling to the surface at odd moments. But she was obviously uneasy with him. He wondered if he had yet met the true Isabel.

"Can you see anything out that window?" he asked.

Isabel whirled around. "How long have you been there? I didn't hear…"

"I only just came in." Sidney advanced into the room and stood beside her.

For a moment, both stood silently, watching the curtain of rain obscuring the garden.

"Well, your garden should be happy with this weather, at any rate," Sidney said, glancing at Isabel.

"We have an invitation." Isabel lifted her left hand and displayed the note.

"Both of us? Curious." Sidney extended his hand and Isabel passed him the sheet.

"Ah, I see. Lady Broadribb, of course." Sidney handed the invitation back to Isabel. "Have you accepted?"

"No."

"Do you wish to go?"

Isabel shrugged.

Sidney could feel the muscle along his jaw jump. "I hoped," he said very slowly, "that we would use this time to get to know one another. You made it quite clear that you would not share your bed, but I don't understand why you refuse to share your thoughts."

Isabel turned from her contemplation of the weather and raised her head to meet his gaze. "Yes," she said. "I would like to attend."

* * *

Sidney leaned against the heavily ornamented column at the edge of Lady Broadribb's ballroom and longed to untie his cravat. The rain had finally given way to the kind of humidity that made summer in London anathema. The air was heavy and the streets rife with unpleasant odor. Lady Broadribb fought back by filling her ballroom with as many ponderously scented flowers as she could find. He imagined it was the kind of evening during which ladies fainted by the dozens.

He tried to imagine another set of circumstances under which he would have willingly attended this ball. Although Lord and Lady Broadribb were quite definitely *haute ton*, it was not the sort of event Sidney enjoyed attending nor, he suspected, were the Broadribbs precisely Isabel's great friends.

After six days immured in the townhouse with an

unwilling bride, Sidney was grateful that his wife wished to attend even though she had refused to give a reason. Perhaps the need to escape the confines of the house was reason enough.

Sidney's eyes narrowed as he watched Isabel hold court against the far wall. The moment they had entered the ballroom, she was besieged by a bevy of gentlemen. She was still surrounded. He could see her smile and imagined her graceful laugh as she responded to a tall, red-headed gentleman who's name Sidney couldn't recall.

Isabel had very politely introduced each one of the gentlemen to her new husband but he was damned if he could remember any one of their names. He shouldered himself away from the column. If he didn't find fresh air somewhere he was going to expire.

"What is it, Lady Ashby?" Archie Mendham leaned as close to Isabel as his considerable height would allow.

"That would be Mrs. Chamberlayne, Mendham." William Bathurst interrupted before Isabel could frame an answer. "Let us not forget our goddess has now a husband," he continued, flashing Isabel a conspiratorial wink.

Isabel felt herself color and thanked the gods of the weather that the heat of this oppressive night had already made her too flushed for the blush to be noticeable. She was growing annoyed that any mention of her new husband produced this unfortunate response.

"Your pardon, Mr. Mendham?" Isabel presented the ridiculously tall man at her side with her most flirtatious smile and almost immediately slid another glance across the ballroom. Where was Sidney? He had been holding up that column not a minute ago. She was determined to enjoy herself every bit as much as she was accustomed to do and she was equally determined that her dour husband should see her doing it.

"You keep looking around the room, Isabel. Are you expecting someone?" Mendham edged closer.

"See here, Mendham. I am sure she will want to see me." George Chiswick joined the small group around Isabel and carefully interposed himself between the lady and her admirer. "Take care that you don't crush Lady Ashby's lovely new gown."

"She's not Lady Ashby anymore," Mendham said sulkily as he moved toward the edge of the group.

"What is this? Married?" George Chiswick turned his handsome face toward Isabel and took her hand. "Have you gone and crushed my hopes?"

"She's married, Chiswick," Bathurst said. "Married Haddon's brother while you were off shooting. What became of Miss MacLean, by the way? Couldn't you get her to the altar?"

Chiswick turned his shoulder to Bathurst and took Isabel's other hand. "You didn't wait for me?"

Isabel clicked her tongue. "I had no intention of waiting for you, George, as you were well aware. And neither had my fortune."

"You wound me." Chiswick dropped one hand and tried to draw her toward him. "Now you must pay with a waltz."

The orchestra was, indeed, beginning a waltz. Isabel had always loved to dance and George Chiswick was an excellent partner. She found she didn't particularly care to dance with the fortune-hunting Adonis tonight, but he had her by the hand and was leading her to the floor.

The music started and Chiswick pulled Isabel close to his body. Closer than Isabel liked. She wriggled her shoulders and pulled back.

"Stop it, George."

Chiswick's grin was unrepentant. "You have broken my heart."

Isabel rolled her eyes. "I know you too well to believe that. It is your purse that needs mending, not your heart. But you well knew I wouldn't marry you."

Chiswick shrugged and swung Isabel into the dance.

"I had to try. One cannot live forever on good looks and dwindling credit. The money must come from somewhere. You and I would have rubbed along tolerably well."

"It's hardly worth discussing now. Why don't you go home and help make your father's estate profitable?"

Chiswick gave a short bark of bitter laughter. "Pry the pile out of Father's spendthrift hands? That's hardly likely this side of the grave. No. I must marry my fortune. It really is too bad you weren't willing. I'm only surprised it wasn't Caenby. I always thought you had your cap set for him."

Isabel looked around the ballroom. Everyone else seemed engaged in dance or flirtation. She smiled disingenuously up into Chiswick's face. "Have I mentioned that my husband is a soldier?" She asked sweetly. "Quite stalwart and rather... er... military."

"Haddon's brother?" Chiswick looked skeptical.

Isabel nodded toward Sidney, who had reappeared at the edge of the ballroom.

Chiswick glanced toward the gentleman and stepped back, regaining what Isabel felt was a respectable distance.

The circle of waiting gentleman had been augmented by at least two while Isabel was on the floor. As she moved back in their direction, she caught sight of the four or five gentlemen looking anxiously in her direction and, hesitating only a moment, spun around and walked in the opposite direction. She could not abide any more talk of her marriage, questions about why she had married Chamberlayne, sly allusions to the fact that she had not brought Caenby up to scratch and dreadful innuendo about her future. There must be something more entertaining in this place.

Sidney stood at the French windows leading out onto the terrace. He had returned from his tromp about the garden in time to witness his wife end her waltz with a well-favored gentleman and decline to return to her circle of courtiers.

Feeling well pleased that Isabel had eschewed her admirers, Sidney pushed off from the door jamb and moved in her direction. They had got themselves out of the house and had a small respite from each other. Surely it was time to go home.

Before Sidney could reach Isabel, she was intercepted by another man, one who had not been among the original group. Sidney frowned and slowed his steps, disappearing into the crowd around the edges of the ballroom.

The gentleman stopped directly in front of Isabel and, lifting her gloved hand, placed a lingering kiss on the knuckles.

"Look at that." Sidney could hear a feminine voice behind him.

"Shameless," another voice answered. "She is newly married, I hear. And she just finished a waltz with Chiswick. I can hardly credit he's still pursuing her now that her fortune has been claimed by someone else."

"I do not mean Lady Ashb... er... Mrs... Oh, who is the new husband?"

"Major Chamberlayne. Haddon's youngest brother," the second voice said.

Sidney winced at the sound of his name on strange lips.

"Well, I don't mean Mrs. Chamberlayne, then. She may be a bit too coquettish, but she has always been welcome among the *ton*. But what is Gosden doing here." The first voice dripped with distaste. "I cannot imagine he was invited."

"He is a baron, Amelia," voice two whispered. "And he is wealthy. I am certain Lady Broadribb would not refuse him."

"Yes, probably so. But look at him. He is shameless. Oh, I know he was part of Lady Ashby's little circle.

Another of her conquests. Isn't it enough that she led that fast crowd around by their noses, chased Caenby until he disappeared into the wilds of Lincolnshire and then somehow got herself married to Haddon's brother? Surely she does not mean to continue that... uh... association with Gosden."

The back of Sidney's neck prickled. Association? What had the man been to his wife? And what was he now?

"Is the husband here?" The whisper behind Sidney continued relentlessly. "I wonder what he thinks."

"I saw him earlier," the friend answered.

Sidney could hear the sound of rustling silk as the whisperer looked around. A stifled gasp followed by a sudden stillness told him she had found the husband.

This was almost unbearable. How could a man who had faced 60,000 French troops at Vitoria have such an overwhelming desire to flee the presence of two gossiping females? Sidney straightened his shoulders and turned to the tabbies.

"Were you looking for me?"

A gray-haired woman in puce satin grabbed her companion's arm and quickly turned the color of her gown. "N-n-no, sir...Major...Mr. Chamberlayne."

Her friend, younger and more composed, was, nevertheless, exceedingly pale. She patted the older woman's hand and looked directly at Sidney. "I beg you forgive us for our small-minded chatter," she said, looking chagrined. "There is no excuse for it."

"Very bravely said, ma'am." Sidney gave the woman as much of a bow as the crowded corner would permit. "And now I shall forget I heard it."

Sidney edged his way out of the crush and looked toward the spot in which he had last seen his wife. She wasn't there. The dancing had resumed and he searched the sets, looking for Isabel's tawny curls. Where had she gone?

Sidney felt a tentative tap on his shoulder and turned to find the lady to whom he had spoken not moments ago.

"They went out there," she said in a small voice, gesturing toward the French windows. Then she blushed violently and merged back into the crowd.

For just a moment, Sidney stood alone in the midst of the heated crowd. He put one hand to his face and massaged the bridge of his nose with his thumb and forefinger. Should he go look for Isabel? Right at this minute, he was dreadfully tempted to go home or perhaps straight back to his regiment.

* * *

"Very well. I am here. Now what do you want with me?" Isabel stood at the edge of the terrace with her hands on her hips, glaring at the man before her, a silhouette against the light from the ballroom.

"Don't you know, my girl?" Lord Gosden's velvety voice seemed to brush against her skin.

She repressed a shiver of revulsion. "I do not," she said, tersely. "And I expect that you will tell me and then allow me to return to the ballroom."

The baron approached Isabel, one hand outstretched. Her eyes never leaving the baron's, Isabel backed up until she arrived against the stone balustrade surrounding the terrace. Her hands went back to support her weight as she hit the coping. In a heartbeat, the baron was by her side, one hand on her arm.

Isabel frowned. Gosden had been part of Isabel's court when she was first married. Lord Ashby had been thirty-five years her senior and frequently infirm. He recognized the difficulty of the age difference and encouraged his new bride to engage in social discourse on her own. Isabel had found herself in what was probably known as a "fast crowd." She'd embraced the experience, finding the whirl exhilarating while striving to maintain decorum and not bring any opprobrium to her husband. Not any an easy balance, but she thought she was largely successful. Now, she regretted much of the time she'd spent dancing with rakes like the one who was currently accosting her.

Gosden, still gripping her arm, leaned down and put his lips close to her ear. "Now you are wed, my dear, perhaps you will consider my earlier proposition," he whispered.

Isabel twisted her arm free and glared at the man before her. "You are impertinent. I desire your *carte blanche* no more now than when I was a widow."

"Ah, but now you have a husband. And one, I hear, already busily engaged at Whitehall. Think of the opportunities spread before us." He drew the word *spread* out with salacious relish.

Isabel's expression hardened. "You do not have leave to speak to me thus, Lord Gosden. You never have and you never will," she said coldly, turning back toward the ballroom.

"Now, Isabel. Do not be like that."

"Mrs. Chamberlayne." Isabel turned once more toward the baron, feeling rather proud of the way she was handling this encounter.

"Is there some problem here?"

Gosden's head jerked up and Isabel whipped around to face her husband. *Drat!*

"Ah, Isabel. There you are." Sidney moved calmly to his wife's side. He gave the baron a perfunctory nod and returned his gaze to Isabel.

"Sidney," she said tightly. Why did he have to appear right at this moment? Another moment and she would have dispatched Gosden handily and returned to the ballroom. She could only imagine what he thought she was doing out here.

She did not quibble, however, when Sidney slid his

arm around her shoulders. "It's time to go home, my dear." His voice was unperturbed and oh so reassuring. As was the rock solid muscle of the arm that surrounded her.

"Yes, Sidney," she said, relieved to hear his reasonable tone. "I believe it is."

* * *

The silence inside the Chamberlayne carriage was as thick as the sultry summer night through which the sleek grey horses drew them.

Isabel burrowed into the corner, regretting her choice of leather for the seats. At this moment, however, not even the discomfort of her body against sticky upholstery would pry her away from her refuge and closer to her husband.

She peered at him beneath half-lowered eyelids. What was he thinking?

Isabel had leapt at the invitation to Lady Broadribb's ball. She might be married, but that was no reason to give up her life. And this was where her life was lived: in the ballrooms and drawing rooms, the gardens and parks of the *haute ton*.

Married.

She glanced again at the opposite corner of the carriage where her husband sat motionless except for the swaying of his body as the vehicle moved over the cobbled streets and around the corners.

Isabel turned her head to gaze out the window, letting her thoughts wander to the evening's events. Her doting cadre of admirers... Aside from Lord Caenby, what would her marriage alternatives truly have been?

Gad! Who were these men, then? George Chiswick? Handsome, surely, and interested. But he was more attracted to her purse than her person. He would have spilt her fortune at the gaming tables and in the brothels.

Archie, perhaps? Very attentive. She twitched. Too attentive. She could not turn around at one of these affairs without treading on the toes of the tall, gangly, red head. She could not imagine dodging him daily.

Isabel suppressed a giggle. Bathurst would more likely be interested in Sidney than in her.

Gosden! Isabel pulled away from the seat and leaned forward, pushing back her hair with both hands and seeking air. The contretemps on the terrace came back with a distressing immediacy. Isabel's skin crawled and she leaned forward to pull the curtain to the side, in search of a stray breeze.

* * *

"Isabel?" Sidney had been observing his wife through his own half-closed eyes. He had not yet decided whether or not he wanted to solve the mystery she presented. But he could not ignore her sudden lurch and her apparent distress.

He eased over to her side of the carriage and leaned forward. Tentatively, he took one of Isabel's hands and peered into her eyes. It was too dark to see anything.

"Are you ill?" Sidney rubbed his thumb over the back of Isabel's gloved hand. "Is there anything I can do?"

Isabel yanked her hand away and shook her head. "The heat," she finally said. "Nothing more."

"Indeed?" Sidney's gaze roamed Isabel's face seeking a better reason. It was obvious that something other than the heat threatened her peace of mind. "Indeed," he repeated, "it has been an oppressive evening."

Isabel's hands, back in her lap, clenched into tight fists and she turned quite deliberately to look out the window.

Sidney subsided against the seat and continued to examine his wife as she all but hung out the carriage window, inexplicably absorbed in their hazy progress through London's fetid streets.

"Is it that bad?" he finally asked.

"What?" Isabel looked around, her eyes wide.

"Are you miserable, Isabel? You know I did not mean to make you miserable."

Isabel sighed. "Let's not discuss it tonight. It's too hot and I am too... miserable."

Silently, Sidney reviewed the events of the evening: Isabel among her court, flirting energetically with three or four men at a time. The voices of the unknown women discussing Isabel's former conquests. The sight of Isabel pressed against the balustrade with Baron Gosden's hand on her shoulder.

"Do you want him?" he asked.

"Want who?" Isabel's voice rose in irritation.

"Gosden. Is he your next conquest or perhaps a previous one?"

"Pardon?" Surprise replaced irritation in Isabel's expression.

Sidney's lips tightened as he recalled the first time he saw Isabel. Or rather, did not see her, but felt her in his arms and on his lips. He had assumed the night in the Caenby library was an aberration and, later, had believed that she had undertaken the seduction as the means to marry Caenby. Was he wrong? Was she a hardened flirt?

Both his mother and brother had mentioned Isabel's reputation. Not that there were any actual incidents reported, but she did run with a fast crowd and obviously was still doing so.

"Do you plan to seduce Gosden?" Sidney's voice was harsh. "The way you tried to seduce Caenby? The way you seduced me? Is he next on your list?" Until he spoke, Sidney had not realized how angry the scene on the terrace had made him.

Isabel stiffened and gasped. "How... How dare you?" she said through her clenched jaw. "How dare you rush me into a marriage I did not want and then accuse me of planning to play you false? What do you know about me? About my plans, my desires, about what is in my heart? What do you understand about what you saw tonight?"

Isabel flung herself back into the far corner of the carriage and crossed her arms over her chest in the perfect image of defiance.

Biting the inside of his cheek to keep from speaking again, Sidney turned his attention to the window and the London night.

CHAPTER 8

Sidney had not even tried to sleep. He disrobed, donned his dressing gown and slumped into a comfortable chair in front of the fireplace. The weather was warm and there had not been a fire in days, perhaps longer, and the grate had not been cleaned. Sidney made a mental note to speak to Wharton. Then he reached for his book.

Minutes later, the book lay unopened on his lap and Sidney stared, unseeing, into the unlit fireplace. One by one, the events of the evening filed through his mind. In his own methodical way, he examined each one as it passed. The parade of gentleman flattering his wife brought him no comfort, nor did the overheard gossip about Isabel's past.

His wife of one week presumably lay in her chaste bed two doors away. She had looked beautiful tonight when she had descended the stairs, her satin gown, the color of moonlight, skimming her enticing body. She had been wrapped in pearls, imbuing the jewels with a sultry allure that never occurred when they graced the necks of debutantes. Sidney's body hardened at the memory.

"Damn." The muted curse disappeared into the darkened corners of his refuge. He rose from his chair and began to pace, his long strides covering the room in four or five steps. What did Isabel propose for this marriage? What did he? Why had he been so insistent that they marry? At this moment, the image of Isabel pinned against Lady Broadribb's balustrade with Lord

Gosden whispering in her ear drove all rational thought from his mind. She was his wife, damn it and she would know it.

Sidney was up and through the door to the small sitting room connecting his chamber to his wife's. He slammed his door behind him and stood for a moment facing the door to his wife's chamber. The heat of his anger propelled him through the door and up against the foot of Isabel's bed.

Isabel sat up, clutching the sheet to her breast and staring wide-eyed at the hand he had wrapped around the bed-post.

"Sidney?" Her voice was strained and barely audible.

Sidney tightened his grip and tried to remember why he was there. He took in deep draught of air and expelled it along with some of his anger. "We must talk."

"Now?" Isabel's voice had risen and taken on an edge of outrage. "In the middle of the night?"

"Now." Sidney came around the side of the bed, snatching up Isabel's dressing gown in passing, and pulled back the sheets. "Here?" he, "or in the sitting room?"

Isabel scrambled out of bed and snatched the dressing gown. "The sitting room," she said.

"I might have guessed." Sidney inhaled the womanly scent that was distinctly Isabel and gave a passing look of longing to the rumpled bed.

"Well?" Isabel had already taken a seat near the window in the small room that divided her bedroom from her husband's. "What is so important that I must be awakened to discuss it?"

Sidney stood stock still in the center of the room. Isabel's back was to the window and the hazy moonlight created a mesmerizing aureole around the gold curls spilling over her shoulders. She looked like a medieval saint until his glance moved to her expression.

Eyes narrowed, lips thinned, arms folded across her chest, Isabel's expression was anything but saintly. She looked angry. In fact, she looked furious.

"What," she repeated through her clenched jaw, "do you want?"

What did he want? Or rather, what did he want that Isabel might be willing to agree to? Sidney shook his head. "I want to know what was going on tonight on Lady Broadribb's terrace. I want to know whether you intend to honor this marriage. I want to know what you expect from me and what I should expect from you. I want to know if I should pack my bags and return to my regiment"

By the time he was done with this recital, Sidney's head was pounding and his fists were clenched.

"Do you mean to hit me?"

Sidney looked down in surprise and relaxed his hands. "I would *never* hit you, Mrs. Chamberlayne," he said quite deliberately. "You may rest assured on that account."

"And how am I to know that?" Isabel's eyes sparked.

"I am an honorable man." Didn't that go without saying?

"How am I to know anything about you?"

Sidney was nonplussed. He had never, ever, had this kind of a conversation with anyone. He talked about strategy and tactics. He talked about guns and horses. He never talked about marriage and feelings.

"I suppose," he said, shaking his head, "through continued acquaintance."

"Very well." Isabel shrugged. "Let's talk."

The silence stretched out for an uncomfortable length of time. Isabel stared at a portrait of the late baron's great-aunt on the far wall and finally said, "I must replace that with something cheerier."

"What?" Sidney followed his wife's gaze over his

shoulder. He did not know what he had expected her to say, but it certainly had not been about decorating.

A spurt of amusement leavened Sidney's anger. He pulled a chair opposite his wife, but remained standing, worrying his lower lip with his teeth, wondering how to proceed.

"Have you had an affair with Gosden?" He had never found subtlety particularly useful.

Isabel jerked upright in her chair. "How dare you?"

"I am your husband. I have the right to know."

Isabel shifted in her chair, her eyes never leaving his. "Men! Always concerned with their rights. Always exerting their authority. How would you feel in my place? Questioned about your every move. Tied in place to…"

"Yes?" Sidney's voice was deadly calm. "Tied to?"

"Tied to a husband you did not want," Isabel finished, her expression daring him to gainsay her.

"So." Sidney crossed his arms and looked down at his wife. "Is Gosden a husband you would have wanted?"

Isabel stood abruptly, nearly colliding with Sidney's considerable nose and glared up at him. "You—are—impossible," she said, punctuating each word with a poke at his chest. "If you had been the least bit perceptive tonight, you would have seen that Gosden is the last man to whom I would want to be wed, even did he not already have some poor mousy baroness stashed away in Gloucestershire."

"But what…?" Sidney was stunned by Isabel's unexpected rant.

"Exactly!" Isabel said. "Exactly what you should have done. Asked me 'what.' But, no. You must act like a man. Worse, like a soldier! Make an assumption and proceed as though it is correct. It is a miracle any of you came back from the Peninsula at all."

Isabel flopped back into the chair, breathing heavily,

her expression mutinous. Sidney lowered himself slowly into his own seat.

She was right. Sidney silently examined his wife. He had made an assumption about what he'd seen. But she was also wrong. That was not how he usually acted. He was a very logical and careful thinker. It was why he and most of his regiment returned from Spain. What was it about this particular, stubborn woman that made him forget how to think?

Sidney dropped his eyes and studied the pattern on his dressing gown. He suspected an apology was in order.

"Yes," he said after a long pause. "Yes, you are quite right. I shouldn't have assumed... the worst."

"No you should not have." Isabel looked as though she wanted to say more, but clamped her lips together and simply nodded.

"Is this marriage so repugnant to you?" Sidney asked suddenly, harking back to his wife's earlier statement about being tied to an unwanted husband.

Isabel sighed deeply and closed her eyes. "How can I tell?" she asked when she had opened them again. "We have been married a week and I have not known you for much longer. All I know is that we tiptoe around each other in this house and you seem to believe me a wanton. I wonder why you married me."

"It is a conundrum, is it not?" Sidney smiled a half-apologetic smile and stretched out his hand. "Shall we start afresh?"

Isabel hesitated and then put her hand in Sidney's.

His hard, calloused fingers closed around her soft, slender ones and Sidney started at the surge of desire that moved through him at the contact. Rising, he drew her from her seat and toward him.

Sidney could feel the hesitation in Isabel's body give way as she allowed herself to be pulled into his arms. He gently wrapped one arm around her waist and, with his other hand, tilted her chin so that he could look into her eyes.

Her cheeks were flushed and her amber gaze was unfocussed. Her soft lips were parted, but Sidney could not tell whether in indecision or invitation. If he had learned anything in the last hour, it was to ask if he had a question. "Isabel?"

Her attention sharpened and he could feel the tension return to her body as she became aware of her position. To hell with it. He wanted only one answer to this question.

Lowering his head, Sidney took her mouth in a kiss of raw desire. Surprisingly, Isabel did not pull away, but returned the kiss, tentatively at first and then with increasing passion, welcoming his tongue with hers and sliding her arms around his neck to bury her fingers in the over-long hair at the nape of his neck.

They stood in the middle of the room, surrounded by the detritus of Isabel's former life and the wash of pale moonlight and engaged in an ages-old battle. Strangers met on the field of passion. Hesitation fenced with urgency. Desire surged over doubt.

Sidney's hands moved over Isabel's body, sliding over the sweet curve of her waist and coming to rest high on her ribcage. Without breaking the kiss, he shifted his hands until they cupped both her breasts, resting his thumbs lightly against her nipples. Immediately, he felt the flesh harden beneath his thumbs and his body responded with a breathtaking rush of arousal.

He gently squeezed the soft mounds, running his hands repeatedly over Isabel's pliant body, dragging the delicate silk of her night rail over her heated skin, relishing her whispered moans. As Isabel's moans turned to soft cries, Sidney slid his hands to the equally inviting globes of her derriere. He kneaded the firm flesh and then pulled Isabel hard against him, easing the pounding of his body against her silk-clad skin.

"Isabel." Sidney broke the kiss long enough to breathe her name against her lips and then bent again to plunder her mouth.

"No!" Isabel tensed the moment she felt Sidney's erection against her stomach and now placed her palms against his chest and pushed. "No. I said you would not share my bed and I meant it."

Drawing a deep breath, Sidney dropped his hands and stepped back, reaching out at once to steady Isabel when she swayed at the sudden loss of contact. "So I recall," he said, his dry tone belied by his labored breath.

Isabel sank into the chair behind her and wrapped her arms around her body, shuddering slightly as the silk of her night rail slid over her still stiffened nipples. "I am sorry," she said in a small voice, running her hands up and down her arms. "I shouldn't have…"

"You shouldn't have responded to me?" Sidney gazed down at the slender fingers and pale arms. "I take it, then, that you made a conscious decision to… er… succumb to my kisses."

Isabel blushed and squirmed in her chair. "I don't believe that is an appropriate topic for conversation."

"Indeed?" Sydney raised an eyebrow. "I am no expert on these things, but I cannot but think that between husband and wife, such a topic might be quite acceptable."

Isabel's countenance froze. "I am for bed," she said, refusing Sidney's proffered hand to rise from her chair without assistance. Without a second glance, she swept into her chamber, closing the door behind her with a decisive click.

After Isabel left Sidney stood at the window for a long while and stared into the moonlit back garden. His wife was a puzzle. Cool and haughty one moment, heatedly passionate the next. Granted, he had married the cool and haughty Lady Ashby, but their rather unorthodox introduction in the Caenby library had hinted at the fire smoldering beneath her façade and their few subsequent encounters had done nothing to dispel that impression.

The niggling doubt that there was another remained. If not Gosden, then some other of her coterie. Was that why was she so determined to refuse his overtures? They were man and wife. They were both obviously attracted to each other. And there was no doubt that she was a passionate creature, no matter how much she might deny it.

Sidney turned and studied the door leading to his wife's bed chamber, wondering what she would do if he stormed it again. Might he catch the passionate Isabel and be invited to her bed? He still ached for the fulfillment her sinuous body had promised.

A sound like a moan emanated from behind the closed door. Sidney took one step forward, his hand outstretched toward the doorknob. He caught himself before he took another step and, hesitating for only a moment, spun on his heel and returned to his own room.

* * *

Isabel fell into bed and buried her face in her pillow. Her body still thrummed in the aftermath of Sidney's lovemaking. Why had she called a halt to it? Even now, she half-wished he would follow her in and fulfill the promise of his kisses.

The other half remembered that she had not asked for this marriage, that Sidney was not the husband she had sought and that she was furious with him for creating such havoc in her life.

She remembered the ignominy of the baron's attempts in the bedroom: the well-meant fumblings, the painful act, the embarrassing result, her repeated failure to produce the requisite heir.

But Sidney was certainly not the baron. She recalled

the sensation of Sidney's hands exploring her body and slid her own hands along the same path. No. He was not the Baron. Isabel sighed and rolled over, giving herself the pleasure she had refused to allow her husband to give her.

CHAPTER 9

Isabel dragged herself out of her warm cocoon of linen and sleep and squinted at the window. The curtains were still drawn and the room was dim. It must be too early for the maid. She sat up and slipped out of bed, padding across the room in her bare feet to fling open the apple green damask covering the windows. She blinked. The sun that hovered over the horizon was a pale disk, unlike the red haze of last night's sunset. Perhaps, the weather would be more tolerable today.

Had the sultry weather and interminable rain of the past week contributed to the uncomfortable beginning of her marriage? Surely even the most devoted of couples might irritate each other trapped in a townhouse during the dog days of London. How much worse was it for strangers, both uncertain of the wisdom of their alliance?

Isabel knelt on the window seat and peered down into her beloved garden. She remembered first entering this house as the bride of an aging baron. The garden had been thin and her hopes had been no less so. And yet she had made a comfortable life around the necessity of her marriage, giving her husband the respect that was his due, even if the memory of some of her obligations still set her teeth on edge.

Her garden thrived and so did she. Why then was she finding this new marriage so difficult? Granted, it was not quite so simple to ignore Sidney Chamberlayne. He was not a fading peer, sitting in his bookroom, drinking port and dreaming of his salad days.

Sidney was virile and vibrant. He filled the spacious townhouse to the very corners. During the week of rain, Isabel had longed to flee to the garden simply to find air she could breathe that was not saturated with the essence of her husband.

She could not ignore him. Did she want to? The memory of last night's encounter rose vividly in her mind and lingered. How could a man who made her so angry provoke such clamoring in her traitorous body? She snapped back into the present when her maid crept into the room with Isabel's tray. Isabel took a last look out the window and discovered her husband standing by the arbor in his shirtsleeves, a coffee cup in one hand and a sheet of paper in the other.

*　*　*

Sidney was surprised when Wharton placed a letter by his plate as soon as he sat down to breakfast. It had not occurred to him that he would receive post at Bruton Place. But, now that he had the letter in his hand, he felt rather silly in that expectation. He did not break the seal until he had finished eating, but turned to it immediately once the last bite of toast was in his mouth. Sidney recognized his mother's fine hand at once. He flattened the page and skimmed the contents. A last minute invitation. He folded it back up, picked up his coffee and strolled toward the garden.

Once the daily rain had abated, Sidney took a great deal of pleasure in a morning turn in the back garden. Today, he went directly to the arbor under which he had proposed to Isabel, set his coffee on a convenient ledge and took up his letter.

"Is it something interesting?" Isabel's voice floated through the sound of water tinkling in the small fountain.

Sidney swung around in time to see his wife, strolling down the path, dressed in a light summer muslin and looking particularly fresh and appealing. He shook his head. "I doubt you will think so. Will you join me?" He gestured toward the bench. "I believe the sun has banished most of the damp."

With a bright smile, Isabel lowered herself gracefully onto the seat. "Are you well this morning, Sidney?"

Sidney eyed Isabel with suspicion. This sunny lady did not seem very much like the one who had pushed him away and fled to her chamber last night. "What have you done with my wife?"

"What?"

"My wife. She looks a good deal like you, I'll admit, but she rarely smiles at me."

Isabel blushed. "Sit with me, Sidney and tell me what's in your letter. Not a message from a lady, I hope."

Sidney lowered himself to the bench beside his wife and opened the paper "Indeed it is from a lady," he said, handing it to Isabel. "It's from my mother."

"May I?" Without waiting for permission, Isabel took the missive and smoothed it out on her lap.

"Ah, an invitation. You are to escort Lady Haddon and Julia to Lady Cheever's rout?" She looked up at her husband who was still examining her with some doubt.

"Of course," he said. "I would not dream of denying my mother."

"No, you wouldn't. Would you?" Isabel contemplated Sidney's somber countenance. "You care very much for your mother and sister."

"Of course I do." Sidney was surprised that Isabel would find that fact noteworthy. "Do you go with me?"

Isabel turned the paper over and studied the direction. "It's addressed to you."

"You are my wife." Sidney leaned forward and stared into Isabel's amber eyes. "You *are* my wife," he repeated and took her hand.

Isabel dropped her gaze, but left her hand in his. "That doesn't mean I must live in your pocket."

"Nor does it mean you must seek your entertainment without me." He hesitated a moment and then raised her hand to his lips. "Join me, Isabel," he said, softly brushing his lips over her knuckles. "I would enjoy your company."

Isabel's gaze returned to Sidney's as if trying to ascertain the truth of his statement. "I'm promised to Mr. Mendham this evening."

"Indeed?" Sidney's voice rose a notch as did his color and he leaned back on the bench, observing his wife. "When was this… er… engagement arranged?"

"Archie sent a note yesterday afternoon."

"And you did not think to tell your husband?"

Isabel bridled. "It is not unusual. We have gone about together frequently over the past two years."

"You were not newly married over the past two years." Sidney released Isabel's hand and watched it slip back into her lap.

"There is no need for you to take that attitude, Sidney. In society, it is not at all unusual for husbands and wives to go about their own lives."

Sidney looked down at his now empty hand. "I am sure what you say is correct, but I cannot like it."

"Oh, you'll become accustomed to it." Although Isabel grimaced, Sidney thought he read something like a plea in her eyes.

"Very well. I'll not ask you to break a commitment — this time." Leaning forward again, Sidney examined Isabel's expression. She looked upset, but he was at a loss to determine the cause. Was it because he had expressed displeasure at her plans or had she hoped he would insist? He didn't ask.

"I shall inform my mother then," Sidney said. "And, if you do not object, tell Julia that you will take tea with her soon."

"Yes, please. I will be sorry not to see Lady Julia."

With a small sigh, Isabel turned her attention to the garden.

*   *   *

Sidney eyed the assemblage gathered round the sideboard on which the drinks were lavishly set forth. They were all there, even Gosden, gathered in a pack like the hunting dogs they resembled. Sidney wondered what they were doing at this genteel rout. They appeared rather ill at ease in Cheevers' drawing room.

Sidney had escorted his mother and sister and Lady Louisa to the rout, leaving Isabel to whatever entertainments she proposed to attend with Archie Mendham. They had been in the Cheevers' over-heated townhouse for more than an hour and Sidney had just managed to locate some chairs near an open window.

"Isabel!" Sidney, turned at the sound of his sister's voice and found her embracing his wife. He temporarily abandoned his attempt to forge a path to the window and glanced over at the pack still lingering in the corner. He knew it would not be long before they scented their quarry. Was it too much to hope that they would not claim his wife's attention? Sidney noticed that Isabel, engrossed in a whispered conversation with Julia, did not once look in their direction.

So, Isabel was here with the pack in pursuit. And he had brought Julia into their orbit. He watched carefully. Would they approach Isabel? Were they interested in his young sister? No good could come of this.

His observation was interrupted by a sharp tap on his arm. "Move aside, Major." Lady Louisa, eased by Sidney to greet her niece.

"How glad I am you are here, Isabel. I thought we would not see you tonight." Lady Louisa stepped back to look at Isabel and briefly glanced over her shoulder. "Oh dear. I believe you are about to be accosted."

* * *

Isabel looked up in time to see George Chiswick making his way through the crush thronging the Cheevers' expansive drawing room. She groaned under her breath. She imagined Sidney would not be happy to see any of these men and she was certainly did not relish the idea of introducing Sidney's family to them.

"Is something wrong?" Julia clutched Isabel's hand.

"No," Isabel said. "Just someone I would rather not see.

Isabel's wish was to remain unanswered. Like a lodestone, Chiswick made his way through the crowd to her side.

"Mr. Chiswick," she said, her tone flat. "I did not expect to see you here tonight."

"Isabel…"

Isabel frowned.

"Mrs. Chamberlayne, rather. I hoped to find you here."

"Indeed?" Isabel lifted a delicate eyebrow.

"Oh yes. These things are always so much more entertaining when you are present." Chiswick made a slight bow and glanced toward Julia. So that was the way the wind blew.

"Yes. Thank you." Isabel said, looking back toward Sidney who had gathered up his mother and Lady Louisa and was shepherding them toward a seat by the windows.

"May I have the honor of an introduction to your lovely companion?"

"You must excuse me, Mr. Chiswick. Mr. Chamberlayne and Lady Haddon are waiting for us." Taking Julia's arm firmly in hers, she led the way toward the far corner of the room where Sidney had finally found his mother as comfortable a chair as was to be had.

"Who was that?" Julia looked back over her shoulder at the attractive man who stood where they left him, a charming smile on his face.

"No one you should know." Isabel clenched her jaw, trying not to sound like Julia's mother. "Don't pout," she added, casting a quick glance at Lady Julia's face and giving up any hope of not behaving like a chaperone.

"But…" Julia regained control of her expression and turned her ingenuous smile on Isabel. "Won't you at least tell me who he is?"

"I will tell you later. But you must trust in me when I tell you if a particular gentleman will not do. Can you do that?" Isabel examined her sister-in-law. Her youthful beauty and guileless expression were entirely too appealing. She would be mobbed by suitors if the family was not careful.

"Yes." Julia nodded. "I will always take your advice, Isabel."

Isabel rolled her eyes. If only it were so. She glanced around the large room. The glow from scores of candles highlighted the gilded leaf on the carved columns and cornices, as well as the brocade wall covering. The deep red draperies tied back with gold cord added to the room's rich warmth, making the surroundings resemble a vizier's palace, except for the very English company crowding the expansive floor.

And, as Isabel well knew, among the crowd were many gentlemen with whom she wouldn't wish Sidney's innocent sister to become acquainted. She also knew that several of them were men with whom she had attended many an entertainment. She could feel the muscles in her neck tighten. She didn't like the realization that her former intimates were not people she felt comfortable introducing to her new family. What did that say about her?

*   *   *

Once his mother had taken the seat he'd procured for her, Sidney turned to find that his wife was no longer by his side. His expression darkened and he scanned the room in grim silence. He was preparing to plunge back into the mass of people to look for Isabel when she popped out of the crowd with Julia in tow.

"Where were you?" Sidney glared into Isabel's amber eyes.

"I was trying to evade George Chiswick," Isabel said between tightened lips. "It would have been easier if you had not marched ahead without us." She glowered at her husband.

"My apologies." Sidney said, glancing from Isabel to Julia. He should have taken greater care of his family.

"Accepted." Her nod was curt, but she seemed to recognize the sincerity in his apology.

Lady Louisa plumped down into the chair next to the countess and began plying her fan. "Something wet would be welcome, Major.".

"It would be my pleasure." Sidney bowed to the senior ladies and departed on his errand.

* * *

"Shall we take a turn about the room?" Julia was scanning the crowd, taking in the array of silks and satins, the rainbow of colors and the jewels glittering around every neck.

Isabel scanned the room as well, looking for trouble. She had attended enough of these affairs to know that there were more dangers than Chiswick lurking in the alcoves and on the darkened society's terraces.

"Very well," she said, slipping her arm through Julia's. "But let's go in this direction."

Unfortunately, Isabel's progress did not go unremarked. No sooner had she and Julia arrived at the other side of the crowded room than they were surrounded by a knot of gentlemen, including not only Isabel's usual hangers-on, but several younger gentlemen she knew only by reputation.

"Won't you introduce us to your lovely friend?" Not surprisingly, George Chiswick was the first to step forward.

Out of the corner of her eye, Isabel could see Julia blush and cursed herself for putting Lady Julia Chamberlayne in the position of being introduced to a fortune-hunter like Chiswick. Only her own association with the Earl's daughter would give such a man the excuse to seek an introduction.

And even worse, Isabel couldn't help but feel a twinge of residual jealousy that the gentlemen besieging her were here not for her attention but for Julia's.

Squaring her shoulders, Isabel proceeded to provide both introductions and protection. "Yes," she said. "Lady Julia, may I present…" and she named one after the other, dismissing those she did not know and refusing to give them a chance to be introduced by anyone else.

As she performed each introduction, she managed, in one way or another to impart the information that Lady Julia was above their touch.

At one point, she heard herself say, "Lady Julia's brother, the Earl of Haddon, you know, would never forgive me if I let the young lady out of my sight. Nor would her other brother, my husband Major Chamberlayne. You have heard, I am sure, of his volatile temper." She suppressed a small grimace at this prevarication and prayed that Sidney would understand the reason if this Banbury tale ever got back to him.

She was in the midst of assuring George Chiswick that Lady Julia would not be at home to him if he came to call at Haddon House when Sidney appeared at her side.

"Am I interrupting?" The gravelly voice murmured into her ear.

"Not at all." Isabel flashed a grateful smile and moved back to stand at Sidney's side. "Gentlemen, have you met my husband?"

As the group around Isabel and Julia nodded noncommittal greetings and melted back into the crowd, Isabel slipped her hand through her husband's arm and gave it a squeeze.

Sidney looked down on his wife, surprise evident in his gaze. "Are you all right, Isabel?"

"I'm glad to see you, Sidney. That is all."

Sidney looked puzzled. "I have been away from you but a quarter hour. And it would not have been that long had you not wandered off while I went for wine."

"Oh, that was my doing," Julia interjected. "Isabel would have been perfectly happy to stay with Mama and Lady Louisa, but I insisted."

"Never mind." Taking one last look at the gentlemen with whom she would have had previously spent the evening, Isabel shook her head dismissively. "Come, take us back where we belong."

Back with the rest of their party, Sidney handed a glass of wine to Isabel. "Where is the Honorable Archie Mendham?" he asked.

Isabel waved a careless hand toward the crowd. "In there somewhere, I imagine."

"I must admit, I am surprised to see you." Sidney said, scanning the crowd.

"But pleased?" Isabel shot her husband a wry smile. "I made Mr. Mendham bring me," she continued without waiting for an answer. "He was not particularly happy about it."

"I imagine not." raised his glass. "But, yes, I am pleased and so is Julia."

"Oh good heavens!"

"What is it?" Sidney cocked his head.

"Chiswick is talking to Julia. Drat his impudence." Isabel handed her glass to Sidney.

"Just a moment." Sidney put the glass down and grasped Isabel's arm. "Who is Chiswick?"

"Well, he's not Gosden, thank goodness. And he's of good family; his father is Viscount Oakhurst. But the whole family is pockets-to-let and he's the worst kind of fortune hunter. We mustn't let Julia spend any time with him." Isabel twisted out of Sidney's grasp without acknowledging his private smile as she started toward Julia and deftly extracted her and returned her to the safety of the family party.

CHAPTER 10

Isabel experienced a sense of comfort when she realized she would be returning to Bruton Place in the Haddon carriage. When Archie Mendham had insisted they attend the Cheevers' rout, Isabel had been surprised at first, but then relieved when she spied her husband and family. Leaving Archie happily regaling his friends with tales of his latest success at the gaming table, she hurried to join her husband. It was not so long ago when she would have stood beside Archie, smiling and laughing at his stories and yet, she thanked her stars she had a more agreeable option. Everything was different now. And a little confusing.

After several glasses of the Cheevers' abundant wine, the gentle rocking of the well-sprung town coach caused Isabel to fall into a fitful doze.

When the carriage halted, Isabel's eyes snapped open and she jerked her head from its comfortable position on her husband's shoulder.

"Oh." The syllable floated breathlessly into the darkened interior of the carriage. Isabel felt Sidney's hand slide from her shoulder and briefly mourned its loss.

"We're home," Sidney said in a low voice.

Home. Oh Lord. Home with Sidney Chamberlayne whose hard body felt so comforting in all the places it touched hers. Home with her husband whose presence was at this moment awakening a variety of interesting sensations.

Disoriented, Isabel looked quickly around the

carriage, her glance falling at once on Lady Louisa whose head nodded against the squabs of the seat opposite.

Isabel touched Louisa's hand. "Aunt... Aunt."

Lady Louisa opened her eyes a slit and glared at her niece. "Drat. I was enjoying that dream."

"Aunt, we are home."

"What?" Lady Louisa pulled herself upright and tugged back the curtain. "Your home," she said, settling back.

"Our home. You have been with the countess a week, aren't you ready to return?"

"M'things are still at Haddon House. I'll come later." Lady Louisa leaned forward, gave her niece a peck on the cheek, and curled back into the corner of the carriage.

Isabel's gaze swept the interior and came to rest on her husband. It was obvious that no one else was about to encourage Louisa to return to her bed on Bruton Place this night.

The Haddon footman opened the door and Sidney descended to the street and extended a hand. With a last word of thanks to the countess and an affectionate smile at Lady Julia, Isabel took the proffered hand and allowed her husband to usher her into their home.

The door closed behind them and Sidney nodded to Wharton and told him to go to bed.

"Good night, Walton," Isabel smiled at the butler.

"Do you do that intentionally?" Sidney took Isabel's shawl and placed it on a bench in the entry hall.

"Do what?" Isabel trailed Sidney into the garden room and settled into her accustomed chair, unbuttoning her kidskin gloves and peeling them off her arms with a sigh of relief. The night was warm and there was no fire, the only light from the moon and the candles still burning in their sconces. The recesses of the room looked jungle-like in the darkness.

Sidney sat beside Isabel and absently took up her hand. "Call Wharton by the wrong name," he said.

"Wharton? My butler? Do I do that?"

"You just called him Walton." Sidney examined his wife's white hand, running his thumb over the topaz set in the modest betrothal ring he had given her less than a month ago.

"Did I?" Isabel leaned her head against the back of the chair and gazed toward the garden. Her thoughts were still a bit muzzy from that last glass of wine. "I must remember to ask Wharton if it bothers him." Smiling, she closed her eyes.

Sidney, still in possession of her hand, stood and urged Isabel to her feet. "Shall we take a turn in the garden before we retire?"

The intense humidity that followed the long week of rain had abated and the night was soft and warm. Pale moonlight filtered through the laburnum turning the flowers into ghostly pendants. A light breeze moved along the top of the stone wall, ruffled the leaves of the pear trees and broadcast the scent of the late roses.

Her head swimming, Isabel experienced a sudden, intense urge to take off her clothes and bathe every one of her senses in the glorious summer night. Deciding that the impulse had as much to do with the wine she had drunk and the tantalizing proximity of her husband's exceedingly male body, she simply moved closer to Sidney, leaning her head against his shoulder.

The evening had been confusing. When Isabel left Bruton Place with Archie Mendham in his uncle's borrowed carriage, she recalled the many evenings spent in the company of Archie, Chiswick, Bathurst and others of the fashionable fribbles who populated her set. Of course, Caenby had been part of it then—she took a moment to wonder why—and that, she now realized, had made a difference.

Was she still pining after Caenby? Isabel snuggled

closer to Sidney and sighed softly as he slid an arm around her waist. No. He was simply the best of the lot and the one with a title. Isabel felt her face heat at this realization and was glad that the moon was not full upon the garden. She had acted the fool and where had it got her? She tilted her head and glanced up at Sidney.

He wasn't as handsome as the Earl of Caenby, or as rich, nor did he have a title or even an estate. But there was something very comforting about having his strong arm around her and something very provocative about leaning against his solid, vigorous body.

Isabel slipped her arm around Sidney's waist and leaned closer, inhaling deeply the scent of sandalwood and starched linen overlaid with the tangy aroma that was his alone. The scent of the summer night fled into the background and Isabel experienced a second impulse. This one also involved ripping off her clothes, but she had found a new stream in which to bathe.

"Mmmmm." A murmur of appreciation slipped from Isabel's lips.

Sidney's arm tightened about her and he looked down into her face.

Isabel reached up and, with one finger, outlined the groove that framed his mouth. "So harsh," she said. "Do you never smile?"

Sidney held Isabel's gaze with eyes so dark and compelling that, for a long moment, she forgot to breathe. Finally, Isabel tore her gaze from her husband's and scanned his face, settling on his mouth.

She moved her finger from its station along his cheek and ran it softly over his lips. Although they looked firm and forbidding, their surface was like silk. When Isabel's finger touched the seam between them, they parted slightly and Sidney's tongue darted out to taste her skin.

Intrigued, Isabel brazenly insinuated her finger a little farther into his mouth. Sidney welcomed the invasion and sucked lightly on her fingertip. The gentle suction sent a sensation streaking through Isabel. Suddenly, her breasts tingled and a liquid warmth bloomed between her thighs. She gasped and clutched Sidney's arm with her free hand.

Sidney nipped at Isabel's fingertip and slid both hands around her waist, turning her to face him. He raised a hand and slowly removed Isabel's finger from his mouth. Returning his hand to her waist, he pulled her to him.

Isabel closed her eyes and let her head fall back, concentrating all of her senses on her husband—the strong bite of his hands through her silk gown, the warmth of his breath, the ineffable scent of a man at the end of a long day, the smoothness of his lips contrasted with the rough growth of a face that had not been shaved in hours.

His lips! Sidney was kissing her and suddenly she wanted to kiss him back. Isabel slid her hands up Sidney's chest and around his neck. She buried her fingers in the thick, dark hair that curled over his collar and drew his head closer. Her lips parted and she flicked her tongue against his mouth.

Sidney groaned and released her waist only to ease his hands farther down her body to cup her buttocks. Seizing her bottom in his large hands, he shifted her body as close to his as possible and laid claim to her mouth, invading its silky depths with tongue and teeth, nipping at her lips and engaging her tongue in a warm, wet duel.

Isabel could feel her knees give way and welcomed the opportunity to press more tightly against her husband. Without breaking their kiss, she grasped Sidney's shoulders and wedged herself against his legs, finding purchase on one rock-hard thigh and noting, as she did so, that his thigh was not the only rock-hard portion of his anatomy.

Sidney's grip tightened and he hauled Isabel up against him so that her toes were barely touching the ground. "Do you mean to do this?" he growled.

Isabel could not think about what she meant to do.

She could only feel—feel Sidney's hands hot upon her bottom, feel his tongue teasing hers, feel the tips of her breasts, more sensitive than she could ever remember, crushed against Sidney's chest. And feel that point of contact where the juncture of her thighs, astride Sidney's satin-covered leg, throbbed with every breath she took. She tried to wriggle closer and the friction sent hot sensation rushing through her.

Winding her arms around Sidney's back, Isabel forced herself against his leg. Sidney increased the pressure of his hands, holding her hard against him as he plundered her mouth. Isabel clung tightly to her husband, returning his kisses with ravenous need.

Sidney shifted her body, lifting her higher and pressing her onto his thigh. He grasped her hips and rocked them in a gentle undulation. She broke the kiss to bury her head against his shoulder, trying to stifle a scream as the throbbing at her body's core escalated into unbearable tension and then spiraled to a place no man had ever taken her.

* * *

Ignoring his own unquenched passion, Sidney examined Isabel's bewildered face. "You bit me." His tone was vaguely amused.

"What?" Isabel's knees buckled and Sidney caught her up and carried her to the arbor bench.

He settled her on his lap before responding. "What?" he said. "Do you not know what? Have you never…? You're not a…? Surely not."

Isabel slapped weakly at his shoulder. "I am not a virgin," she said. "I was married for ten years. How ridiculous."

"Well…" Sidney was at once perplexed and gratified. Isabel had responded to his caresses as no woman had ever done. His body was still thrumming with the hunger his wife's avidity had evoked. But, her uninhibited response held a hint of wonder, as if passion was new to her.

"Yes?" Isabel yawned, dropping her head back on his shoulder.

"Well, when you…" Sidney could feel his face heat. Damnation! When was the last time a woman had made him blush? He must have been no more than fourteen. "When I…"

Isabel's body became a dead weight and a soft snore issued from between her well-kissed lips.

Sidney sighed, hefted his wife into a more manageable position and carried her to her room.

*   *   *

Sidney paced the floor for a long time after he had deposited Isabel on her bed and summoned her maid. She had left him in a rare state. He had not had a woman since he'd returned from Spain and, although he felt the usual urges associated with so long an abstinence, he had not, until tonight, been driven beyond those urges into pure lust. His wife had done that to him.

What was it about Isabel? Such a strange combination of the sensual and the innocent. When he first held her in his arms at Caenby Castle, he would have sworn she was a courtesan. She was all flirtation with a generous hint of things to come. And since—he could not deny her reluctance to marry, but there were moments when he thought they were coming to terms. And yet, she continued her flirtations with the set of useless bucks with whom she associated.

Tonight was raw with a sensual hunger, but he could have sworn that her release had taken her by surprise. At the memory of it, he became hard again and took his pacing to the cupboard to pour himself a sizeable portion of brandy.

After several miles and a second glass of brandy, Sidney finally climbed into his bed and fell asleep.

The dream was vivid, right down to the perfumed skin of the woman. She wore Isabel's scent and that was just fine with Sidney. For was it not Isabel who had wound him up to the point where he was seeking surcease in his sleep?

She was naked and, as she slid her body over his, her skin was as smooth as Devon cream. Sidney ran his hands over her plump breasts and murmured in appreciation. Her skin was warm and dewy and, when he slid his hand to the crux of her legs, he found that dewy as well. His dream woman straddled him and he groaned and eased himself into the welcoming warmth between her thighs.

"Sidney." On a sigh, his name issued from the lips of his dream. His eyes flew open and he found himself gazing up into the clear, amber eyes of his wife, in whom he was deeply imbedded.

Sidney wanted to ask what she was doing there, but could only think about how she felt above him—the soft curve of her stomach, the more emphatic curves of her enticing breasts, and, not least, the warm, welcoming concavity in which he was enclosed.

Isabel wound her arms around his back and her legs around his hips and covered his neck with the soft suction of open-mouthed kisses.

Sidney was beyond stopping, beyond speech, beyond thought. He slid his hands around his pliant wife and pulled her toward him as he thrust into her, slowly until she caught his rhythm and then more urgently, driving them both to the peak she had reached by herself in the garden.

Isabel rode him, her breath coming in ragged gasps, her fingers clutching his shoulders. Sidney drove deeply into her and then, as he had done in the garden, held perfectly still. This time, he could feel her inner muscles tense around him as the force of their joining produced the moment of exquisite equilibrium. He held her on the fulcrum for an eternity of seconds until the counterpoise shattered and Isabel fell into the sparkling pool of release. With a final thrust Sidney followed her.

Sidney rolled onto his side, pulling Isabel against his chest. She nuzzled his shoulder and drew an "S" on his chest with her finger.

Sidney placed a knuckle under Isabel's chin and raised her head so that he could see her eyes. "What are you doing here?"

Isabel blushed. Sidney was charmed but not deterred. "Well?"

Isabel sighed and drew another letter around one of Sidney's flat nipples.

"Do not try to distract me," Sidney said, thoroughly distracted.

Isabel looked up. "In the garden... Before I... ah... fell asleep..."

"Yes?"

"Well, I knew that you were..." Isabel ducked her head.

"Ah." Her meaning became clear.

"I told you I was not a virgin." Isabel gave a little shrug with one naked shoulder.

"That much is obvious." Sidney bent his head and placed a kiss on her shoulder. "But, if you do not mind, I would like to verify that once more."

CHAPTER 11

The morning breeze wafted birdsong and the heavy scent of her Gallica summer roses through the open window. Isabel stretched luxuriously. The offering precisely suited her mood.

"Hmmm." Isabel's feet met a sinewy leg. Her husband murmured and wrapped a warm arm around her pulling her flush against him. She snuggled her back against his solid chest and, for a moment, lay in contented abstraction, enjoying the sanctuary of her husband's arms and the musky scent that whispered the secrets of the night just passed.

"Oh!" Something stirred against her bottom and she was quite sure it was not Sidney's other hand.

"Indeed." Sidney's sleep-roughened voice hummed in her ear. Then, his lips slid away and nuzzled the delicate skin of her neck. Isabel arched her head back onto the cool linen of the pillow, presenting the entire length of her neck to her husband. He took full advantage and, before Isabel had caught her breath, she found herself on her back with her husband buried deep inside her.

Yes. This felt extraordinarily right. Isabel sighed in voluptuous surrender, riding the tide of pleasure to its conclusion and then burrowing back into Sidney's embrace for a lengthy nap.

Fulfilling. Had she been asked, that was how Isabel would have described the ensuing week. She wasn't asked. Lady Louisa, newly returned to Bruton Place, had taken to giving Isabel satisfied little smiles that seemed to indicate she had drawn her own conclusions. Fortunately, Isabel was too much in charity with the world to be properly annoyed by her aunt's complacent countenance.

Although Isabel looked forward to the nights with endless anticipation, the days held their own kind of pleasure.

Without intending to, Isabel found herself spending more and more time in her husband's company. When Sidney was not at Whitehall, he was with her. Rather than annoying her, as she had once thought it might, Sidney became a soothing presence in her day. He was not voluble, but his silences were comforting in their own way, particularly after the noise and confusion of her social life. Isabel had come to think of these small moments with Sidney as an oasis to which she might retreat when she needed calm.

The door to Isabel's morning room clicked open and Sidney poked his head in. "Would you care for a ride in the park?"

Isabel looked up from her household accounts and smiled. "Now?"

Sidney nodded toward the window. "It is a beautiful day and I'm not expected at Whitehall. I fancy a turn through Hyde Park with my wife."

He stopped and glanced at her writing table. "But if you are busy…"

Isabel put down her pen and closed her ledger. "Not at all. Pray give me a moment to change."

She rose from her desk and, passing close to Sidney in the doorway, trailed her hand lightly over his sleeve.

The day was mild despite the strong sunlight of midsummer. Carefully outfitted in her new Devonshire brown habit and matching hat, Isabel maneuvered her mare alongside her husband's strapping chestnut gelding.

In silence, they rode into the park and continued for several minutes. It was not yet the fashionable hour and they were only stopped three or four times to exchange greetings.

When they reached a stand of trees near the Serpentine, Sidney pulled his horse up. "Shall we stroll?"

Isabel answered with a nod and Sidney slid from his saddle and tossed his reins to the groom.

She lifted her leg over the pommel as Sidney grasped her waist and plucked her from the saddle. A tiny frisson of pleasure ran through Isabel at her husband's touch. She put her hands on his shoulders and managed to slide to the ground nearly flush against his body.

Isabel saw his eyes flash in answering awareness of the spark between them before he stepped back and offered her his arm.

Sidney led them toward the lake, maintaining a leisurely pace and humming softly to himself. Isabel strolled easily at his side, her hand comfortably tucked in his elbow. Turning her face up to the sun, she inhaled deeply.

"I believe I am missing the country."

Sidney looked down, surprise evident in his eyes. "Are you indeed?"

"You need not look so shocked, Major Chamberlayne," Isabel said with a cheeky grin. "I was born and raised in Hampshire. In my heart, the country girl still breathes."

Sidney raised an eyebrow. "Interesting." Sidney's tone was skeptical. "You seem very much at home in the city."

"Do I?" Isabel frowned. "Yes, I suppose I do." She shrugged. "On days like today I miss the country."

"Tell me about your childhood, then," Sidney asked. "It seems there is much I don't know about you."

"Oh." Isabel continued walking, her eyes on the lake in the distance. "There is not much to tell. I am the only daughter of a country squire. I lived quietly in Alresford until I married and then I lived quietly outside Basingstoke except for the occasional visit to London."

"But…" Sidney looked puzzled.

"You must stop looking so surprised," Isabel said, giving Sidney a tap on his wrist with her free hand. She sighed and looked away. "Shall I ask the question, you're thinking of then? Why was I living such a… ramshackle existence when you met me?

"There is no reason to look so chagrinned," she continued. "I know how I am seen among the *ton*."

She stopped speaking and gazed into the trees for what seemed like a long while before she spoke again. "I really don't know why I chose that path, Sidney. I truly don't. Perhaps it was because I had been immured with the baron for so long that I thought I must make up for lost time. Perhaps it was not."

Memories of the years since Lord Ashby's death flooded through Isabel's mind in a series of tableaux. Each scene held an element of desperation. She seemed to be on a perpetual quest for the thing that would make her happy.

Isabel leaned her head against Sidney's shoulder. Had she been searching for a tall, quiet man with a deep streak of honor all along?

As if sensing her mood, Sidney released her hand and wrapped an arm around her shoulders. Isabel hesitated and then slid her arm around his waist and they walked on in silence.

"Shall we sit?" Sidney gestured toward a stone bench at the water's edge.

Isabel looked out over the lake. The smooth surface was broken only by a few boats bearing what she took to be courting couples. The stone bench had been warmed by the sun and Isabel was further warmed by the proximity of her husband.

Once they were seated, Sidney dropped his arm and

lapsed into silence. Isabel wondered if he had found her story distasteful.

"What about your childhood, Sidney?" She asked, finally. "You never talk about your family."

"It was a happy one, I suppose." Sidney shifted a bit and Isabel wondered if he would put his arm around her again.

"I have an excellent mother and got along well enough with my father and older brothers. I'm sure it was a childhood like many other boys." Sidney had not moved his arm and Isabel read tension in the set of his mouth. Was it the memory of his childhood that made him uneasy or was it the proximity of his wife?

"Brothers?" Isabel could only recall meeting the earl.

"Yes. Thomas is in the church. He and his wife and sons are happily ensconced in their vicarage."

"And Julia?" Sidney had not mentioned his sister.

Isabel could hear the smile in her husband's voice and sense the easing of his posture. "Ah, well, Julia is something special. I remember the day my mother first put her in my arms. I was only ten years old, but I knew I had received an extraordinary gift."

Isabel could feel her eyes fill at Sidney's admission of affection. She blinked her tears away and changed the topic.

"Did you always want to be a soldier?" She asked, imagining a young Sidney setting up lines of lead infantry in his nursery.

"It was what I was expected to do."

Isabel raised her head and twisted slightly to look up at Sidney. "Do you always do what is expected?"

Sidney was quiet for a moment, as if considering his answer. "I do what I think is right," he said finally.

"That is why you married me." Isabel could feel the warmth draining out of the afternoon.

"Yes," Sidney said, "it was. But that is not why am still here." He placed one finger under her chin and turned her face back to his. "I'm still here because I have discovered that I like surprises."

* * *

Sidney, Isabel, and Lady Louisa clustered around one end of the table in the formal dining room for the family dinner that had become a familiar part of the day.

"So, Haddon will take you to the fireworks display?" Sidney had been relieved when Isabel accepted his mother's invitation to view the fireworks in Green Park. She genuinely wanted to see them and he found the spectacle a deal too much like the real thing. A week ago, he might not have objected to her attending with Mendham or Chiswick, but things were different enough that he was gratified with her choice.

"Yes." Isabel's response was distracted and Sidney followed her gaze down the long expanse of polished mahogany toward the head of the table. A bowl of deep crimson Portland roses sat halfway down the table, their large blossoms reflected in the gleam of the wood.

"We should eat at the other end of the table," she said. "It would save the servants so much time."

Sidney looked up from his fish as the conversation veered into domestic arrangements.

His wife raised her face toward the fading light, her gaze lingering on his. Sidney noticed for the first time that the amber of her eyes was flecked with browns and golds. How astonishing that he had not seen that before. He forgot the subject of the conversation.

The clattering of Lady Louisa's fork against her plate recalled her dinner partners to their surroundings. "Haddon will call for Isabel tomorrow evening," she said.

"Have you chipped that plate, Aunt?" Isabel craned forward to examine the delicate Wedgwood onto which Louisa had dropped her fork.

"I have not chipped the plate, girl. I was merely trying to remind you two that you are in the dining room, not the boudoir." Louisa sighed extravagantly and reclaimed her fork.

"Nonsense." Isabel blushed and Sidney could feel his own face heat.

"Well..." Lady Louisa forked up a portion of the flaky fish and kept talking. "The major asked if you had an escort for tomorrow and you were obviously in some other part of the house. And looking at you two, I had very little trouble guessing which part of the house it was." She popped the fish into her mouth and smirked at her niece.

Sidney sat back to allow the footman to remove his plate, then watched the man trek down to the far end of the room where the door led to the servants' hall. Isabel had a point about the seating arrangements.

"Are you not going as well Lady Louisa?" Sidney raised an inquiring eyebrow.

"Go to a damp park, stand packed cheek by jowl with heaven-knows-who and be assaulted by loud noises? Hmmmm..." Lady Louisa tapped her cheek with one finger as if contemplating the possibility. "No," she said crisply, "I shall not be at Green Park. I have an engagement elsewhere."

Sidney turned a concerned expression on his wife. "Who else is accompanying you?"

"Besides Lord Haddon, you mean? Should he not be sufficient?" Isabel took a small sip of her wine and placed the crystal glass back on the table. "Is there some problem?"

He shrugged. "There is no problem. I feel certain you will enjoy the evening."

"Go to your club, Major, and enjoy an evening with the gentlemen. You must be longing for a respite," Lady Louisa said with a cheeky grin.

"I have no club," Sidney said. He looked down at his

plate, wondering how he really felt about Isabel attending a social event without him now that their marriage had truly begun.

"Well get yourself one, boy. You're the brother of an earl, for heaven's sake. Go find a club. You cannot sit around this house forever."

"You might still come with us." Isabel said, her smile an invitation in itself.

Lady Louisa groaned and rolled her eyes. "I will be in the drawing room." She scrutinized the couple still at the table. "That is if you are not too tired to take tea."

CHAPTER 12

Rather than take Lady Louisa's advice that he go to a club, Sidney elected to spend the evening behind his desk at Whitehall.

He had constructed a job for himself, processing paper flowing between the Foreign Office and Vienna, where the congress was to be held to set the future boundaries of the continent in the wake of Bonaparte's defeat. It was, for the most part, excruciatingly dull. But, he had recently begun to notice indications that there might be a problem.

Although, he had yet found nothing explicit, Sidney had pieced together a picture of a group of men working to restore the Corsican to the French throne. And they appeared to have agents in London.

Sidney examined the latest dispatch. It contained a copy of a message that had been intercepted in Vienna and was marked as having originated in London. He read it again. The sender was not a military man and, quite likely, not even in government. He was most probably an errand boy, useful to the conspirators for his ability to move about London unremarked.

Who was he? Sidney had taken his surmises to his superiors and had been gratified when they authorized him to pursue the investigation. This was much to be preferred to the interminable sifting of papers that constituted most of his days.

Sidney pulled out a sheet of foolscap and began a list, starting with the names and places that appeared in the dispatches. Then he continued with a list of all the names he could recall from his recent forays into the drawing rooms of London's elite.

Sidney dropped his quill and looked at the list. What had caused him to start with the *ton?* Surely illicit money was more apt to change hands at the level of society he rarely frequented. He skimmed the list one more time. But, conspiracy was a pursuit of the privileged, wasn't it? Perhaps it was just a feeling.

The list was growing quite long and he was certain he hadn't even skimmed the surface of possible conspirators among the *ton.* And he didn't know London well enough to guess who they were. Sidney sighed deeply and pushed back from his desk. He would need more evidence than this.

However, he hadn't succeeded in the army by giving up. He retrieved his pen and began the tedious process of cross-checking what he did know.

The clock struck eleven. Sidney began clearing his desk. Isabel would likely return from the fireworks display soon. He folded the intercepted message and locked it securely in his desk.

*   *   *

Isabel could not remember when she had last seen the Earl of Haddon. She thought it must have been last season. The earl had not attended her wedding, but Sidney had never said why and Isabel thought it best not to ask.

Now, as she stood next to him in the crowd milling around Green Park, she realized that he had not come because he disapproved of her wedding his brother. And she recognized that the earl hadn't changed his mind.

His demeanor had been stiff and perfectly correct from the moment he took her up into his carriage with his sister and mother, but his countenance bespoke disdain. In her wilder days, when she had flirted outrageously with any handsome man thrown in her path, when she had so vigorously pursued the Earl of Caenby, when her actions seemed not to matter, she would not have given a fig for how Lord Haddon saw her.

So, Sidney's brother had no use for her. Perhaps she should show him just how fast a woman his brother had married. As Isabel looked about, hoping to find someone with whom to flirt, Julia came up beside her and took her arm. No, that wouldn't do. She would not expose Julia to such behavior. Isabel abandoned her thoughts of revolt and, smiling warmly at Sidney's sister, moved off in the wake of the earl.

As she had expected, Lord Haddon had arranged for a good site from which to view the festivities and Isabel was relieved not to have to stand in the dense crowd.

Isabel listened idly as Julia chattered about the show they were to see, but her eyes were on the earl and his mother. As always, Lady Haddon was the height of elegance. Something about her caused the crowds to part before her. Isabel thought that it was her regal carriage and privileged air more than her, obviously dear, satin cloak.

Beside the countess, the earl looked remarkably unprepossessing. Mentally, Isabel compared the earl to her absent husband. As she watched Haddon's stocky figure, accompany his mother's graceful progress, she wondered that her tall, hawk-like husband should have such a sparrow of a brother.

"Are you paying attention?" Julia squeezed Isabel's arm.

"Your pardon, Julia." Julia pulled Isabel's thoughts away from her husband and back to the present.

"I said, that handsome man is trying to call your attention." Julia nodded to her right.

In fact, two handsome men were shouldering their way through the crowd. Isabel had expected to see them and, indeed, at one time would have engaged in a flirtation with one or more of them. Now they were here, she wished they weren't. Julia didn't need any further exposure to the likes of them, nor did Isabel relish the censure of the Earl of Haddon.

"Lord. Not tonight."

Lord Haddon swung around. She had spoken too loudly and could have bitten her tongue.

"What is that, Mrs. Chamberlayne?" the earl asked.

Oh God. She hoped he hadn't seen the pair. She hoped he didn't know Chiswick.

"I was just regretting my husband's absence tonight, my lord." Isabel inhaled deeply, hoping that the earl would let this pass.

Lord Haddon glanced to his left in time to see Chiswick moving in their direction. He looked back at Isabel and raised an eyebrow. Both her hopes dashed. He had seen the men and obviously recognized one or both of them. Her remaining hope was to attain their box before they could accost her.

"Shall we proceed, my lord?" Isabel took up Julia's arm once again and stepped forward.

The countess, who had been inspecting the crowd, turned back and urged her son on.

The two men intercepted the party just as they reached their destination, Chiswick in the lead. Isabel's last hope vanished.

"Lord Haddon." Chiswick performed the appropriate bow.

Haddon nodded. "Chiswick. Hadn't expected to find you here, tonight."

"Hmmmm. Perhaps. But the entire country is celebrating the peace and I could not bear not to have my share." Chiswick slid a sly glance at Isabel.

"Very commendable." The earl glanced around. Isabel could not decide whether or not he was oblivious to her distress. "Join us. Plenty of room."

Isabel shook her head at the earl, a shiver of distaste running through her.

"We would be honored." Will Bathurst extracted himself from the crowd and bowed to the earl.

"Oh." Haddon looked startled, but recovered quickly. "Yes," he said, looking over the second man, and then frowning at Isabel as if she were to blame for this incursion. She tended to agree that she might be.

By the end of fifteen minutes of fireworks the park smelled of sulphur and camphor. Isabel admired the brilliant display of light against the night sky but wondered how anyone could bear the noise over a protracted period. She was relieved when the display stopped for an interval.

Lord Haddon took his mother and sister on each arm and led them off to stroll around the gardens until the fireworks resumed. Bathurst and Chiswick took themselves to some unspecified destination. Isabel elected to stay in the box, cherishing the few moments alone. Minutes passed during which the smell of the fireworks dissipated and Isabel soaked in the relative quiet of hundreds of people talking and laughing.

The soothing murmur of the crowd was suddenly punctuated by a giggle that had become familiar to Isabel since her marriage. She lifted her head, expecting to see Lord Haddon returning with his party. Peering into the darkness, Isabel picked out Julia under a tree with a man who was definitely not Lord Haddon. Squinting, Isabel recognized Chiswick. Great heavens! Where was the earl and his mother? How could this have occurred?

Isabel whirled around and fairly ran out of the box. In five strides she had crossed to the tree, ignoring the dew soaking her evening slippers. In another thirty seconds she had inserted herself between George Chiswick and Lady Julia.

"Julia, I did not realize you had returned." Isabel

turned her back to Chiswick and faced Julia. Her expression reflected utter disapproval of finding Sidney's sister in such company.

Julia ignored the implicit criticism in Isabel's expression. "There you are, Isabel. Mr. Chiswick offered to escort me back to our box. Was that not kind of him?"

"Indeed," Isabel said, grimly. "Perhaps you can explain to me then, why you are not *in* the box."

"I believe I can do that," Chiswick interrupted, moving out to the side where he could see both women. "Lady Julia... hmmm... needed to stop and catch her breath." He winked at the younger woman. "And how could I deny this lovely face anything it requested?"

Julia gave the gentleman a playful slap on the wrist. "What nonsense. You were the one who suggested we stop here so as not to bother Isabel."

"Well, perhaps I did, but who could blame me?" Chiswick winked again.

"Go to the box, Julia. We will speak later." Isabel gave the younger woman a small push and Julia flounced off.

"Jealous, my dear?" George Chiswick's eyebrow quirked upward.

Isabel ignored the question. "Let me make myself completely clear, sir. You will stay away from Lady Julia from now on."

"Will I indeed? I hardly think you are in a position to dictate my activities, my dear Mrs. Chamberlayne." Chiswick ran a finger along Isabel's jaw line. "You forfeited that opportunity when you wed the soldier."

He shifted again so that he was only inches from Isabel. His benign smile was belied by the intent Isabel read in his eyes.

"She is not for you, Chiswick." Isabel put her hands on her hips and hardened her gaze.

Chiswick's handsome face assumed a cold smile. "My very dear lady, surely you know me well enough to realize that ultimatums are not nearly so effective as reward. Pray tell, what will be my reward if I do as you request?"

"You will have the reward of having done the proper thing," Isabel said.

"Oh no," Chiswick answered, his hand alighting on Isabel's arm. "I rarely find that rewarding. And at the moment I fear that I am only interested in one kind of reward."

Isabel's eyes widened and she took a step backward.

"Oh. Did you think I meant your charming person? No, my dear. As lovely as you are, you are no longer in the position to put blunt in my pockets. I do regret it, however." Chiswick's smile broadened and he ran his hand provocatively up Isabel's arm to her shoulder.

"This is interesting." The Earl of Haddon's voice sounded from Isabel's left. Her heart sank and her stomach clenched. Disregarding the possible damage to her gown, she tore herself out of Chiswick's grasp and whirled to face the earl. "My lord, I... you..." The earl's brown eyes, so like Sidney's but lacking the glint of humor, were narrowed in appraisal. Isabel shut her mouth with a snap and marched toward the box. She could tell from the earl's expression that it was useless to explain.

The party was uncommonly quiet for the rest of the evening. No one spoke either of the incident or of anything else. Without saying a word, Julia managed to communicate that she was exceedingly displeased with Isabel. Every time she turned around, Isabel found the earl staring at her, his gaze cold and assessing. The countess simply looked confused by the sudden silence.

The entertainment ended and, as the Haddon party left the box, Julia took her mother's arm and moved ahead, leaving Isabel with the earl. Her stomach immediately developed a severe case of knots.

The earl offered his arm and Isabel simply shook her head, leaving her own arms stiffly at her side.

"My dear sister," the earl said, reaching down to take Isabel's hand and tuck it into the crook of his arm. "Do not say you have taken a disgust of me. Certainly that would be too ironic for words."

"I beg your pardon?" Isabel could feel her blood pounding in her ears and knew that her face must be redder than her Portland roses. She could hardly believe that Sidney's brother would make such a comment without bothering to learn the truth of what he had seen.

"No need to do that, my dear. I believe it is my brother's pardon you must beg."

Isabel tried to pull her hand away, but Haddon tightened his grip and kept her close to his side.

"Do you not want to know what happened with Mr. Chiswick?" she asked.

"I have eyes, Mrs. Chamberlayne, and am quite capable of understanding what I see."

"Appearances may be other than what they seem," Isabel said quietly, her gaze fixed on the backs of Lady Julia and the countess, several feet in front of her.

"Oh come now." The earl spoke as if to a child caught in a lie. "I know your reputation. You were out for a title and settled for the brother of one. You have no scruples. Why should I not believe that you arranged an assignation with Mr. Chiswick?"

Isabel was silent. It was plain the earl had taken her in dislike. It was useless to try to explain the event he had witnessed. She made the rest of the journey to the carriage without uttering a word, biting back tears of anger. As she waited while he handed in his mother and sister, she prayed that other members of his family would not be so quick to judge.

* * *

As he rode up Whitehall toward Charing Cross, Sidney wondered if Lady Louisa was right. Perhaps he should join a club. He tried to imagine himself spending his evenings like the one just past.

Would he spend the rest of his life poring over papers in a dingy office while his wife flitted about town in the company of the loose fish who had previously formed her court? Would a club be any better?

Unsettled by his thoughts, Sidney climbed the stairs to his own chamber, climbed into bed and blew out the candles. Sleep didn't come, nor did he expect it to. His mind reeled with questions about his marriage and his future.

He had heard a certain amount of talk when he returned to London from Lincolnshire. Isabel's two years of widowhood had not been spent in sedate retirement, and it was well known that she wanted to marry the Earl of Caenby. But, no one had ever produced a bit of evidence that Isabel had compromised herself during those two years.

Oh Lord! Sidney sat up and pummeled his pillow so vigorously that feathers flew. Of course she had compromised herself and with intent. As he was here to testify. He flung the pillow across the room. Then, disgusted with himself, scrambled out of bed to retrieve it.

Plumping the pillow with a bit more care, Sidney considered what had unsettled him most about the evening. Reluctantly, he admitted that it might be the image of himself behind a desk, day after day, essentially living on his wife's fortune, allowing Isabel to live a life apart from him. No. A life without an active occupation would drive him mad. And Isabel had already made inroads on his sanity.

After an eon of fruitless musing, Sidney was distracted by the sound of footsteps behind the far door. He thought he could hear the rustle of Isabel's silk dressing gown as she moved about the little room. And, staring into the gloom of his bed hangings, he thought he could smell the jasmine of her perfume and picture her dark gold curls, unbound and cascading down her back.

His body became immediately alert. The longing to gather Isabel in his arms and part the painted silk of her dressing gown overwhelmed him. The image of Isabel padding around in her dressing gown was quickly replaced by one of Isabel naked, body aglow with the effects of vigorous coupling. Only prodigious effort kept him abed. He did not wish to go to Isabel tonight, while his mind was in conflict with his body.

* * *

As Willington removed the pins from Isabel's curls and began the gentle brushing that always soothed her, Isabel's gaze strayed to the closed door separating her room from her husband's. This was the first time in over a week she had not found him in her bed or been invited to his. Her heart fell at this indication that her honeymoon had reached its end.

As soon Isabel heard her maid close the door softly behind her, she shrugged into her dressing gown. For a long moment she stared at the door to the small sitting room that stood between her chamber and her husband's. Was Sidney in it or was he abed?

Finally, Isabel turned the knob and entered. She hesitated on the threshold, allowing her eyes to grow accustomed to the dark. Sidney wasn't here.

She peered at the door on the far side of the room. No sound issued from behind it and no light appeared under it. If her husband was at home, he was asleep. She wondered why she had not thought to ask Wharton when she entered the house. Isabel smiled a private smile. Sidney would be pleased she had remembered her butler's name.

Isabel longed to open the door and crawl into her husband's bed. The events of the evening had been distressing. What promised to be vastly entertaining had turned into a disaster.

Julia was obviously vexed with her, and Sidney's brother believed her the worst kind of flirt. Only the countess had bid her a kind good night. But Isabel did not doubt that Lady Haddon would soon be informed of her new daughter's flaunting of propriety.

Isabel felt Sidney would comfort her if only she walked into that room and sought his arms. She reached for the door.

Why was he in his bed? Some doubt stopped Isabel from touching the latch. In truth, despite the delicious nights spent in his arms, her husband was, in many ways, a stranger to her. With a pang of regret, Isabel retracted her hand and retreated to her own, cold bed.

As Isabel tossed, trying to find slumber, the memory of Lord Haddon's countenance when he found her with Chiswick kept running through her mind. There was little question that the earl was predisposed to doubt her. Would he tell Sidney? Should she?

CHAPTER 13

Sidney sat behind the desk in the Bruton Place library and turned the letter over in his hands. He had read it several times, wondering whether or not he was glad of the commission it contained. Wondering what he would do about it.

He folded it up and leaned back in his chair. In the weeks since his marriage, he had come to think of this desk, this room, perhaps this house, as his. The library displayed the style that pervaded the rest of the house—his wife's graceful choices. Every room reflected her tastes and every room was warm and welcoming.

But it was not his. Like every one of his possessions, other than his military gear and his beloved horse, the house was brought to the marriage by Isabel, a legacy from her first marriage and a painful reminder that he had nothing to contribute but his presence.

Lost in the miasma of passion that followed the beginning of his marriage, Sidney had had little inclination to consider what his life had become. But it was time to contemplate what he was meant to do. Although his job at Whitehall kept him busy and made him feel useful, he could not imagine a life of administrative duties.

He had always thought that the army would be his life, but the longer he spent away from it—the longer he spent with Isabel—the less anxious he was to return.

He looked down at the desk. The message lay by itself, a stark island of white in the center of an expanse of highly polished mahogany. He was a soldier. It had always been a simple answer and his place had always been dictated by duty. Suddenly, nothing was simple. Sidney picked up the letter and re-read it.

"Lord Haddon, sir." The butler appeared in the doorway and Sidney could see his brother behind him.

"Thank you, Wharton." Sidney rose from the desk and met the earl in the middle of the room.

"Just in time for tea," Sidney said, gesturing to the table before the fireplace. "Or perhaps a bit late. That pot has been cooling for a while. Well, the biscuits are still good. Will you have sherry?"

Lord Haddon accepted a glass from his brother and moved to the window that looked out onto the garden. "Lovely house," he said, absently.

"Yes. I was just thinking as much." Sidney crossed to stand beside his brother. He had half-expected to see Isabel in the garden, but it was empty save for two or three birds pecking at the grass.

"Was it worth it?"

"I beg your pardon?" Sidney swung around to look at his brother.

"Was it worth it?" the earl repeated.

"I am afraid I have no idea what you mean." Sidney was completely baffled by the question.

"This house, the fortune, whatever it is you derived from this travesty of a marriage. Do you think you have sold yourself for a reasonable price?"

Sidney felt as though his blood had frozen, beginning at the back of his neck it moved through his body like a glacier. He clenched his hands at his sides to still their trembling and walked very deliberately to the other side of the room lest he injure his brother.

Sidney stopped in front of the fireplace and stared down at the cold grate, willing the ice to leave his veins before he answered.

His brother remained at the window, looking supremely unaware of the effect of his words on Sidney. Or, looking as though he didn't care.

Sidney prolonged his silence until the earl was forced to turn from the window to face him. Once he had his brother's full attention, Sidney spoke very slowly and distinctly, the ice in his veins clearly manifesting itself in his tone.

"This marriage was not a financial transaction."

"Nonsense," the earl interrupted. "All marriages are financial transactions."

Sidney waved his hand, dismissively. "Yes, yes, very well, I suppose that's true. But I did not contract this one for material gain."

"That raises the question, then, of why exactly you did contract this marriage." The earl's flat drawl grated in Sidney's ear and he could feel his hands once again coiling into fists.

"I do not believe that is any of your business, Harold." Sidney raised an arm and laid it along the mantelpiece in a gesture he hoped looked nonchalant.

"I beg to differ, little brother. As head of the family, it is every bit my business."

This statement was so patently in concert with Harold's pomposity since he became earl that Sidney was momentarily distracted from his anger. Momentarily. His brother's next statement was like a match to tinder.

"Your wife is a slut."

Sidney pushed away from the mantelpiece and crossed the room in three long strides. By the time he reached his brother, the earl's color had completely drained from his face. This did not stop Sidney from taking him by the cravat and hoisting him against the window frame.

"I beg your pardon?" Sidney could hear himself speaking in the cadence of the battlefield, the cool, uninflected tone that caught and held a soldier's attention.

"Of course you do not want to hear that." Lord

Haddon reached up and pried his brother's fingers from his shirt front. "Do try not to act the soldier," he said. "It looks so uncivilized."

"I am a soldier, damn it." Sidney let his hands drop to his sides, but leaned forward, crowding his brother closer to the wall. "As you are about to find out unless you wish to apologize for maligning my wife."

The earl sidled away from Sidney. He straightened his jacket, adjusted his cuffs and turned back to the spot where Sidney was still seething.

"You are all bluster. How did you ever survive the Peninsula?"

Sidney scowled. "You are my brother, Harold, not my enemy. But I will not brook slander and I will not hesitate to punish it. The apology?"

"There is none," the earl stood still in the middle of the floor, his thickset frame braced for a blow and his chin jutting at a belligerent angle. "Your wife is engaged in at least one dalliance. For all I know, there may be more."

"You have come to tell me that you think my wife is unfaithful?" After seven years fighting Napoleon, Sidney finally realized what it meant to see red. His voice rang like cold steel and his brother flinched.

"Not at all, dear boy. I have come to tell you that I *know* your wife is unfaithful. I found her under a tree at Green Park with George Chiswick and, I might add, he had his hands all over her. I have come to ask you what you mean to do about it."

Sidney crossed the room once more and this time, grasped his brother firmly by his upper arm. "Here is what I mean to do," he said, propelling the earl toward the door. "I mean to eject you from—

"Sidney, I would…" Isabel stopped in the doorway, her eyes wide and her complexion blanching.

"Later, Isabel. I must see my brother out," Sidney said through gritted teeth. "Wait here." And he was gone, his brother levered before him like a puppet.

"Oh no." The whispered words slipped from Isabel's lips as she watched her husband frog march his brother toward the front door. This could only be about her, about the previous evening at Green Park, about Chiswick.

Feeling behind her, Isabel sank into the large chair at her back and wrapped her arms around herself. She should have come to Sidney right away. Now that he had the story from his brother, anything she might say would sound like an excuse. "Oh Lord." She closed her eyes and leaned her head against the brocaded back of the wing chair.

The door thumped and Isabel's eyes flew open. She stumbled up from her seat and stood, frozen with apprehension, staring at her husband.

Sidney's eyes were dark with an emotion Isabel could not identify. "Is there something you wish to say to me?"

Isabel reached back to steady herself against the chair, her mind awhirl. There is little doubt that Haddon had come to tell Sidney about the previous evening. And little doubt that Sidney was not happy about it. If only she had not gone to the fireworks. If only she had not run into Chiswick and his cronies. If only she had come to Sidney right away.

She straightened her back. No. She would not act the submissive wife. Sidney knew who she was when he insisted they marry. Why should he look like a thundercloud upon receiving word that she had been seen with one of her friends?

"Yes, Sidney. I have. But I'm obviously late." Isabel was proud of her cool delivery. Let Sidney think what he would. She would never be the wife he wanted and, for that, he had no one to blame but himself.

Sidney said nothing and the long silence seemed to fill the room, twining itself through the fading afternoon sun and tugging at Isabel's limbs. Suddenly enervated, she sank back into the chair and looked up at her taciturn husband.

Isabel broke the silence. Sticking her chin out, she said, "May I assume that Lord Haddon has come bearing tales about my behavior at Green Park?"

"You may." Sidney took one step forward and then continued past Isabel to the desk on the other side of the room. He sat on it, one lean hip propped up on the edge, one gleaming boot, swinging against the dark wood.

Isabel shifted in the chair, never taking her eyes from her husband. "Perhaps you should tell me what story the earl has told before I explain what happened."

"Perhaps you should tell me what happened." Sidney's voice was dead calm, and oh so cold. Isabel could not begin to fathom what he was thinking. She felt her face heat and cursed herself for allowing him to make her blush.

"I will not." Neither Sidney nor his pompous brother would force her to feel as though she had to defend herself when no defense was necessary. Had it not been for their sister, she would never have found herself alone with Chiswick in that cursed park.

"I see. Then I shall assume that you subscribe to the version of the incident that my brother told." Sidney's face was a mask of infuriating calm. How could he look so unemotional when Isabel's heart demanded either anger or justice?

"You may assume no such thing." In the back of her mind, Isabel knew her behavior was completely irrational, but the entire situation made her furious. She was in no mood for anything but a good fight.

"Very well." Although he spoke quietly, Sidney's expressionless voice seemed to fill the room, to wrap itself around Isabel like a tensile web. She felt bound and gagged by her anger and Sidney's flat, reasonable voice.

As if exploding from the bonds, Isabel rose from her

seat and stormed across the room toward Sidney, who slid his leg off the desk and stood at her approach.

Isabel intended to slap him and, if necessary, to continue slapping him until he showed some kind of emotion. At that moment, it made no difference what kind of emotion he exhibited as long as he reacted in some—human—manner. But when she reached her husband, slapping no longer seemed sufficient.

Raising both hands, Isabel launched herself at Sidney and shoved mightily against his broad chest. It was like hitting a wall. Stunned by the impact, Isabel stepped back and then flung herself back at the immovable object she had married.

This time, Sidney moved. But not as Isabel had expected. As she made contact with his hard wall of a chest, his arms came around her, pinning her hands between her own body and his and lifting her feet from the floor.

Isabel did what any self-respecting woman in a fury would do in such a situation. She kicked him for all she was worth, her flimsy slippers beating a fruitless tattoo against his gleaming Hessians.

Finally, finally, the odious man reacted. Finally, Isabel had provoked him to emotion. As he held her, squirming with pique against him, a lazy smile spread over his face, accentuating the deep grooves on each side of his mouth and warming the brown depths of his eyes.

Isabel's jaw dropped in astonishment and the next moment, Sidney's lips were upon hers, taking full advantage of her parted lips. He was kissing her!

Isabel made one more feeble kick against Sidney's shins and then, working her hands into position, grabbed the front of her husband's jacket and kissed him back.

She had never known a man as infuriating as this one, a man so hard to provoke, a man she understood less. She was simply glad that he had finally given her some kind of response. Wasn't she?

Sidney deepened the kiss and Isabel gave up wondering why she was kissing him back. The effort to think was too intrusive when all she wanted to concentrate on was the sensations his kiss was causing to course through her body.

Relaxing into her husband's powerful embrace, Isabel gave herself up to the voluptuous pleasure of his mouth. The hard kiss with which he had captured her lips had transformed into something more subtle, more seductive, as if he was no longer demanding her compliance, but luring her into complicity with the promise of what was to follow.

Sidney held Isabel against his body with an ease that made her feel nearly weightless. Her slippers had fallen off sometime during the kiss and the feeling of her stockinged feet gliding over her husband's boots sent yet another frisson through her body. She gasped slightly against Sidney's mouth.

Sidney slid his hands to her waist and, swinging around, sat her on the desk. He did not release her, but tightened his grasp as he nudged her thighs apart and stepped between her legs. He lowered his hands to her bottom and, placing a large palm against each hemisphere, edged her forward so that she was flush against him, painfully aware of the aroused state of his body.

They groaned as one, swallowing each other's sound as their mouths met in heated desire. Sidney's hand moved to Isabel's thigh and began inching her dress upward.

Isabel ripped her mouth from his and gazed into the endless cavern of his eyes. "Lock the door."

CHAPTER 14

Sidney slid out of his bed and turned to tuck the covers around his wife. Isabel slept the sleep of the sated, but Sidney had awakened with the first light and rose to the birds twittering outside his window. He padded across the floor to his dressing room and quietly closed the door behind him. He needed time to think and Isabel's proximity made that effort difficult.

Eschewing food, Sidney made for the mews behind the house where he found Chiron engrossed in his own breakfast. Sidney stroked the beast's shiny coat and decided that perhaps a walk was just what he needed. Striding past Berkley Square, Sidney headed toward Piccadilly. His mood demanded activity.

The streets were empty but for tradesmen beginning their day and gentlemen ending theirs. Sidney paid little heed to either, his head full of traitors… and of Isabel.

Nothing about his life in London had turned out as he'd expected. The end of the war had left him at loose ends. He had been meant for the army and, when he bought his first commission, it seemed a natural fit. He loved the camaraderie and took pride in the performance of his battalion. He did not like war—no sane man would —but he was good at it.

Then the war was over. He thanked God for it, but wondered what he would do now. He could not imagine himself in the militia nor did he care to cross any oceans to find adventure. The post at Whitehall had been a good stopgap; at least it gave him something to do other than pace the corridors of the house on Bruton Place and accompany the women in his life to social events.

But the moment the tedious paperwork revealed the presence of treason, the stopgap occupation became another way he could be useful. And he hoped that he might be good at this as well.

Sidney crossed Piccadilly, avoiding the carts disgorging goods in front of the shops and entered Green Park. He strode down the Queen's Walk, avoiding the ground scarred by the peace festivities and into a dense stand of ash. He stopped amid the trees and inhaled deeply. The pervasive scents of summer growth and moist loam overtook the more pungent smells of the London streets. Thank God for the men who thought of parks.

From this spot, he could only hear the muffled voices of people passing in the distance. Sidney considered finding a place to sit, but his body demanded activity and he kept walking, emerging eventually on the Mall near St. James Park.

Sidney shuddered at the sight of the burnt ruin of the Chinese pagoda spanning the canal. Thank heaven Isabel had been at the display in Green Park rather than here.

Isabel. Would that the puzzle of his wife was as straightforward as the hunt for traitors. His "marriage of honor" was not nearly as simple as he had thought it would be. When he offered marriage—indeed, insisted on it—his one idea had been to save the lady's reputation and establish an agreement whereby he might continue with his life while his wife continued hers.

When had that changed? If he closed his eyes, Sidney could still feel Isabel's soft curves snuggled against him, could smell the jasmine in her hair, could invoke her saucy smile when she teased him, her fiery temper when he angered her. No. Marriage to Isabel was a good deal more complicated than he had imagined.

This business of marriage, of women, of emotion, was completely foreign. He had no idea how to go about any of it. And yet, he could not stop himself from thinking about it. About Isabel.

They fought. Oh how they fought. And, oh how they reconciled. His wife was passionate in everything she did. Sidney flushed, thinking of last nigh—the argument in his office, followed by the interlude on his desk, followed by the interlude in his bedchamber.

Gazing over the canal, Sidney shook his head in befuddlement. Despite their rocky beginning, he quite liked his fiery wife. She met everything about life head-on and was not afraid to speak her mind. She had the kind of character he would value in a comrade in arms.

Everything about his marriage was so unexpected. He felt a strange compulsion to be with Isabel, to share his life with her. But, he held himself in reserve, unsure what he could trust.

Sidney rounded Duck Island and found himself at Whitehall. He stood stock still, stunned by the conjunction of ideas that had formed during his walk. Isabel, passionate and straightforward, had never made a secret of her objections to the marriage or of her expectation to maintain social engagements as she had before she married. She had never lied to him. Why should he think she would lie about what happened in the park? He shook his head at the vagaries of the human heart and turned his steps toward his office.

As had come to be the case, the corridor off which Sidney's office stood was deserted when he arrived. Did no one else in the ministry rise before ten? Sidney sifted through the papers on his desk and then pushed himself back. He was in no mood to work.

"Sir." The blond head of a junior clerk peered around the door jamb.

"Curtis." Sidney looked up from his desk, dragged from his thoughts by the arrival of the morning post. "What have we today?"

The young man advanced into the room and dropped a pile of correspondence on the desk. "Nothing pressing, sir, except for this." He fished a heavy packet off the top of the pile. "Colonel Peabody said to bring this to you straightaway when you arrived."

"Hmmm?" Sidney took the packet and dismissed the clerk with a nod.

Breaking the seal, Sidney removed an assortment of papers and spread them out on his desk. He sat back and surveyed the collection: fragments of letters, singed pieces of parchment, obviously fished out of a grate, bits of what appeared to be a list. Where had these come from? He picked up the packet and turned it over. Colonel Peabody's seal. The package must be the remnants that had been gathered during the raid on the Queen Street rooms yesterday. Sidney examined each document with care. His effort to unearth treason was so different from his life as a cavalryman, yet the endeavor had captured his imagination. He had found an occupation that seemed to suit him and at which he thought he might make a difference.

Scanning the list, he came upon a partial sketch of a seal. He lifted the paper and carried it to the window to examine it in the flood of midmorning light.

The paper had been ripped and a third of the rough sketch was missing, but something about it looked familiar. Sidney returned to his desk and pulled open the bottom drawer. Reaching into the back, he removed a wooden box. He pulled out his fob and unlocked the box with a small key that dangled from it.

Sidney took an enameled snuffbox from the box and set it beside the ripped paper on his desk top. The snuffbox had been collected yesterday during a frustrating search of a house where he had expected to find some of the men they sought. They had found only hastily vacated rooms, devoid of any indication of who had been there except for this elegant snuffbox.

He turned the box several times until he had what he wanted. Yes. The sketch could very well be of the same seal that decorated the snuffbox. He picked up the snuffbox and opened it carefully. It was half full of a rich brown powder.

Sidney leaned over and sniffed the contents. It smelled like tobacco and… what? . He knew little about tobacco, but the snuff smelled unusual, faintly floral and faintly foreign. He took a clean sheet of paper out of his desk and tipped a small amount of the powder onto it. He folded the sheet tightly. Someone with more expertise might be able to identify the blend.

"Curtis!" Sidney pulled his head back in from his office door and returned to his desk. He had yet to figure out a more efficacious was way to summon the clerk. Shouting seemed to work. Within minutes, the door opened and Curtis entered, stopping just inside and waiting with an expectant look on his face.

"There you are." Sidney tried not to smile. There Curtis always was. He removed the small packet of tobacco he had poured out of the mysterious snuffbox and folded it into a note he had just written. "Take this to Friberg and Treyer," he said, "and wait as long as you need to for an answer."

"As long as I need to?" Curtis looked down at the packet Sidney had just put in his hands and back up.

"Pack a lunch," Sidney said, returning to the work on his desk.

"Um, sir." The young man shifted his feet.

"Yes, Curtis?" Sidney peered up at the clerk.

"What am I waiting for, sir?"

"Oh." Sidney shook his head at his own preoccupation. "You are to wait for an answer to that letter and bring it directly to me. To my home, if I am not here."

As the door clicked closed behind Curtis, Sidney leaned back in his chair and examined the cracks in his office ceiling. Would the tobacconist provide the information the investigation needed?

* * *

Isabel stretched and yawned. Without opening her eyes, she rolled toward Sidney's side. It was empty. She reached out and felt the pillow. Cool. Sidney had been gone for a while. Where, she wondered, and why? She thought he had planned to spend the day at home so that there would be no rush preparing for the ball his mother was to give that night.

Isabel grabbed the pillow, pulled it to her and buried her nose in the cool linen, imbibing the scent of her husband. She lay embracing the pillow and squinting at the sun beating against the windows. She had expected to wake in Sidney's arms.

The passion of their fight in the library had quickly turned to another kind of passion. They had missed dinner and most of the night's sleep. As was always the case, when she and Sidney were in each other's arms, all conflict faded. She wondered if they could not extend that charity to the moments when they were not in bed.

They circled each other like wary dogs; they fought with an excess of energy. Isabel knew that Sidney still did not trust her. Despite all this, she feared that she was beginning to look forward to the moment when he entered a room, to depend upon the comforting strength of his presence in her life, to love him.

Isabel rolled over and kicked at the sheets. Damn. She rolled again, taking the sheets with her and grimacing as her stomach roiled at the motion. Double damn. Wrapping a sheet around her, Isabel sprinted for her own chamber and her own chamber pot.

Isabel was rinsing her mouth and contemplating her fate when Willington scratched on her door and entered with a tray of dry toast and tea.

Isabel shuddered. "Remove that food."

The maid set the tray down on the little writing desk by the window as Isabel collapsed into a chair feeling like a wet rag.

"This will settle your stomach, ma'am, when you're ready for it."

"Does the entire staff know?" Isabel imagined the

gossip in the kitchen when Willington put tea and dry toast on the tray instead of her usual chocolate. Her stomach lurched. She thought she might never drink chocolate again.

"No ma'am." Willington poured fresh water into a basin, moistened a cloth and handed it to Isabel. "No one is about when I fix your tray. Your... ah... health is no one's business, I'm thinking."

Isabel took the cool towel and buried her face in it. "Thank you," she mumbled into the damp cloth. Lifting her face, she repeated her thanks, thinking that she was entirely too likely to say the important things when they could not be heard.

Her maid look startled and Isabel smiled. "I don't thank you enough for putting up with me."

"Oh no, madam." Willington's face flushed and she turned away to busy herself at the wardrobe.

Isabel took one more swipe at her face with the cool cloth and, rising, stretched and edged cautiously toward the tray. Once a piece of toast and some tepid tea sat tentatively in her stomach, she turned to address the issues of appearance.

"Has my new gown been delivered?" Isabel poured another cup of tea and returned to her chair.

"It's right here, ma'am." Willington reached into the clothes press and removed a creation of ivory satin and amber gauze shot with gold. "It's lovely, if I may say so." She carried it carefully to where Isabel sat.

"It is." Isabel reached out and stroked the delicate fabric. "And the slippers?"

"Here as well."

"See that they are made ready. We leave for Haddon House at eight."

The day was long. Sidney had not returned to Bruton Place and Isabel wandered through the rooms, feeling strangely bereft. Inevitably, her steps took her to the garden. Settling herself in the arbor seat, Isabel opened the book she had picked up during her prowl through the library.

It was a useless endeavor. She couldn't concentrate on the story. Sidney's face, his hands, his body kept interposing themselves between Isabel and the pages. With a sigh, she closed the book and put it aside. Closing her eyes, she gave herself up to wondering whether her husband would like her new gown, would be proud to escort her to Haddon House, would ever believe that she wanted to be his wife.

"There you are, dear heart." Lady Louisa trotted down the path toward the arbor, a violet parasol over her head and lace flounces bouncing over her ample bosom at every step.

"Aunt. I have been looking for you." Isabel swung her feet to the ground and patted the bench beside her. "Join me."

"Looking for me?" Louisa lowered herself onto the seat and furled her parasol. "Where? Under the bench?"

"Earlier. In the house." Isabel leaned over and kissed her aunt's soft cheek. "I... I wanted to be sure you had everything you needed for tonight."

"Tonight? Do we have an engagement tonight?" Lady Louisa put her finger to her chin and looked puzzled.

"Aunt!" Isabel's head swiveled toward Louisa.

Lady Louisa grinned. "I am teasing, my dear."

"Well do not. I beg you." Isabel slumped back against the bench in relief.

"Of course I'm ready for the countess's ball. I am looking forward to it," Louisa said. "But you seem to be in a rare taking. What is bothering you?"

Isabel did not speak for several minutes. She took her aunt's hand held it on her lap, looking off toward the back of the townhouse.

"What is it, dearest?" Lady Louisa asked softly.

Isabel could feel her eyes well up and shook her

head angrily. "Oh. Oh bother. What do you think it is? Sidney's family has no use for me. And I have no idea how Sidney feels."

"Have you asked him?" Louisa squeezed Isabel's hand.

"Asked him?"

"Asked him how he feels. It is a time honored method of gathering information." Lady Louisa cocked her head at Isabel and twinkled.

"Don't be absurd." Isabel dropped her aunt's hand and stood, pacing a few steps away from the bench and back.

"What do you fear?" Louisa asked.

"Nothing. That is a foolish question." Isabel paced back and forth once more and then dropped back down on the bench.

"Well, perhaps, I am afraid to know what he feels," she said, shrugging.

"Perhaps you are. But, I do not think you should be, Isabel. I think that you might be pleased at the answer to that question."

CHAPTER 15

Isabel sat at the right hand of the Earl of Haddon and wished she were somewhere else. Anywhere else. But, the ball Lady Haddon was giving this evening was to honor Isabel's marriage to the countess's youngest son. There was no question that Sidney and Isabel would be at the family dinner before the ball.

A family dinner. Isabel contemplated the appointments of the grand room in which they sat. Surely this was not the family dining room. The room extended the entire width of the house and the gleaming rosewood table took up nearly two thirds of it. The sideboards at either end were supported by gilt carvings that echoed the elaborate cornices topping the damask covered walls.

A fire burned in the massive fireplace, but Isabel could not seem to get warm and she had not brought her shawl to table. Lifting her glass, she tried to ingest enough claret to warm her. It didn't work.

Isabel squinted at her plate. The terrine had been sitting, uneaten, for some time and the pieces of game birds in congealing sauce looked even more unappetizing than the earl's scowl. She took a deep breath and glanced down the table.

Sidney sat beside his mother, peering up the table at her with some concern. She could feel her face heat and prayed that the dish would be removed soon and spare them all the embarrassment of her delicate stomach.

Quickly, Isabel inspected the rest of the party to see if they noticed her state. Lady Julia was leaning toward her dinner partner and Aunt Louisa was trying to catch the eye of a footman to refill her wine glass.

"Do you not like the food, Mrs. Chamberlayne?" After two courses, the earl had chosen this moment to break his silence.

Isabel swallowed convulsively. "I am sure everything is delightful, but I find I am not very hungry this evening."

"Indeed? Perhaps it is the excitement of the evening." Lord Haddon leaned closer and dropped his voice. "Or is it a guilty conscience?"

Isabel's hands clenched into tight fists. She dropped them into her lap, and compressed her lips to keep herself from causing a scene at Sidney's mother's table. The blood rushing to her head caused the room to swim before her eyes. She swayed slightly and reached one hand up to grasp the edge of the table.

The earl produced a chilly smile, but the countess, at the other end of the table broke protocol to ask, "Are you unwell, Isabel?"

Isabel shook her head and glanced down the table, registering with a sickening certainty that every eye was upon her.

Taking advantage of the moment, the earl jumped to his feet and took Isabel's hand. "Unwell?" he asked, his face a mask of polite concern. "Why didn't you say so, my dear sister? Allow me…"

Before Isabel could protest, Lord Haddon waved away his mother and brother and escorted Isabel to a small withdrawing room.

Once they were out of sight of the family Isabel tore her arm out of the earl's grasp and whirled to face him. "Don't touch me," she said through gritted teeth.

"I shall treat you as you deserve." The earl let his arm drop and walked away from Isabel.

"You don't know me, my lord. How can you know what I deserve?" Isabel sank onto a chair. She no longer felt ill, but she was drained, exhausted by the tension she suffered whenever she was in Lord Haddon's presence.

"I think I've heard enough, seen enough to know the kind of woman you are." The earl spoke with his back to Isabel.

Isabel felt all the insult intended by Lord Haddon's posture and, gathering her resources, stood and crossed the room.

She stepped around the earl and stopped directly in front of him. "Have the courtesy to face me when you are insulting my character, Lord Haddon." Her back straight and her chin up, Isabel trembled. She knew that the Earl of Haddon had the power to demolish her reputation and, likely, her marriage, but she was not prepared to let him do so unchallenged.

"Isabel?" Sidney stepped through the drawing room door and strode to where Isabel stood facing his brother.

Isabel glanced away from the earl as her husband moved to her side. She wasn't certain she was glad to see him. His presence was comforting, but some part of her wished to resolve the problem of Lord Haddon's rabid dislike on her own. If, indeed, it could be resolved.

"Is something amiss?" Sidney's eyes flicked from Isabel to his brother. "Are you feeling ill, Isabel?"

"I... I was a bit faint at the table. It must have been the heat." She shivered.

Isabel swayed slightly and Sidney placed his palm against her back. She drew in a deep breath and straightened, trying not to rely on the strength of her husband. She was determined to settle this contretemps without Sidney's help.

Sidney's gaze moved between her face and his brother's. "There's more going on here than faintness. What...?"

Isabel could see he was distressed. "It's nothing," she said quietly. "A misunderstanding between Lord Haddon and me. Please don't..."

"A misunderstanding?" The earl's voice reverberated off the high ceiling, causing Isabel to flinch. "There is no misunderstanding, Sidney," he continued, turning to his brother. "I merely confronted this woman with what I know about her."

Sidney's hand slipped from Isabel's back to her waist and he drew her against him. "Your pardon, Haddon? What is it you know about my wife?" He asked in a voice so chill it should have made the earl's blood freeze.

The earl drew himself up to his full height, his eyes easily meeting Sidney's chin. "You know as well as I do. I told you what I know."

"You told me what you *think* you know," Sidney said, his arm tightening around Isabel. "You told me what you *think* you saw."

The earl maintained his stance, refusing to look away from Sidney. "I'm not blind, man. I saw this woman—" he nodded toward Isabel—"with Chiswick."

"Yes, so you said."

"So I did," the earl's voice took on an insistent note.

"He did, Sidney," Isabel whispered. She and Sidney should not be discussing this here. She should never have let her temper prevent her from telling him what happened.

"I am sure he did, Isabel." Sidney looked down at her for a moment and she was startled to perceive a sort of tenderness in his gaze.

"But." Sidney looked back at his brother, his expression hardening. "But, it was not precisely what he thought he saw, was it?"

"No." Isabel leaned against her husband's solid form as the warm realization that he might trust her rolled through her.

"I thought not." Sidney looked down his nose at the earl. "I will have an apology now," he said.

"But—but…" The earl's ruddy complexion turned an alarming brick color and his neck seemed to swell over his collar. Isabel thought he looked like a rouged frog. She suppressed a nervous giggle.

"Do you trust me, Harold?" Sidney's voice thawed and his expression warmed minutely.

After what seemed to Isabel an interminable interval, the earl nodded.

"Then you must trust my wife."

When the earl would have spoken, Sidney raised his hand. "I know," he said. "I know how things are done in the *ton*. But I will not have that in my family. Do you understand? And I will not have Isabel's name bandied about for no reason. Particularly by my own brother. She is part of your family now, Harold. She is your sister. Treat her as such."

The earl inhaled, his chest expanding to reveal a broad expanse of peacock blue silk waistcoat decorated with an elaborate chain. "Yes," he said, finally. "I take your meaning" Turning to Isabel, he lifted her hand and saluted it with his lips. "I beg your pardon, Mrs. Chamberlayne."

Isabel glanced up at Sidney as if asking what she should do. Sidney lifted a dark eyebrow but said nothing. She lowered her head for a moment, examining her gloves and, when she raised it again, met the earl's eyes. They were as cold and hard as they had been before Sidney arrived, but he did not seem to be inclined to press the matter. Then neither would she. "Thank you, my lord. I accept your apology."

Sidney drew Isabel closer. She felt that perhaps everything would be all right. She hoped that were true.

The earl nodded, spun on his heal and left the room without another word, without so much as a nod to his brother. Isabel shivered again.

"Let me have someone fetch your shawl." Sidney removed his arm from around Isabel and moved toward the door.

"No, Sidney." Isabel reached out and touched his sleeve. "I'm not cold."

"You're shivering, my dear. You *are* ill. Shall we

leave?" Sidney had stopped and turned, looking both concerned and confused.

"No. We must stay. I'm neither ill nor cold. My conversation with Lord Haddon was a bit upsetting. That's all." Isabel knew that leaving the countess's ball would destroy any chance she might have of being accepted by Sidney's family.

Sidney looked skeptical. "Did my brother say anything else to you? Shall I speak with him further?"

Isabel's eyes widened. "No," she said urgently. "Please leave this as it is. You must trust me."

Sidney raised his eyebrows and Isabel knew on the instant that he did not yet trust her. But he had come to her defense. Was it possible that he wanted to trust her? Isabel sighed. Anything was possible.

* * *

Sidney led his wife into the opening quadrille. She had regained the color that had drained from her face during dinner and was, in his opinion, in her best looks. She glowed against the amber and ivory of her new gown, a creature of warmth and charm, so different from the cool lady in blue who had stood by his side at their wedding.

As they made their way down the set, Sidney observed he was not the only gentleman captivated by his wife's beauty. But that was nothing new. Isabel had cut a wide swath through London before Sidney ever met her, or so the stories went.

Sidney had seen Isabel sparkle in ballrooms and drawing rooms throughout Mayfair, but as they progressed down the dance, he noticed that her sparkle was different, warmer, less diffuse. She was not flirting with every gentleman in the set. In fact, every time Sidney looked up, his wife's gaze seemed to be on him.

As they came together in the dance, Sidney smiled into her eyes and was warmed by her sudden blush. He turned to the next lady with a shake of his head. How ridiculous that a blush from his wife should make his heart beat faster.

The dance ended. Sidney bowed to Isabel and offered his arm. Rather than lay her hand on his sleeve, Isabel slipped it into the crook of his arm, allowing her to step closer to him as they crossed the room. Sidney tightened his arm a bit, squeezing Isabel's hand against his ribs. She giggled softly and Sidney felt very well, indeed. If he could keep his brother from displaying his animosity toward Isabel, it promised to be a successful ball.

Sidney seated Isabel between the countess and Lady Louisa. When he would have taken a position in back of her chair, his mother tapped his arm.

"You must dance with the other ladies, Sidney."

"Must I?" Sidney tried a plaintive smile that had always worked on his mother in his youth.

The countess rolled her eyes. "None of that. You can't sit in your wife's pocket tonight. Now go do the pretty with that nice Miss Prescott. No one has yet asked her to dance."

Sidney took Isabel's hand and kissed it before moving off to rescue Miss Prescott from the status of wallflower. The young lady was grateful for his attention and Sidney was grateful that she was not unduly clumsy. She was not as graceful a dancer as Isabel, certainly, but she was young and would probably learn. When he returned her to her chaperon, he was gratified to see that a young gentleman was waiting to solicit the next dance.

Before he could return to Isabel, he found her at his elbow.

"What is Chiswick doing here?" She asked *sotto voce*, her expression fierce.

Sidney glanced across the room. "He must have been invited. Is he not a friend of yours?"

"He does not belong here." Isabel gripped his arm. "We must ask him to leave."

"Isabel, this is my mother's ball. If she invited Mr. Chiswick, we cannot ask him to leave unless he has done something out of the way." Sidney peered down at his wife. "Is this about the incident in Green Park?"

"No. Yes. Oh, come here." Isabel slipped her hand into Sidney's and led him toward a small side door.

Sidney allowed himself to be towed up the stairs and into the small gallery overlooking the ballroom. He peered down onto the floor where Chiswick was greeting his mother and sister.

"Tell me what happened in the park, Isabel."

"Will you believe me?" Isabel did not look at him. She stood at his side, scrutinizing the activity below.

Sidney did not answer immediately and could feel Isabel's arm tense against his as she waited for the answer.

"Tell me," he said.

"Chiswick is a fortune hunter. I told you that before." Isabel slid her hand from Sidney's arm and gripped the balustrade so tightly that he could see her knuckles whiten.

"Yes. You did tell me that. And I assumed it was your fortune he was hunting."

"He was." Isabel's voice rang with impatience. "Of course he was, when he thought he had a chance of winning it."

"And in the park?" Sidney tried to keep his tone cool, unwilling to let Isabel know how bothered he was by her erstwhile flirtations.

"Surely you don't think he was after my oh-so-desirable self," Isabel said derisively.

Sidney glanced down at Isabel's lush body, its every curve limned in ivory satin. Desire rushed through him. How could any man not be after this woman? He cleared his suddenly dry throat.

Isabel looked up at him and then gestured toward the floor where Chiswick was leading Julia toward the dance. "Do you see?"

"I see my sister dancing with Mr. Chiswick."

Isabel breathed out an exasperated sigh. "You see your <u>well-dowered</u> sister dancing with Mr. Chiswick."

"Really, Isabel. Chiswick cannot be so stupid as to think my brother and mother would let him anywhere near Julia's dowry."

"Chiswick is not smart," Isabel said flatly. "And I caution you that he might be desperate. His entire family is on the River Tick."

"The River Tick?" Sidney snorted. Isabel's occasional use of cant always amused him.

"Don't laugh, Sidney. I have a bad feeling about this." Isabel looked so solemn, Sidney stopped to reconsider her words. He took her arm and urged her away from her station. "I promise I will have a word with Haddon... and with my mother."

"Good." Isabel threw a last glance at the dance floor before allowing Sidney to escort her back down the stairs.

CHAPTER 16

Relieved to be free of engagements, Isabel rose from the dinner table. "Will you be staying for port?" She asked Sidney this question every evening. By now it had become a joke.

"Why, yes, my dear. The gentleman and I will join you ladies in…" —Sidney took out his watch as he did every evening— "say half a minute?"

Isabel smiled. She loved these small glimpses of Sidney's humor and knew that she perpetuated the joke for the sole purpose of evoking that response.

On the occasions they dined at home, Sidney and Isabel had formed the habit of taking their after dinner tea in the library rather than the more formal drawing room.

Frequently Lady Louisa joined them. Tonight, she excused herself and took tea in her room. "Too tired, my dears. You must do without me."

"Chess?" Once the door closed behind her aunt, Isabel moved toward the board set up in the far corner of the library. Neither was a particularly accomplished chess player, but they had, on occasion whiled away an evening at home with laughable attempts at strategy.

Sidney shook his head. His hand moved to his jacket and removed a folded document. He turned it over several times as though wondering what to do with it.

Isabel abandoned her position by the chess table and took a seat by the fire. She considered Sidney for several moments, her gaze lingering on his lean face.

"You are very solemn tonight." Isabel could not

imagine what the problem was. But there always seemed to be one. Their moments of charity and nights of passion always seemed to be interrupted by the vicissitudes of life in London. Not for the first time, Isabel thought of luring her husband away to the relative quiet of the country estate the baron had left her.

Sidney, intently studying the paper in his hands, did not seem to hear her.

"Sidney!" Isabel had risen from her chair and was crossing toward her husband when she was interrupted by the familiar scratching on the door that always preceded a servant.

"Come," she called, stopping in the middle of the carpet and turning toward the door.

The door eased open and a footman stepped over the threshold He scanned the room and, finding Sidney almost seemed to come to attention. Fleetingly, Isabel wondered if he had been in the military

"Mr. Curtis to see you, sir." The footman bowed and backed toward the door.

"Eh?" Pulled from his reverie, Sidney placed the paper on a table and nodded to the footman. "Finally. I will be there in a moment."

As Sidney passed Isabel, she reached out and touched his arm. "What is it?"

"I am about to find out," Sidney said, nodding toward the door.

"Not that. The paper." Isabel pointed to the letter Sidney had left on the table.

"We shall talk about that when I return." And he was out of the room.

Isabel walked over to the table and stood looking down at the paper. It was, indeed, a letter, addressed to Sidney in a bold scrawl. She reached out one finger and touched it, drawing back immediately as if scalded. The second time, she slid the paper along the smooth surface of the table, noticing that the wood had been newly waxed. As the paper skidded along its surface, she could smell the beeswax and lavender.

One more prod and the sheet slid off the edge of the table and fluttered to the floor. Isabel bent to retrieve it and, as she straightened, the folded letter fell open. Isabel held the letter between thumb and forefinger, slightly away from her body. It took her a moment to acknowledge that the paper had not strictly fallen open; perhaps that little shake she had given had encouraged it.

Now what to do? Sidney had not returned and the letter was calling her name. Had Sidney not said he would talk to her about it when he returned? Would it not smooth the way if she had already read the letter and he didn't have to take the time to tell her what as in it?

Isabel rolled her eyes. She recognized an excuse when she heard one, even if it was of her own devising. As she was going to end up reading it, anyway, Isabel carried the letter toward the window and opened it fully.

Despite the scrawled direction, once opened, the document looked rather official. The writing was small and neat as if done by someone whose job was to write. The signature alone repeated the scrawl on the outside. This was from the army. Isabel's hand shook as she shifted her position to hold the letter up to the fading light.

The door opened just as Isabel had gathered that the letter recalled Sidney to his regiment.

"Isabel."

Her heart, already pounding at the news in her hand, seemed to double its rhythm. "Sidney." Her voice was no more than a whisper.

Sidney barely glanced at the paper in her hand. "I must leave."

"Now? So soon?" Was this it? Did Sidney intend to tell her he had been recalled and then just leave? She had thought that he might treat her with a bit more respect than that.

Sidney looked confused. "Right away," he said, slowly, as if trying to fathom her panic. "But I should not be gone long."

"What?" It was Isabel's turn to feel confused. "How long?"

Sidney pulled his watch out of his waistcoat pocket and opened it. "I dare say I'll be home before you retire."

"Wait." Isabel waved the letter she held and Sidney blanched.

"Oh, Lord." He snapped his watch shut and replaced it. "This is something else. The messenger was from Whitehall. We will talk when I return. Tomorrow if I'm back too late."

And he was gone, leaving Isabel adrift on a sea of questions.

Sidney was still gone when Isabel went to bed. Sleep did not come easily. She tossed for at least an hour, one ear cocked toward the door, listening for the return of her husband. And when she finally drifted into a half-sleep, her mind roiled with images of Sidney in battle, attacked, bloodied, maimed.

With a gasp, Isabel sat bolt upright in her bed, clutching her sheets, tears streaming down her face. Sidney was dead. She blinked and looked around the room. Trying to draw in a deep breath she collapsed back onto her pillow. Of course Sidney wasn't dead. The war was over, Bonaparte in exile. Sidney may be rejoining his regiment, but he was not going to die.

Isabel rolled over and buried her face in her pillow. Sidney was rejoining his regiment. He might end up anywhere. The idea of her life without Sidney seemed bleak. How long had he known? Why had he not told her earlier? And where in the name of the almighty was he right now?

Isabel sat up again and punched her pillow. Damn the man. She had been married to him for less than two months and here she was mooning over him in the middle of the night. Major Chamberlayne, half pay officer. No, she corrected herself. Major Chamberlayne, full pay officer. Damn!

Sidney was gone when she awoke the next morning. She poked her head into his room and could not tell if his bed had been slept in. Her staff was much too efficient. She wasn't sure whether to be pleased or annoyed.

"Good morning Wharton. Is Mr. Chamberlayne at breakfast?" Isabel knew that Sidney was not in the house, but could not bring herself to ask if he had returned last night.

"Mr. Chamberlayne left word that he would return for dinner, madam." Isabel marveled at Wharton's ability to speak without moving his lips.

"Thank you." Isabel wandered off toward the breakfast room. So, he had come home and had not awakened her. The thought left her dispirited.

* * *

"Mrs. Chamberlayne, sir" Mr. Curtis stood in his doorway.

"I beg your pardon?" Sidney thought he must have misheard.

"Mrs. Chamberlayne is here and wishes to see you. Shall I show her in?"

Sidney was out of his chair and to the door before the clerk finished asking his question. "Of course you should show her in, Curtis. Do not leave my wife loitering in the hallway."

Sidney flung open the door and leaned out. Isabel was, indeed, in the hallway. She wore a pale pink day dress and a deep orange spencer and looked like a brilliant butterfly trapped in the dingy halls of officialdom.

"Isabel. Come in." He held out a hand to his wife as Curtis scuttled away down the hall.

Her head held high, Isabel ignored Sidney's hand, proceeded into his office and took a seat.

Sidney sat opposite her and leaned forward. "What are you doing here?"

"I expected to see you last night." Isabel stared out the window, her lips a thin line.

"The sun was nearly up when I came in. I did not think you would thank me for waking you."

"Didn't you?" Isabel finally turned to face Sidney so that he could see the anger glinting in her amber eyes.

Sidney rose and fetched his hat and gloves. "How did you get here?" he asked.

"Samuel drove me in the curricle." Isabel looked quizzically at his hat.

"Excellent. Let us go for a drive." Sidney walked to the door and put his hand on the latch.

"A drive? I came here to talk." Isabel did not move.

"We will not discuss domestic matters in my office." Sidney's surprise at seeing Isabel was giving way to annoyance. "Now, let us go."

Isabel's groom was happy to relinquish the curricle for charge of Sidney's horse and Sidney soon had the carriage headed down Piccadilly.

Neither had spoken since they left Whitehall, but when they passed the entrance to Hyde Park without turning in, Isabel put her hand on his sleeve. "Where are we going?"

Sidney nodded toward the road ahead. "Kensington."

"Kensington?" Isabel took her hand off Sidney's arm and turned on the bench to look at him. "There is nothing in Kensington."

"Precisely."

The curricle tooled past the imposing mansions on Kensington Gore, evidence that there was, indeed, something in Kensington.

Sidney headed straight for the Queen's Gate and turned down the South Carriage Drive. Before long, he brought the curricle to a halt and, jumping down, tethered the horses to a post. He lifted Isabel from her seat and offered her his arm. She was left with little else to do than take it and enter the Lancaster walk with him.

Although it shared a border with Hyde Park, Kensington Gardens did not attract the traffic that the larger, public green seemed to. Sidney was fairly certain that he and Isabel could find a place to talk away from interested ears.

But Isabel said nothing as they walked and remained quiet when Sidney had found a hideaway among the trees not far from Round Pond.

Sidney sat quietly, listening to the breeze rustle the leaves around him and watching the birds of late summer, hunting dinner in the grass. He thought he could also hear his wife grinding her teeth.

"Here we are, Isabel," he said, finally. "What is it you wished to say to me?"

"Here we are?" When Isabel finally spoke, her voice was at least an octave higher than its usual musical timbre. "Why are we here?"

"I brought you here for your argument." Sidney knew his conversational tone would only further aggravate his wife, but he could not keep from using it. He was right. Her color rose and her eyes sparkled. Sidney grinned. He found her almost irresistible when she was angry.

Isabel grimaced. "Why do you think I want to argue?"

"Isabel." Sidney turned to look down at where Isabel was seated on a stone bench. "You did not come to Whitehall to bring me my lunch."

"I want to talk about the letter."

There it was. Of course, Sidney knew why she had

come, why she was upset. It was the very reason he had chosen not to awaken her when he returned last night.

He had known she would be angry, but he was not quite sure why. Of late, he thought she might have forgiven him for marrying her, might even be coming to enjoy the marriage. But she had given no positive indication that would make him sure this was so. Unless her anger was the sign he had been looking for.

All he said was, "Very well."

Isabel rose and stood facing away from him. Sidney could see her slender back tensing beneath her light spencer. She drew a deep breath and turned around. "Why didn't you tell me about the letter?"

Sidney had not moved, but his eyes sought his wife's. She could not know what his decision had cost him. He remained still, considering whether to relate the long hours he had spent contemplating his future, the arguments he had battled through with his colonel, the confusion that his new life presented. "I intended to. I intended to tell you tonight."

"How long have you known?" In an instant the anger drained from Isabel's voice and she sounded defeated.

"Known?"

"Known that you were returning to your regiment?" Impatience flashed in Isabel's eyes.

"I received the letter last week."

"And you waited this long to tell me you were leaving?" Isabel paced away from Sidney and then returned to stand in front of him, her arms folded under her breasts, her lower lip forming a belligerent pout.

Sidney suppressed a lascivious grin. Her anger was beyond beguiling. "I'm not leaving," he said.

"The least you could have done... What?" Isabel stopped in mid-sentence and goggled at him.

Sidney was gratified by Isabel's astonishment. Isabel would never understand the anguish he felt on relinquishing a way of life he had thought to be his future, but his recalcitrant wife figured prominently in his decision. "I decided to sell my commission."

"How dare you?" Isabel pulled back her right arm and punched Sidney in his shoulder—hard.

"What?" Sidney's question emerged in a yelp of pain. His wife could teach Gentleman Jackson a thing or two.

"How dare you keep this a secret from me? Did you think I would not care. Did you think I would want you to leave... London?"

Sidney opened his mouth to answer, but Isabel did not give him the opportunity. "Well, go ahead. Go away. Take your commission. Sail off to India or Canada or wherever your beloved regiment is going. What do I care?"

"Isabel." Sidney gentled his voice and tried to put his hands on his wife's shoulders. She shrugged away and moved off several paces.

"This has not been an easy decision for me," Sidney said.

"Oh, I am sure not. The choice between a wife and a colonel must be arduous." Isabel would not look at him.

"I need to feel useful." The words expressed one of the most elemental parts of Sidney's being and he prayed that Isabel would hear that.

"You are useful," she whispered, finally, blinking her eyes rapidly.

"I have concluded that I can be," Sidney answered, grateful that she might at least understand his need.

"Without the army?" Isabel asked.

"Without the army." Sidney reached out and traced a tear down Isabel's cheek.

Isabel sniffled and faced Sidney. "Why are we here?" she asked, repeating the words with which she had begun the conversation.

"I told you. I brought you here so we could argue."

"We have a home for that," she said with a flash of her characteristic humor.

"Oh no." Sidney smiled slyly at his wife. "When I fight with you near a bed, we never seem to finish the argument."

CHAPTER 17

"Dover?" Isabel swallowed her tea around the lump that had formed in her throat then carefully returned the cup to its saucer and placed it back on the table.

Sidney, elegant in a stark, black coat and pantaloons, sat across from her, quiet and solemn. He nodded. "Yes."

The lump in Isabel's throat plummeted to her stomach and she wondered for a moment if she was going to be ill. One hand clenched in front of her middle, she rose from her chair and walked to the windows. It had been only days since Sidney had told her he had resigned his commission. Now he was leaving for Dover. What was he about?

They were in the garden room. The afternoon sun flooded the walls with a warm light and yet Isabel felt inexplicably cold, as if all the blood had drained out of her. She stared out into her garden, but saw none of the flowers and shrubbery that usually calmed her. She had eyes only for the bench under the arbor where Sidney had offered her marriage, where he had held her in his arms and taught her passion, where, just this morning, he had taken his leave for Whitehall without ever mentioning that he would soon be leaving London.

Turning back toward the room, she said, "Dover? When? Why? How long will you be gone?" Isabel could hear her own voice rising to a querulous pitch but seemed unable to control it.

Sidney crossed the room and took Isabel's hand. "Sit with me, my dear."

"No!" Isabel's heart was pounding wildly. She slapped Sidney's hand away. "I will not sit anywhere until you tell me why you are going and how long you will be gone. You told me you had resigned your commission."

"I am not going to my regiment. This has to do with my Whitehall assignment." Sidney looked down and began to strip off his gloves.

"This journey is important to my work—to the matter I am investigating." Sidney hesitated and then continued. "I will not be leaving right away and I think I will not be gone long."

"You have an administrative position. You have a desk. It does not require" —Isabel made a sweeping gesture— "travel. You asked for this—asked to leave... here." Isabel looked wildly around the room. She could not seem to stop babbling and cast about for something to anchor her.

"Why?" she said. Finally clenching her teeth to dam the questions piling up behind them.

"I am needed," Sidney said. "I need to find... to find some people."

"You are needed here." Isabel clasped trembling hands over her abdomen. It was increasingly apparent to her that he was needed here. That she needed him and that it was impossible that he should leave her just as she was discovering it.

Sidney placed a finger under Isabel's chin and tilted her head up so that she was looking directly into his eyes. "That is good of you to say, Mrs. Chamberlayne. But I think you exaggerate. You have very little need of me."

"I... " Isabel grasped Sidney's hands and held them between her own. She shook her head. "I do," she said very quietly. "I know you cannot believe it, but it is true."

"Oh, Isabel." Sidney gathered Isabel to him and slid her onto his lap.

"You will come back?"

"Of course."

Isabel wrapped her arms around Sidney's neck and kissed him soundly. He was returning. He did not want to leave her. Her heart leapt and her blood pounded through her veins.

Sidney's arms came around her, but he did not return the kiss. "I take it you are pleased, madam."

"Pleased?" Isabel drew back to look at her husband's face. It was still somber and nearly expressionless. "Yes, Sidney. I am pleased." Isabel cocked her head in puzzlement and examined the austere countenance before her.

"And you?" She removed one of her arms from her husband's neck and massaged the crease between his eyes with a gentle finger. "Why do you look so downcast?"

Sidney closed his eyes and sighed. "This is not a pleasant assignment, my dear. And, truth be told, I would rather remain in London than hie off to the coast." His head fell back against the chair and Isabel took this as permission to tuck her own head into his shoulder and curl up against him.

*   *   *

Sidney slid his arms around Isabel, enclosing her in a loose embrace. He had not raised his head or opened his eyes, but all of his other senses were attuned to the woman in his arms. Her soft hair brushed his cheek and he inhaled the faint scent of jasmine and sandalwood, a fragrance he now recognized as uniquely hers. And his arms recognized the soft contours of the body nestled so sweetly against him.

There was none of the passion that characterized most of their encounters, only an elusive sense of comfort, a feeling that he and Isabel fit together in some indefinable way.

Isabel murmured wordlessly against his shoulder and he dropped his cheek to the top of her head. Some distant part of his mind rehearsed Isabel's words: *You are needed here.* He acknowledged that his desire to quickly discharge his task and hurry back to London was tied, at least in part, to the woman in his arms. Indeed, it seemed as though most of what he did these days took Isabel into account.

Sidney hadn't been able to fathom exactly why Isabel's presence exerted such a force. Granted, she was tantalizing when roused and a sweet armful when she was compliant. He slid one hand around her waist and she wriggled comfortably against him. Their passion was astonishing. He had never before bedded a woman who responded with Isabel's ardor and he had never before left a bed wondering when he could return to it.

Their life outside the bedroom was anything but comfortable. Sidney opened his eyes and smiled down at his wife. She had closed her eyes and her lashes lay in a golden crescent against her cheeks. She looked perfectly comfortable at this moment. His smile turned wry. They had much to learn about each other and the learning promised to be as challenging as any military campaign. He wanted to trust her. In many ways, he did trust her, but so much militated against it.

A soft snore interrupted Sidney's train of thought. His wife seemed to make a habit of dozing off in his arms. He could not blame her today; it had been a late night. Sidney shifted the weight of his sleeping wife and rose with the facility of a man used to bearing burdens. Easing the door open with his shoulder, he carried Isabel to his room.

* * *

Isabel lay curled on her side in Sidney's bed, her eyes almost closed, trying to keep her breathing even. She had awakened as Sidney slid her onto his bed, but had been unwilling to let him know. Embarrassed at having fallen asleep in his lap again, she was also fascinated to learn what he meant to do now that he had brought her upstairs.

Isabel snuggled into the pillows and thought about her secret. For more than a week, she had been convinced that she carried Sidney's child. She had told no one, wanting first to determine her own feelings.

Amazingly, the likelihood of a child warmed Isabel in a way she had not thought possible. She supposed that, at one time, she would have resented the interruption of her activities. But now, it felt like a symbol of the strength and permanency Sidney had introduced into her life.

How extraordinary she should discover that the security she craved resided not in a title and wealth, but in nobility of character. Isabel peered through half-closed eyes at her husband. She would tell him her secret when he returned from Dover. Today, she would show him how she felt.

Feigning sleep was difficult as Sidney freed the tapes at the back of her gown and eased the muslin off her shoulders. It was almost impossible when he unlaced the light stays she wore under the bodice. Carefully, Sidney eased the stays apart and loosened the drawstring on her chemise. Isabel bit the inside of her cheek to keep from squirming as he ran his fingers over her shoulders.

Sidney sat quietly on the edge of the bed and then stood and strode across the room. He closed the door and then shrugged out of his jacket, placing it carefully over the back of a chair. He stripped off the rest of his clothes in less than a minute, folding each garment as he removed it. When everything was in a neat pile, Sidney turned toward the bed,

Isabel watched every movement through the veil of her lashes. She had little experience of the naked male body, but she felt quite sure that Sidney's was a superlative example. The smooth play of sculpted muscle over his long frame made her breath quicken. Each time a muscle tightened or relaxed, she could almost feel it under her hand, against her body. When he turned around, she gulped.

"How long have you been awake?" Sidney's glare was belied by the alert state of the rest of his body.

Isabel rolled over on her back, allowing her bodice to fall aside, letting the sagging neckline reveal her breasts, nipples already crinkled with excitement.

Isabel could feel Sidney's scrutiny of her body, warm as flesh, arousing as a touch. She could sense the second his gaze fastened on her breasts. At that moment, warmth rushed through her every vein in her body, converging between her legs. She stifled a groan.

Sidney's very presence did things to Isabel's body that she had never experienced with any other man. Despite her less-than-spotless reputation, despite the scores of flirtations she had conducted since the baron's demise, despite the brittle façade she still tried to wear, she had previously shared a bed only with the elderly Lord Ashby. And no stolen kiss or furtive caress in the shadows of a garden had ever produced the kind of thrill she felt at a single glance from her husband.

And he knew it, the devil. She could tell by the gleam in his dark eyes that he knew what he was doing to her just standing beside the bed.

She reached out a hand and caught one of his. "Come here." Her voice was already husky with desire.

Sidney sank to the edge of the bed, retaining Isabel's hand and bringing it flush against his chest. His gaze had moved from her body to her face. He looked as though he was trying to read her mind through her eyes.

"Sidney?"

Without a word, Sidney leaned over and kissed her. His lips were soft and pliant against hers, a gift rather than a demand. Gently, he outlined her lips with his tongue and, gently, teased her mouth open.

On a sigh, Isabel wound her arms around her husband's neck and pulled him fully onto the bed, welcoming him with the warmth of her mouth and the softness of her body.

They lay together for what seemed an eternity, kissing in a myriad of combinations, tongues dueling, lips caressing, breath mingling, moving from one delight to another, tasting each other as if for the first time.

As each kiss melted into the next, Isabel's body ignited. Her breasts ached for Sidney's touch, her core turned to liquid fire. She tangled her legs with Sidney's and pressed close, seeking to ease the desire burning through her.

Finally, Sidney slid his hand over her breast. She gasped in relief. And then he stopped.

"What?" Isabel opened her eyes and stared up at her husband who was regarding her with an amused smile.

"You are wearing far too many clothes."

Isabel looked down and blushed. "I forgot."

She sat up and began struggling with her bodice.

"Allow me." In a moment, Sidney had the gown, stays and chemise, pushed over her hips into a bundle at the foot of the bed.

"You are quite good at that," Isabel said, unable to control the quaver in her voice.

"At what?" Sidney resumed his position and gathered Isabel into his arms.

"Never mind." Isabel reached up and ran her hand through Sidney's thick black hair, brushing aside the forelock that always seemed about to fall over his eyes. She drew his head down to hers and kissed him, deepening the kiss as his arms tightened around her.

Isabel wriggled against Sidney. The friction of flesh against flesh was unbearably pleasurable. As her nipples brushed against the rough hair of his chest, Isabel expelled a susurration of exquisite enjoyment. Then she buried her nose in the crook of her husband's neck and greedily inhaled the pungent odor that was his alone, sharp and bright, overlaid with the musk of sweat and arousal.

Winding her legs through Sidney's again, Isabel nipped at his neck. She slid down his body, nipping and kissing until she came to his nipples. She lingered there, running her tongue over the flat areolae, nibbling at the risen flesh, blowing gently over the crisp hair.

When he groaned and gripped her shoulders with both hands, Isabel stopped nibbling and lay her cheek against Sidney's chest. The beating of her husband's heart sounded against her ear and it seemed as though her own heart picked up the rhythm and began to beat in time. She nuzzled Sidney's chest and then slid back up to his shoulder, content, at that moment, to simply lie in his arms.

Contentment quickly returned to desire as Sidney explored her body with his clever hands. As he skimmed one hand down Isabel's back and began to massage her bottom, the other lifted a breast and kneaded it in gentle emulation. Isabel arched in luxurious acknowledgment, and her husband bent his head to her neck, fastening on the delicate skin at the base of her throat and drawing it between his lips.

Isabel sighed and stretched farther, encouraging Sidney to slide his lips downward where her breasts were afire with anticipation of his mouth. Sidney moved toward Isabel's breasts, in a rain of kisses. She knew her fair skin would be marked by his beard and by the soft suction of his lips. She didn't care; she arched her back, offering herself to him.

When Sidney reached Isabel's breasts, he released her bottom and took both breasts in his hands. Raising them, he blew across the reddened tips and Isabel shoved her hand into her mouth to keep from screaming. Sidney rubbed his cheek against her nipples, the day's beard abrading the sensitive skin.

And then, when Isabel thought she might expire from sheer yearning, Sidney took her breast into his mouth and drew deeply. Isabel moaned, arching into his mouth, and twining arms and legs around his body. The urgent need for his mouth, his hands, his body escalated with every touch and Isabel moved sinuously against him, impelling him toward the ultimate moment.

Sidney drew the moment out, prolonging the play, setting her ablaze. Isabel yearned toward him, wanting his touch and, today, wanting something more. Their moments in bed were wonderful, but until this moment, seemed to have been the mere satisfying of a mutual lust. Not that Isabel minded. Sidney had taught her the joys to be found in the joining of bodies. But, now, for the first time, she yearned to join more than her body to his. She yearned for their union to truly make them one entity. She wanted to be part of him. Now. Tomorrow. Next year.

Taking Isabel's waist in both hands, Sidney raised her slightly and tucked a pillow under her bottom. Isabel wriggled to find a comfortable placement in this unlikely position. "What are you doing?" she asked in a breathless murmur.

"Improving things." Sidney dropped a quick kiss on Isabel's nose then placed his mouth on hers as he positioned himself between her raised knees. "Now hush," he breathed against her lips.

Cupping Isabel's bottom in his large hands, Sidney slid slowly into her. He raised his head and their eyes met and locked. The liquid chocolate of his gaze became almost black as his eyes fastened on hers and Isabel swore she would fly apart if he continued looking at her like that.

Without breaking eye contact, Sidney began a languorous rhythm. Isabel watched his eyes as he moved within in her and felt that her wish had been fulfilled, that this joining was of more than their bodies, that

Sidney was giving her a glimpse into his soul as he drove her toward fulfillment.

Desire built with each thrust and Isabel's body rose to meet her husband's, her fingers clutching his shoulders in desperation. At last, with a final, powerful surge, Sidney buried himself deep within in her and, wrapping his arms around her, held her tightly against him until she reached culmination in a wave of warmth and light unlike anything she had ever experienced.

Isabel could feel Sidney follow her over the edge and then collapse on top of her. She wound her arms around his back, digging her fingertips into the quivering muscles, and buried her face against his shoulder. Her face hidden, Isabel placed her lips against Sidney's damp skin and silently whispered her secret. "I love you."

CHAPTER 18

"When does Sidney return?" Lady Julia Chamberlayne leaned forward and scooped a biscuit off the tea table with deft familiarity.

Isabel shook her head. "His last letter indicated that he had not completed his task. I do not know when to expect him." She sat back in her chair and folded her hands over her stomach, an attitude that had recently become second nature.

She looked down and quickly moved her hands to reclaim her teacup. She knew that no one looking at her would suspect that she was *enceinte*, but she had seen enough pregnant women to recognize that the protective position of her hands would raise speculation she was not yet ready to have raised.

"I don't understand why Sidney must dash off to Dover during the season. He must know how valuable he is as an escort. I am really quite vexed." Julia frowned into her teacup.

Isabel fiddled with the teapot. The memory of how badly she had reacted to Sidney's departure was fresh in her mind, as was the memory of the long night that followed it. She could feel her face heat at the recollection and spoke quickly to cover it.

"Sidney didn't leave in order to thwart your social plans. He has work to do."

Julia rolled her eyes. "Soldiers! All they see is duty. Can't Sidney find some better excuse to go haring off across the countryside?"

Isabel bridled. "Do you think he was looking for an excuse?"

"Dover?" Julia shook her head in disbelief.

Isabel could feel the blood rush to her face and knew she must look exactly like an irate wife. She couldn't seem to help herself. "Think what you will," she said. "But Sidney is gone on official business."

"Yes, of course." Julia examined her teacup.

Isabel let out an exasperated sigh.

"Really, Isabel. I heard that Sidney was investigating snuff. I can hardly believe that forced Sidney to leave London." Julia set her cup down with a clatter, her chin set at a stubborn angle and looking like nothing so much as a child about to have a tantrum.

"Where did you hear that?" It didn't seem very much like Sidney to discuss official business with his eighteen-year-old sister. Although he had eventually explained his entire investigation to Isabel, he had done so reluctantly and with many exhortations to secrecy.

Julia shrugged. "At your ball, I think, when Sidney was closeted with that man in the divine regimentals."

"You were spying on Sidney when he was talking to Colonel Peabody?"

"I was not spying." Julia shifted in her chair, looking particularly chagrined. "I was... well, I hoped Sidney might introduce me to the Colonel. But he never did. And now he's gone, deserted me to make my way to the next ball without him."

"I assure you, my dear girl, that Sidney would not have left unless he had an important reason." Although Isabel had become very fond of her husband's sister, she occasionally grew impatient with the girl's propensity to relate everyone's actions to herself. She supposed that at eighteen she had been the same.

"Hmph!" Julia picked up another biscuit. "I still don't understand. Sidney shouldn't be acting like some common runner. He has a position that requires filing papers, doesn't he? Are there papers to file in Dover?"

Isabel had wondered the same thing. Until the

moment Sidney told her he was leaving and why, she had not given his Whitehall assignment a second thought. Now, she knew that he had got himself embroiled in something that might be dangerous and she didn't like it at all.

"Your brother has spent the past seven years in the army, Julia. You can't expect him to be happy idling around London waiting to take us to our next rout. He's a man who needs to be active, to have a purpose." Isabel's voice sounded preternaturally admonitory to her own ears and she wondered if acting like a mother began with conception.

"Oh, pooh. Sidney is glad enough to be home. What can be so important that it would pull him away from his sister? And his new bride," she added quickly.

"Your brother is a man who keeps his commitments," Isabel said, thoroughly annoyed with Julia's harping on Sidney's duty as an escort. "His mission is important to England and, indeed, to the continent. Don't you think this is slightly more important than your next ball?"

Julia colored at the rebuke, but clung to her disgruntlement. "It makes no difference," she said with a shrug. "I will simply ask Chiswick to escort me. He is willing enough to look after me."

"Chiswick!" Isabel nearly vaulted from her chair. Instead, she sat forward and looked intently at Julia. "Do not say you have been seeing George Chiswick."

"And if I have? I dare say it's none of your business." Julia brushed imaginary crumbs from the skirt of her white muslin afternoon dress.

"Oh, Julia. Haven't I warned you about Chiswick? You must trust me that he will look after you as long as he might also look after your dowry." Isabel frowned and raised a hand to rub her temple where a headache was threatening to form.

"Nonsense, Isabel. Chiswick is a perfectly delightful man and has only my best interests at heart."

Isabel rolled her eyes and then winced as the movement made her head begin to throb. "Don't you recall that you agreed to let me be your guide when you entered society? That you would always do as I said?"

"That was before I realized you would be jealous of my friendships with your former beaux." Julia tossed her head in an exasperated flounce, sending her chestnut curls quivering around her face.

Isabel leaned forward, catching Julia's eye and looking as earnest as she possibly could. She spoke calmly and slowly. "Listen to me, Julia. I am not jealous of you and Chiswick. I am concerned. The man is a gazetted fortune hunter and you are a lovely young woman of fortune. I only ask that you be careful."

Julia drew her hands away. "Yes. Very well." She looked away, scanning the room and then back at Isabel. "I didn't mean what I said about you being jealous. Truly. I know you mean well, Isabel But you must trust me to have a care for myself."

Isabel smiled weakly, her head now truly pounding and her belief in Julia's ability to look out for herself shaky. She had grown to love her husband's sister and felt an unfamiliar desire to protect her. She recognized many of her own traits in the young woman and this did nothing to comfort her.

* * *

Sidney sat in the common room of the Three Horseshoes in Buckland and lifted his glass of ale. He felt as though he'd been on the coast forever and was no closer to identifying the cabal he had come all this way to find. The weathered timbers of the ancient building were beginning to feel familiar. It could not be a good thing to feel at home in a public house.

He pulled Isabel's letter from his jacket pocket and smoothed it open on the pocked surface of the table. The paper still held the faint scent of jasmine and Sidney's nostrils flared appreciatively. *Isabel.*

There had been an indefinable change in the way he and his wife dealt with each other in the days preceding his departure. Almost as if some barrier they had both erected had been breached by unspoken mutual consent.

Sidney did not need to read the letter. He had fairly memorized it since he received it two days ago, but holding it provided some sort of visceral connection to its sender.

Running his hand over the creamy vellum, Sidney could almost feel Isabel's smooth skin, could almost taste her scent. Their last night together had been a revelation. Isabel was a passionate woman, a lover eager for experience, generous in her desire to please him. But, she always held something back.

Until their last night together. The change was subtle but significant. For the first time, Sidney had felt that every aspect of his wife was engaged in the loving, that he had touched more than her body. Sidney felt a pang in the neighborhood of his heart. Had he and Isabel begun to love each other? It was a startling notion and one he was not at the moment prepared to examine. He folded the letter and replaced it in his pocket.

The door to the inn opened and Sidney could hear the rush of the Dour River as it coursed past the old building. He had chosen to stay in Buckland rather than in the barracks in Dover as he could have. His search demanded some stealth and berthing with the army seemed like announcing his purpose as official.

The little man who slipped into the room would have gone unnoticed had Sidney not been expecting him. His worn brown jacket and weathered face blended into the background until he seemed to disappear. It was only when he turned his pointed face and piercing eyes toward the room that he seemed at all corporeal.

Sidney pulled out a chair and, without a word, the little man slid into it.

"What do you have?" Sidney pushed a mug of ale toward his visitor.

The man picked up the mug and drank deeply, wiping his mouth on his sleeve before speaking. "Well, me lord, I've been followin' 'em fellows just as ye asked."

Sidney rolled his eyes. He had informed Mr. Withers that he was no lord, but it had made no difference to the man. Sidney had given up. "And…?" he prompted.

"And ye was right. They be meetin' in the old abbey."

"The abbey?" Sidney had not been in the environs long enough to know all the landmarks.

"Aye. The one they call Bradsole."

"The ruins you mean, outside of town?" Sidney could dimly recall a rather substantial complex of ruined walls remote enough from town to make a reasonable meeting place if the weather was good.

The little man nodded and took another gulp of his ale. "Do ye want me to follow them?"

"No. By no means." Sidney fished in his pocket and removed a guinea. "You have been very helpful. I will send word if I have further need of your services." He placed the coin on the table and left Mr. Withers to his drinking.

Sidney's long strides took him out the door and onto the bridge that spanned the Dour. Not long ago, travelers had to ford the river where the bridge now stood; built thirty years ago, the structure made it possible for Sidney to establish his camp in the quieter Buckland.

Leaning over the edge of the sturdy bridge, Sidney studied the river and contemplated what he should do next. If he was to learn anything about the men he sought, he would need to either infiltrate their group or arrange to overhear their meetings.

Sidney rolled the possibilities over in his mind. He needed to identify them so they could be arrested, but he wanted to do it as expeditiously as possible. At the forefront of his mind was the thought that the sooner he accomplished his task, the sooner he could return to London, to Isabel. Sidney chuckled into the distance. Sidney Chamberlayne was anxious to go home to his wife.

Sidney slapped his hands down on the rail and turned on his heel. It was time to do some reconnaissance, something he had not done since he'd left Spain. He felt a small thrill at the idea of working in the saddle once again.

The hostler brought Sidney's gelding out of the stable and stood back to allow Sidney to saddle the huge chestnut himself, a task Sidney never ceded to others if possible. Sidney spoke quietly to the restive animal and blew softly in its nostrils until it stopped side-stepping and settled down to the familiar routine.

The kinship he felt with Chiron asserted itself and Sidney took a moment to lean his forehead against the shiny coat of the horse's neck and inhale the ineffable scent of horseflesh and leather, a scent that until recently, smelled like home.

Sidney took the southwest road, heading toward St. Radigun's Abbey, a Medieval ruin that locally went by the name of Bradsole. The sun was low on the horizon and the air carried the tang of salt water.

The trail to Bradsole Abbey was odd, to be sure. A trail of specially blended snuff that most likely came from France into England somewhere near Dover. He was not even sure he would find his answers here, but Mr. Withers's information was promising.

Surrounded by a large area of unused land, much of it wooded, the abbey ruins appeared an ideal place to hold a clandestine meeting. Tethering his horse a distance away, Sidney crept toward the thick walls on foot.

Sidney had no way of knowing whether the men he sought would be at the abbey tonight. He rather thought not, but was taking no chances. If they were there, all the better. If not, it would give him the opportunity to reconnoiter.

Unwilling to sacrifice the fading daylight, Sidney entered the walls of the ruin, picking his way over fallen stone and underbrush. He moved quietly and paused frequently to listen for others. There was no one there, but, toward the center of the abbey, he found evidence of a recent fire.

Foolish to signal their presence with a fire. But it had been foolish to leave a snuffbox at the house in London. They were getting careless and Sidney worried that this might mean they were close to their goal. He shuddered to think what Bonaparte's escape would mean to England.

Sidney faded back into the shadows surrounding the fire. He would wait to see who turned up.

CHAPTER 19

"I wish Sidney were here." Isabel gazed into the mirror on her dressing table.

"Madam?" It had taken some doing, but Willington had finally given up calling Isabel "my lady." It surprised Isabel that she was relieved to have done with the title.

"Nothing." Isabel shook her head and made a face at her reflection. Talking to herself. If Sidney didn't return soon, the gossip below stairs would probably turn to Isabel's peculiar fits and starts. She could hear the maids telling the cook that "the mistress has started talking to herself when no one's about."

"Do you think my skin is blotchy?" She turned to her maid and angled her head so that the morning sunlight illuminated her cheek.

"No madam, you look as lovely as you did before…" Willington's voice died out, her expression stricken.

"Before? Yes, I suppose there is now a before and since." Isabel's stomach clenched, not an unusual occurrence these days.

She turned back to the mirror and peered at her maid's image behind her. "Never mind. I could not deceive you and soon I will not be able to deceive anyone else." Isabel winced at the memory of Willington rushing in with a basin on several recent mornings.

"What will you wear today, ma'am?"

Grateful for Willington's practiced detachment,

Isabel turned to the bed where three gowns had been laid out. "The peach muslin, I think. And the brown morocco slippers. I meet Lady Haddon and Lady Julia for shopping today."

When had shopping ceased to be entertainment? Isabel was amply provided with shoes, bonnets, stockings and dresses. Although she suspected she would be requesting something new from her dressmaker soon, she still fit comfortably into her gowns and she saw no reason to brew gossip by ordering the clothes needed by an expectant mother.

Not long ago, she would have considered a day in the shops a day well-spent, regardless of the state of her wardrobe. Until recently, a new bonnet provided as much entertainment as a day in the country or an afternoon at Astley's. Sometime in the last several months, it had lost its charm.

Nevertheless, within two hours she was on Pall Mall, arm-in-arm with Lady Julia Chamberlayne, exchanging views on various merchants with Lady Haddon and trailed by two footmen already laden with purchases.

As they approached the modiste favored by both Julia and Lady Haddon, the countess excused herself.

"You will not mind going on without me?" She addressed Isabel, who would have to take on the role of chaperone in Lady Haddon's absence.

Isabel groaned inwardly. The day was already too long and her legs ached from the constant walking and standing. But she smiled and shook her head. "Of course not, my lady."

"Oh, thank you." The countess beamed in real gratitude. "I simply must put my feet up. I will send the carriage back for you." She signaled to one of the footman and, without another word, was gone.

Bubbling with energy, Julia led Isabel into the shop. Isabel tried to suppress a sigh as she sank down into a comfortable chair in Madame D'Arlemont's showroom.

Julia had already spread out a length of pale primrose silk and was holding up fashion plates next to it and discussing trims and furbelows with the shop's owner. Isabel was only grateful for the chance to sit. She put her head back and closed her eyes for a moment.

As was frequently the case since Sidney's departure, Isabel's thoughts went directly to her husband. She eased her feet half out of her slippers and wriggled her toes under the cover of her hem. Her hands crept over her still-flat belly. Isabel sighed deeply. She wished she had told Sidney about the baby before he'd left.

They had made love long into the night and fallen asleep in each other's arms. For the first time, Isabel had felt the bond between them, had felt that it was more than pleasure, more than passion, that, in some part, she was irrevocably connected to Sidney.

When she awoke in the middle of the night, curled contentedly into Sidney's hard body to find her husband's hand right over the spot where their baby rested, her body had thrummed with the desire to share her secret.

She had turned over to face him, but he had been sleeping soundly, the harsh lines of his face relaxed into a boyish innocence. She couldn't bring herself to disturb him and simply settled against his chest and drifted back to sleep.

Neither had she been able to form the words to tell him she loved him, at least not out loud. But, this—this incredible secret would have spoken for her. Why had she not told him?

"What do you think?"

"What is that, dearest?" Isabel straightened in her chair and shoved her feet back into her slippers.

Julia held up a length of red silk. "Wouldn't this be stunning?"

"Julia!" Isabel's eyes widened in disbelief. "You can't wear that color, as you well know."

"And why not?" Isabel jerked around at the smooth tenor voice issuing from the doorway. George Chiswick leaned against the doorframe, the picture of an elegant gentleman.

Isabel turned back to Julia in time to see the smile of welcome light her face and the flush creeping up her neck. Isabel pursed her lips in disapproval, but Julia, ignoring her, continued smiling at Chiswick.

Madame D'Arlemont gathered up her fabric and scurried into her workroom, leaving Isabel alone with Julia and her admirer. She rose from her chair and moved to stand beside Julia, placing her hand on the girl's shoulder.

"What are you doing here, Chiswick?" Isabel hoped her cool tone carried the message that he was not welcome.

Chiswick smiled broadly. "I was just passing by and I saw you through the window. How could I not pay my respects to two such lovely ladies?" He fixed his gaze on Julia as he asked the question.

Isabel compressed her lips in irritation. She knew Chiswick well enough to have little doubt of his tenacity. He would not be easily dismissed. Nor would Julia be likely to look kindly on the attempt, although that was the lesser of her problems. Yet, one had to try.

"How kind of you to stop in." It was an obvious dismissal. But, as she had expected, Chiswick ignored it.

"My pleasure, ladies. My pleasure. I'm particularly gratified to be in time to counsel Lady Julia on her choice of fabric."

"Yes, that is very kind," Isabel said, a raised eyebrow clearly signaling that she thought just the opposite. "However, I fear that we will not be taking your advice on this matter."

Julia, who had been observing the exchange with some avidity, twisted around to look up at Isabel who still stood beside her, her hand resting on Julia's shoulder. "But, I love the crimson," she said, a plaintive note echoing in her voice.

Isabel tightened her fingers imperceptibly and glared at the younger woman. "It is not appropriate."

"But, Mr. Chiswick—."

"Your pardon, Lady Julia." Chiswick bowed and smirked. "Of course you must listen to your sister. She has long experience of the *ton* and I would not think of contradicting her good taste."

"Very wise." Isabel's mood was worsening by the moment. She wished the man would just leave so that she and Julia might finish their business and she could go home and put her feet up.

Before Julia could complain, Chiswick said, "Naturally Lady Julia will allow herself to be guided by your taste, Mrs. Chamberlayne. No young lady of breeding could do otherwise."

Isabel clearly heard the sneer in his tone and, as she pondered just how badly she had been insulted, Julia responded by clamping her mouth shut. At least that had muzzled her for the moment.

Seizing the opportunity, Isabel turned to Chiswick. "I hope you will excuse us, Mr. Chiswick, but Lady Julia must complete her order here."

Julia stirred and Isabel, sensing the prelude to a complaint, dug her fingers in Julia's shoulders. The girl subsided with a put-upon sigh and picked up her fashion plates.

"Naturally." Chiswick slapped his gloves against his thigh. "Forgive me for interrupting. I know how important the right gown is to beautiful young ladies."

Isabel could have sworn he winked at Julia and, judging by Julia's heightened color, she was probably correct.

"Quite right, Mr. Chiswick." Isabel's tone was brisk. She turned to signal Madame D'Arlemont who trotted back into the showroom so quickly it was obvious she had been listening at the door.

Chiswick paused with his hand on the door knob. "I shall return for you in an hour. Will that be acceptable?"

"What?" Isabel's head snapped up, but, before she could answer, Julia anticipated her.

"That would be delightful, Mr. Chiswick. I thank you." Julia blushed yet again and, before Isabel could say anything, Chiswick was gone. Isabel cursed under her breath.

"I heard that." Julia returned to her fashion plates and signaled to the shopkeeper to bring the fabrics closer.

Isabel glanced quickly at Madame D'Arlemont. The woman was busily holding silk up to Julia's face and making clucking sounds. She might be the soul of discretion, but Isabel was hesitant to discuss personal matters in front of a shopkeeper. Something must be said before Chiswick returned.

"Will you excuse us, Madame?" Isabel knew that dismissing the modiste a second time would probably give rise to as much gossip as conducting the conversation in front of her. But, she was not about to air family disagreements in public if she could possibly avoid it.

The moment the seamstress had closed the workroom door behind her, Isabel moved to stand directly before Julia.

"You heard me curse, Julia?"

"Yes." The girl looked mulishly up at Isabel. "And I cannot think mother would approve."

"I cannot think your mother would approve of your being escorted about town by George Chiswick," Isabel said, crossing her arms over her chest.

"Do sit down, Isabel." Julia flounced in her seat. "I don't like you staring down at me like a nasty governess."

"Don't make me act like a nasty governess. Your willful disregard of my advice will only bring you grief." Isabel dropped to the seat facing Julia.

"I know my own mind." Julia turned her face toward the workroom door.

"And I know the dangers." Isabel reached out and took Julia's hand.

Julia pulled her hand away and got to her feet. "If you don't feel equal to seeing me in Mr. Chiswick's company, you may leave," she said, sounding every inch the daughter of an earl.

"I'll summon Madame." It was obvious to Isabel that she would not win this argument and that the best she could do today was remain vigilant while Chiswick escorted them through the rest of Julia's errands.

*   *   *

Chiswick was punctual, an occurrence that surprised Isabel until she remembered that he had been so with her when her fortune was still eligible. *Until Sidney rescued her.* The thought whispered in her ear, almost making her smile at the ridiculousness of the idea that she had been rescued by a man who she had not wanted and who had not wanted her.

"I have a hackney waiting on the next street," Chiswick said, staring rather pointedly at Isabel's breasts.

Wishing she'd brought a shawl, Isabel glared back. She had observed this morning that her dress was a bit tight through the bosom, but thought that no one else would pay attention. She should have known that someone like Chiswick would notice. Glancing quickly at Julia, Isabel perceived that she was not the only one annoyed by Chiswick's interest in her anatomy.

"Lady Haddon's carriage will be calling for us," she said in a tone that should have frozen Chiswick's toes.

"Well, then..." Chiswick's intonation was as jovial as Isabel's was cool. "Then you must both take my arms so that I am the envy of every man on Pall Mall."

Julia giggled and immediately hurried up to take Chiswick's right arm, beaming up at him as she did.

Isabel gritted her teeth and nodded toward the door. "I am right behind you," she said, hoping it sounded like the warning it was meant to be.

Regaling Julia with details of the play he had seen the previous evening, Chiswick ushered the ladies through the door and onto the busy street.

Isabel found it necessary to take Chiswick's other arm in order to monitor what he was saying to Julia. When Isabel placed her gloved hand on Chiswick's left sleeve, the gentleman smiled down at her with considerable satisfaction. Julia frowned, but soon recalled Chiswick's attention to herself.

The shopping trip seemed endless. Isabel waited at the milliner, the boot maker, the haberdasher. She watched Chiswick help Julia pick out gloves, lace and a fan, but drew the line at boots. Her head ached. Her feet hurt. Her temper grew short.

Isabel sent up a short prayer of thanksgiving when the Haddon town coach appeared as they were leaving Dyde and Scribe's, having placed what Isabel thought was a decidedly premature order for a fur muff. Without a glance at Chiswick, Isabel swept Julia into the carriage and signaled the coachman.

"How rude." Julia's face was livid. Isabel could see that the girl was incensed, but she was beyond caring.

Isabel leaned back against the velvet squabs with a luxurious sigh.

"Did you hear me, Isabel?" Julia leaned forward so that her face was level with Isabel's.

"I heard you, Julia, but I am in no mood for an argument."

"This is not an argument. This is a demand." Julia straightened up and looked down her confection of a nose at Isabel. "Stay out of my personal affairs."

Isabel bit her lip and wondered if she was tired enough to cry. "Julia," she said softly, "I am thinking only of your welfare."

"Well don't!" Julia went from regal lady to petulant child in the blink of an eye. "I can look after myself."

"We have had this conversation before. If you believe Chiswick is not after your fortune, it is obvious to me that you cannot look after yourself." Isabel leaned her head back and closed her eyes.

"I will speak to my mother about your interference," Julia said, her lip still protruding in a pout.

Isabel nodded. "Oh Lord, Julia. I wish you would."

CHAPTER 20

The weather had turned cold and blustery. A stiff wind blew in off the channel. Sidney, shivering in the lee of a battered Dover tavern, turned up his jacket collar and thought with surprising fondness of the heat of the Spanish sun. As he waited for the sailor, his thoughts turned to the even more pleasurable warmth of Isabel's bed.

A door creaked and Sidney peered around the corner of the building. He hastily reminded himself why he was there. Isabel was on his mind far too much of late. It would not do to allow infatuation with his wife to jeopardize the mission.

Several nights of hiding in the ruins of St. Radigund's Abbey had resulted in cold feet, damp clothing and, finally, the opportunity to observe his conspirators at work. At first glance, they were a shabby lot. When they had first gathered around the small fire in the shell of the old Abbey's refectory, Sidney had been hard pressed to credit that one among them had the brains or initiative to mount an attempt to rescue Bonaparte.

Two consecutive nights of eavesdropping had proven that, although they were not stupid, neither were they the driving force. They appeared to be well-informed lackeys, in Dover to act as the conduit to whomever in London was pulling the strings and providing the money. That was what Sidney was here to learn.

They were careful. Sidney sat motionless for what seemed like hours before anyone mentioned a name. And then, it was not the name he sought, but that of the ship that had transported money to France. Still, it was more than he'd had.

A door creaked again and Sidney's contact crept around the corner. Behind the nondescript little man straggled an equally nondescript sailor who peered around as if expecting to be waylaid at any moment.

"This is the gentleman you're to talk to." Mr. Withers gestured toward Sidney.

"Y'said there'd be a pint in it," the sailor said, giving Mr. Withers a belligerent glare.

Withers slewed his eyes toward Sidney who shrugged and led them into the tavern. "The table in the corner," he said.

While Mr. Withers and the sailor drank their ale, Sidney went in search of the innkeeper and paid him enough to keep the door to this small anteroom closed and the occupants undisturbed.

Sidney slid onto the bench behind the table and leaned back against the roughly mortared wall. He had his own tankard and said nothing as he took a first sip from the contents. The sailor applied himself to his ale until Mr. Withers gave the sailor a nudge.

"Tell the gentleman what ye know."

The sailor squinted at Sidney as if trying to decide if he was worth telling. "I might," he said at last.

Sidney glanced at Mr. Withers who rolled his eyes and began his own narration. "Carson is first mate on the Apollo." He stopped and took a long swallow of his ale.

"And...?" Sidney tried to quell his impatience. He was used to direct action, but suspected that would not be an effective course to take at this moment.

"I don't like it," Carson said to his tankard.

Taking a chance that he might know what the man was talking about, Sidney said, "No one likes it, Mr. Carson."

"Aye," the man said, still staring into his drink, "That's God's truth."

"Perhaps you can help to improve it." Sidney clutched his tankard and prayed that the thing Carson disapproved of was treason.

"Mr. Carson was telling me that his captain might be involved in some…er… questionable trade." Sidney was grateful when Mr. Withers decided to prod the conversation along.

"Indeed?" Sidney set his mug down and leaned forward, planting his forearms on the uneven surface of the table. "I would pay well to hear more about it."

The sailor's head jerked up, his sharp gaze meeting Sidney's. "How much?"

Sidney leaned back and detached a bag from his belt. He set it on the table, but did not take his hand from it. "It really depends upon how much your information is worth," he said.

"The captain been carrying blunt to the Frenchies." The bag had a dramatic effect on Carson's tongue.

"So I gathered." Sidney picked up the sack of coins and hefted it. "That news is not worth a shilling."

"Hold on." Carson held up his hand. "I can tell you where he delivered it and describe them as he gave it to."

"And?" This would be helpful to Whitehall, but Sidney wanted to know the names of the men in London who were funding this heinous enterprise.

"And I can tell you what we brought back with us to be delivered to London." The sailor sat back in his chair and smirked. "What'd that be worth to you?"

Sidney opened the pouch and removed a stack of coins. He set them on the table and then covered them with his hand.

Carson took a gulp of his ale and, wiping his mouth with the back of his hand, proceeded to describe the Apollo's journey and his captain's perfidy in precise detail.

"Snuff?" Sidney came to attention in his seat, his heart hammering. "The Apollo carried snuff?"

"Aye." Carson nodded.

"You mean as cargo." Sidney tried to tamp down a wild hope that he had found the trail he needed.

"No. As a special favor to them as sends the blunt." The sailor looked as though he had just won a prize.

And Sidney thought that perhaps he had. "What more can you tell me about the snuff."

The sailor shrugged. "Don't know. It's Frenchie's all I know."

"Can you get me some?"

Carson scratched his chin and eyed the stack of coins. "Mayhap I can."

Sidney extracted several more and added them to the pile. "And can you give me a name?"

"Can't say. Dangerous work, sneaking around the captain's papers."

Sidney emptied the bag on the table and the sailor grinned. "I'll send word," he said, reaching out toward the money.

Sidney clapped his hand over the coins. He removed three from the pile and handed them to Carson. "The rest when you bring me the snuff and the name."

Carson bit down on one of the coins, then, flipping it in the air, placed it and the other two into his pocket. "Fair enough," he said and skulked out of the dingy tavern.

The door slammed shut after the sailor and Sidney turned to Mr. Withers who was silently regarding the exit. "Do you trust him?"

The little brown man shrugged. "He doesn't like treason, if that's what you mean. But he'll look out for his own skin first."

"Will he come back with anything substantial?" Sidney slid the coins back into the bag and shoved it into his jacket pocket.

"Might be he will." Mr. Withers sidled out of his seat and stood. "Do ye need anything else from me?"

"Not today." Sidney rose and handed the man a coin. "But do not let him tarry. I am in something of a hurry."

* * *

"A letter for you, Mrs. Chamberlayne." Wharton placed the silver salver on Isabel's writing desk.

She picked up the heavy paper and examined the seal. From Haddon House. Curious. She broke the seal and smoothed the paper out on her desk. The note was in Lady Haddon's fine copperplate

My Dear Isabel... Her dear? Although Isabel felt as though she and Sidney's mother had reached something of an understanding, she was certain that the countess did not think of her as "dear." This could not be a good sign.

I must beg your assistance in an urgent matter. The letter went on to explain that Lady Haddon's mother had taken ill and that the countess was compelled to travel to Rutlandshire to be with her.

As Haddon is too busy with such things as men must do and, as a man, is no fit chaperone for Julia, I entrust my dearest girl to your care. And I do so with all confidence that you will look after her as if she were your own sister. The letter continued in that vein for several more sentences and ended by informing Isabel that Julia would arrive that morning.

Isabel folded the letter and sat back. Regardless of whether or not Lady Haddon thought of her as "dear," the letter was a watershed in their uneasy relationship. Granted, it was convenient to send Julia to Bruton Place. The fact that the countess had done so rather than pack the girl up and take her to Rutlandshire with her, evinced a certain trust. And that warmed Isabel. Rising, she rang for her housekeeper.

*   *   *

When Julia arrived, she was in an ebullient mood.

"We will have so much fun, Isabel. It will be just as if we really were sisters." She beamed at Isabel who was directing her footman on the disposal of Julia's trunks.

Once the trunks and Julia's maid were safely arranged in the sunny chamber in the family wing that Isabel had selected, Isabel led her sister-in-law into her morning room and sent for tea.

"I am sorry to hear that your grandmother is ailing," Isabel said when the two had made themselves comfortable.

A worried frown crossed Julia's face. "Grandmama is frequently ill," she said. "But it is difficult to tell when it is real."

Isabel raised an eyebrow.

"She always has the megrims and London makes her bilious so she never comes for the season. But, if she wants to see Mama, she tends to have an attack of something. I daresay it's the gout that's got my mother heading for Rutlandshire."

"I hope your diagnosis is correct," Isabel said, passing Julia a cup of tea. She picked up her own cup and inhaled the soothing aroma. There was nothing like a good cup of tea.

Julia, she noticed, had conveniently forgotten her sulks of the previous day. She wondered if the girl had second thoughts about her petulant behavior. Even more, she wondered if Julia had second thoughts about her infatuation with George Chiswick. She didn't dare ask about either, but she did wonder if she had been precipitous in writing to Sidney about her inability to convince Julia to forgo Chiswick's company.

*   *   *

Sidney lay low over Chiron's neck and let his horse have his head. He had been too long in Kent with little to show for it and his patience was wearing thin. It had been two days since his interview with the first mate of the Apollo and there was still no word.

The men he tracked to the Abbey had not ceased meeting, but he could glean no more from them. Their evening gatherings quickly degenerated into roistering drinking parties during which the only information exchanged involved gaming and the local women.

Mr. Withers, who stopped by the Three Horseshoes daily to report his lack of progress, had not heard from Mr. Carson. Sidney was reluctant to have the man return to St. Margaret's Bay, lest his continued presence be remarked upon by those he would rather were not aware of the investigation.

Sidney was sure he had walked every lane in Buckland. At another time, he would have visited the barracks on the Western Heights to meet with fellow soldiers, or gone to view the construction on the new fort. But his investigation kept him away from any society he might have sought. It would not do to be known as a soldier.

His only respite was in the saddle, wind in his face, problems at his back. Only when he was on Chiron did he feel anything akin to comfort.

On the third day, Mr. Withers and a letter from Isabel arrived simultaneously.

"He's ready to talk to you," Withers said without preamble.

Sidney flicked his eyes quickly to the boy who had entered behind Withers holding the letter. Withers clamped his mouth shut and leaned against the box in which Sidney was currying his horse's gleaming chestnut coat.

"Mr. Chamberlayne, sir." The boy outside the stall, pulled a forelock and proffered the envelope.

Sidney took the letter, gave the boy a coin and gestured to him to be on his way.

"When?" he asked Withers as soon as the door stable door banged shut behind the young messenger.

"Tonight. Said he'd meet ye at Bradsole." The little man shouldered himself away from the wall on which he was leaning and made for the door.

"No," Sidney said, sliding the letter into his pocket. "Not the abbey." He had been there too many nights not to know how many places it held in which a man, or a band of men, could hide.

"Tell him to meet me at the tavern in Dover where we met before." Sidney pulled out his watch. "At four o'clock. Can that be done?"

The man looked out the door at the sun. "Yes, sir. I'll have him there."

Left alone in the stable, Sidney laid his hand against his horse's neck. Chiron swung his huge head around and nuzzled Sidney, eliciting a smile and a groan. "Lord, Chiron. I hope this is what we need. I'm ready to go home."

Chiron nickered softly and began searching Sidney for sweets. Sidney dug into his pocket and extracted a dried apple he'd been saving for the horse. Absently, he held the fruit out and, as Chiron daintily plucked it out of his hand, realized that he was thinking of Bruton Place as home. When had that occurred? When he first moved into Isabel's townhouse, Sidney was convinced that he would never be comfortable there, that it was a temporary bivouac until he returned to his regiment.

Sidney muffled a chuckle against Chiron's sleek neck. How could he return to the army when his life had changed so radically since Vitoria? His work at Whitehall had become as engrossing, as important to him, as his work as a cavalry officer and, he hoped, of a less violent nature.

If he were to be absolutely honest with himself,

though, Isabel was a factor. Something had grown between them. When they weren't arguing, there was a warmth of communion that he'd felt nowhere else in his life. And, when they were arguing there was a warmth of an altogether different, but no less interesting, kind.

Chiron, nudging his hand in search of another treat, recalled Sidney to the present. He had to leave for Dover if he was to be on time to meet the first mate.

Carson was already in the tavern when Sidney arrived and, from the look of it, had already indulged in the local ale. Sidney prayed he was still coherent.

Sidney had expected Withers to be there, but was not sorry that he was absent. If things went as he hoped, the fewer people who heard the conversation, the better.

"Carson." He pulled up a chair and assessed the extent of the man's inebriation.

"Aye." The man's eyes were red and his breath reeked of ale, but his voice was remarkably steady and he looked sober enough.

"What do you have?" Sidney asked.

"Did you bring the money?" The man drained his mug and signaled the serving girl who was loitering by the door.

As he had at the first meeting, Sidney placed the bag on the table and kept his hands on it. The man nodded but did not speak again until his ale was served and the girl had left the room.

"Yer going ta owe me that whole purse for what I did," he said.

"That is yet to be seen." Sidney wound the leather straps that held the bag closed around his hand.

"If my captain knows I rifled his papers, he's like to kill me."

"He won't know," Sidney said, trying to sound reassuring despite his growing impatience.

"Well," the sailor said, finally, "he's got some papers hid with his clothes."

"Did you bring them?" Sidney asked.

"Are you daft, man?" Carson looked incredulous. "If I took 'em, he'd a knowed who did it. But I looked at 'em."

Sidney bit his tongue to keep from asking if the man could read. He only hoped he could. "So?"

"So, as I told ye before, he's been takin' money to the froggies for... well you know what for."

"And were there names?" Sidney clenched his hand so tightly one of the leather strings snapped, startling both men.

"There was one." Carson looked at the bag.

One would be enough, if it was the right one. Sidney waited in silence.

"The one that takes the snuff," the sailor offered, digging around in his own pocket.

Sidney thought he might kill the man out of sheer annoyance before he got his information.

Carson slid a small packet across the table, but kept his finger on it.

"The name?" Sidney watched Carson's eyes, feeling sure he would know if the man was lying.

"Chatsworth," the sailor said and then drew a breath. "Or Chittenden." He hesitated again and then said, "No. Chipman."

Sidney raised his hand and pinched the bridge of his nose, his hopes dashed in the face of near-illiteracy.

"The blunt?" Carson asked.

Sidney sighed deeply. "Show me what's in the packet."

The sailor carefully unwrapped the parcel, revealing a small pile of snuff. Sidney took a pinch between his fingers and smelled it. It could be the same. He wouldn't know 'til he got it back to London. And, he at least had the name of the captain and the ship.

Sidney nodded and pushed the bag across the table to the sailor. Pulling the top open, Carson examined the contents and, appearing satisfied, transferred the pouch to his own pocket.

"Will you be needing anything else?" he asked, pushing away from the table.

"Do you have anything else?" Sidney asked, feeling suddenly weary.

Carson shook his head. "If I do, I'll send word."

"You do that."

Sidney turned the conversation over in his mind all the way back to Buckland. There might be something in those names. The man obviously recognized some of his letters. But none of the names he offered sounded even vaguely familiar to Sidney. But still, he had the snuff and he had some information. And it was time to go home.

Home. Sidney suddenly recalled the letter he had received that afternoon. He patted his jacket pocket. It was still there. He put his heels to Chiron's flanks, anxious to get to the inn.

Sidney went directly to his room, put the packet of snuff safely inside his portmanteau, shed his jacket and sat down to read Isabel's letter.

He read it twice, threw his jacket back on and dashed to the stables. He came to a halt in front of Chiron's stall and looked at his horse, peacefully munching the oats the stable boy had put in the bucket.

Sidney wanted to leave that minute, saddle Chiron and ride through the night. He needed to get to London. Chiron raised his massive head and stared back. Sidney could almost read the fatigue in the great beast's eyes. He had ridden him to a lather that morning. He could not ask him to start for London tonight.

Sidney went back to his chamber and threw himself into the sole chair in the room. High backed and upholstered in an unidentifiable material, it was not particularly comfortable, but Sidney had come to appreciate it for what it was.

He unfolded Isabel's letter and scanned it for a third time. Damn! He was going to wring Julia's neck when he finally got to London. What was she thinking? And what was Haddon thinking to allow her to associate with Chiswick after Sidney had warned him about the man's situation?

Chiswick. Sidney's eyes went back to the name. Written in Isabel's graceful, sloping hand, it looked elegant, not at all like the name of a rogue. He stared at it until it stood out from the rest of the page, a hieroglyph with a meaning unto itself.

Damnation! Sidney bolted from the chair and paced to the window. Chatsworth, Chittenden, Chipman... Chiswick? Was it likely? Was it even possible? Sidney had seen him take snuff once or twice, but that did not make him a traitor. Nor did the fact that he was a fortune hunter. But it did mean that he needed money. How badly did he need it? It was going to be a very long night.

CHAPTER 21

Julia had been agreeable throughout the afternoon, more like the young girl who had eagerly welcomed Isabel as her sister than like the moody young lady she turned into once she had experienced the attention accorded her by the *ton* and especially its gentlemen. Isabel was reminded just how green Julia was.

Isabel would rather have not attended the Goodwright's ball. But Julia expected to go and Isabel was not about to let her out of her sight if she could possibly help it. She stood in the middle of her chamber as Willington slipped the apple green satin over her head. Green was not her favorite color, but tonight it didn't seem to matter.

She gazed out the window while Willington adjusted the silver net overdress and fastened the emerald earrings. It was hard to see the garden. It had been hazy all day and the moon was obscured by clouds.

Isabel wondered if her message had reached Sidney. She had dipped into her pin money to send the letter express, but the weather had been so bad, she feared express might be no better than post at this rate. She hoped that Julia's improved demeanor meant that Sidney's intervention would not be necessary.

"There you are ma'am." Willington stepped back and walked around Isabel. "You look very fine, if you don't mind my saying so."

Isabel smiled at her abigail. "When have I ever minded hearing that?"

Julia was waiting at the foot of the stairs, smoothing the creases in her kid gloves and pacing to the window and back.

"You look quite the thing, Julia." Isabel inspected Julia's gown. The pale pink muslin trimmed with cerise ribbon made the girl's complexion glow. Or perhaps that was youth.

"Do I?" Julia looked down with a tiny frown. This gown seems so... infantile."

Isabel gave Julia a long look. Her coltish grace was turning to fluid femininity. The angles were becoming curves and the naiveté a beguiling innocence. Had she ever been that young? She laughed. "My dearest girl, I am afraid you will never again look infantile."

Julia lifted her gaze to Isabel, an eager smile on her face. "Do you think so?"

Isabel reached out and patted her hand. She was pleased and relieved to have the bright-eyed young girl back in her company. "You will be the belle of the ball tonight. I will enjoy watching your success."

Julia gave a contented sigh. "Thank you for bringing me. I promise not to be too much trouble."

Isabel raised an eyebrow. If the last week was any indication, Julia was going to be nothing but trouble. She sent up a small prayer that the evening would continue as it had begun.

* * *

The ladies looked up from the chairs lined against the wall. "Will you be joining the chaperones, Mrs. Chamberlayne?" Mrs. Smythe-Barrington sounded pleased at the prospect.

"Tonight, I am a chaperone." Isabel gratefully subsided into a chair in the midst of the other ladies. The ballroom was already awash with the rustle of silk and the scent of perfume. It looked as though everyone in

London was present. Isabel scrutinized the crowd, looking for anyone who might be trouble. Looking, she had to admit, for Chiswick.

Julia had been quickly absorbed by the group of young women with whom she had made her curtsey. Isabel watched her animated face as she chatted with her friends. She would never be a diamond, but she was a lovely young girl, bright and self-possessed. Isabel would have been happier, however, if Julia was not quite so sure of herself—sure of what she wanted, or thought she wanted.

"Mrs. Chamberlayne."

Isabel looked up to find that, while she was woolgathering, her hostess had appeared before her. She stood immediately. "Lady Goodwright."

"May I introduce my nephew, Mr. Fawley? Francis this is Mrs. Chamberlayne."

The young man bowed. After a polite acknowledgment, Isabel turned back to Mrs. Goodwright in curiosity.

"Francis is the younger son of my brother, Baron Fawley. He would like to be introduced to Lady Julia." Mrs. Goodwright sounded tentative and young Mr. Fawley looked as though he feared Isabel might cut off his right hand rather than grant this great boon.

"Oh, of course," Isabel said, amused as Mr. Fawley broke into a sunny smile. She extended her hand and, with flawless manners, Francis Fawley offered his arm. Oh this was very good. Mr. Fawley was handsome and polite and would surely be a welcome distraction for Julia.

The musicians were beginning another tune as Isabel accomplished the introduction. Julia seemed almost as charmed by Francis Fawley as he was by her and granted him the next set. Isabel retreated to the sidelines with the sense of having accomplished a successful battlefield maneuver.

* * *

George Chiswick hated skulking. He was a gentleman of the *ton,* the son of a viscount, handsome, worldly, attractive to women. He was meant for better things than hurrying through the back gardens of Mayfair in the shadows of an overcast night. In his pocket, he had an invitation to the Goodwright ball and every right to be in the ballroom dancing with the heiress of his choice. But, here he was by the garden wall, waiting for a man he did not want to see.

The man in black slipped through the gate in back of the Goodwright townhouse. Chiswick caught the movement out of the corner of his eye and moved in that direction. The man remained where he was until Chiswick had joined him and then silently turned and led the way back toward the mews.

"Do you have the money?" Chiswick was impatient. He had done his job and now wanted to be paid and left alone.

"Money? Is that all you can think of?"

Chiswick had never seen the man's face, covered as it was with a scarf, and his voice had a false hoarseness, as though he was trying to disguise it. Little chance that he would ever want to identify this man.

"Of course, that's all I can think of. It's the only reason I carried your dirty laundry for you." Although he did not attempt to disguise his voice, Chiswick kept it low. The last thing he wanted was to be overheard.

"Then perhaps my news is of no interest to you," the man said, turning to leave.

"News?" Chiswick grabbed him by the arm.

The man pivoted and, with surprising strength, pinned Chiswick against the garden wall. "Don't touch me."

Unable to speak with the man's arm at his throat, Chiswick nodded. The man released him and he slid to the ground.

"Get up you fool and listen to what I have to say."
The man stood at a distance and waited.

Chiswick clambered to his feet and leaned against
the wall, while his companion paced a few steps away
and then came back to stand in front of him.

"Do you take snuff?" the man asked.

What was this? "Yes," Chiswick said, reaching into
his pocket.

"Put that away. I don't want your filthy tobacco."
The man took one step closer. Chiswick tried to back up,
but found himself flush against the stone wall.

The man continued to speak, his words low and
distinct. "You—left—your—bloody—snuffbox   at
Queen Street.

"No." Chiswick fished in his pocket. "I have it
right..." And then he remembered digging out his old
plate snuffbox when he couldn't find the enameled one
he carried all the time.

The man said nothing as Chiswick struggled to come
to grips with his slip.

"No harm done," Chiswick said finally. "What
difference does it make whether I left it. Who would find
it?"

"Quite probably the Foreign Office," the man said,
his voice rife with disdain.

"What?" Chiswick felt lightheaded. "But... but they
cannot connect it to... to..."

"To treason?" the man asked. "Don't be too sure."

"Well they can't connect it to me," Chiswick said,
hopeful it was true.

"We shall see." The dark man stepped closer and
grasped Chiswick's left arm. "Remember this," he said.
"If any connection is made to the rest of us, you will find
yourself closely acquainted with the river. Do you
understand me?"

Chiswick pulled away and put his right hand where
the man's had been, rubbing the sting left by his hard

grip. "I understand you," he said and fled back through the gate.

Only when he was half way across the garden did he remember that the man had not given him the money he was owed.

Chiswick's heart was pounding so hard that, when he re-entered the ballroom, he thought that those nearest must surely hear it. He scanned the room, hoping that the warning he had just received was for naught. Hoping that, if it wasn't, a solution would present itself.

* * *

"No," Isabel said. "No, I will not dance with you. I don't even want to talk to you. Now kindly remove yourself from my presence."

Lord Gosden's smile intimated that he knew better than to believe she didn't want to see him. It made the back of Isabel's neck prickle. Her night had steadily deteriorated since she took her seat among the chaperones. She hadn't wanted to dance, but could not, in good conscience, turn down Lord Buckley. And once she had danced, she could hardly refuse the next offer.

She had lost sight of Julia and prayed that the girl was in a set in another part of the ballroom or had gone off with her friends to the refreshment table.

She had been on her way to find her when the current frustration occurred. Richard Gosden, in all his lubricious splendor, importuning her for a dance when she would prefer him on a ship to the antipodes or in hell.

"Let go of my hand." She attempted to pull it away without causing a scene, but the baron was intent on detaining her.

"Just the waltz," he said. "It has been too long since we danced the waltz."

"It has not been long enough and it will not be

repeated." Just as Isabel was considering leaving her glove in Gosden's hand and walking away, her host came to her rescue.

"Excuse me Mrs. Chamberlayne. Am I interrupting?" Portly little Mr. Goodwright positioned himself so that he was almost between Isabel and Gosden.

"Yes. We are about to dance," Gosden said.

"Not at all, Mr. Goodwright," she said at the same time.

Goodwright wrinkled his brow. "I was certain you had promised this dance to me, Mrs. Chamberlayne."

"Why so I did." Isabel finally extricated her hand. "I thank you for your excellent memory."

Gosden was left with no choice. Isabel took Mr. Goodwright's arm, relieved to be away from Gosden but resigned to one more set before she could look for Julia.

* * *

It didn't take long for Chiswick to spot Julia in a set with a singularly unprepossessing young man. Chiswick stifled a snort. If that was the best she could do, he felt certain he would prevail.

The young man escorted Julia back to the chaperones, but Isabel Chamberlayne didn't seem to be among them. Chiswick scanned the ballroom once more. Isabel was going down the dance with Lord Buckley.

So, this was what her newly acquired wedded virtue had got her. Dances with stuffy gentleman who might have been her grandfather. Chiswick's eyes lingered on Isabel for a moment. She had been a succulent prize, both physically and financially. Chiswick sighed. He had failed to win her. Now he would win her husband's sister. It should be interesting to see how she liked that.

Chiswick returned his attention to Julia, who was still standing by the chaperones with her erstwhile dance partner. The man looked like he intended to remain with Julia until he could return her to her chaperone. This might be a problem.

Chiswick watched Julia's gaze wander over the crowd and stop when it met his own. She smiled a half-smile and said something to the young man. She dropped a little curtsey in the general direction of the chaperones and headed toward the back of the ballroom, leaving the young man looking dumbfounded.

As Julia approached, Chiswick smiled broadly. He intended his expression to communicate that she was the woman he most wanted to see. He was sure he looked, for all the world, like a man in love.

"Mr. Chiswick." Julia sounded a bit breathless, her smile as tremulous as her voice.

"George," he said, keeping his voice low. "I'm so glad to see you, Lady Julia..."

"Julia," she said. "Just Julia. And I'm glad to see you, as well."

"How glad?" Chiswick asked, looking intently into her eyes.

Julia's eyes widened and she blushed.

"Come into the garden with me." Chiswick had hold of her hand, his voice urgent.

Julia looked around and Chiswick followed her gaze. Isabel was scowling at Gosden. She was paying no attention to what was going on at the edges of the room.

Satisfied that their departure would not be noted, Chiswick led Julia into the night. The torches scattered around the garden did little to illuminate the darkened corners of the terrace or the secluded alcoves carved out of the shrubbery.

Once they had passed the fountain, the sound from the ballroom faded, replaced by the musical splashing of the water. Chiswick looked once toward the back of the townhouse and drew Julia to the carved seat sheltered among the branches.

Julia waited, her eyes huge, her breathing rapid. "Lady Julia... Julia." Chiswick lifted her hand to his lips. "I have not known you long. But some things— some earth shattering events—require no time at all. From the moment I beheld you, I knew that you were the only woman who could complete my life. Will you make me the happiest of men? Will you be my wife?"

Julia's color increased and she swayed on the bench. Thinking she might faint, Chiswick put his hands on her shoulders. "My dear?"

"Oh." Julia could barely speak. "Oh yes. That is... I want to. But, my brothers..."

"There is an impediment?" Chiswick infused his voice with a hint of wickedness. Just the thing to tempt a girl in search of experience.

"No," Julia said, her voice quavering.

"No?" Did she mean no impediment or was she refusing his proposal?

Julia shook her head as if to clear it. "I mean yes," she said, in the same, faltering voice. "Yes." More forcefully. "I will marry you... George."

Chiswick drew her into his arms and kissed her. This was perfect. Marriage to Haddon's sister, to Chamberlayne's sister. A dowry and influence. All would be well. And she was a delightful young thing, if a trifle innocent.

Chiswick pulled away slowly and studied her face. "But your brother..." he said, knowing exactly what would come next.

"We will win him over. I am sure of it." Julia grasped Chiswick's hands and held them in hers. "It just might take some time."

In a quick movement, Chiswick rose from the bench and stared down at Julia. "I can't wait. Do not make me." His voice was a hoarse murmur.

He strode to the fountain, gazed at the cherubs frolicking in its center, and then returned to her as abruptly as he'd left. Dropping onto the bench, he pulled her to him, kissed her again and whispered in her ear. "I must make you mine."

Julia gazed up into Chiswick's face and touched his cheek. "If you mean to... I cannot... I am a..." She blushed again.

"My sweetest girl." Chiswick took Julia's face between his hands and gave her a look calculated to melt her earrings. "I would never dishonor you. How could you think such a thing? No. Never. We must be married. In Scotland. Yes. That would be the thing."

He kissed her again and held her against him, crooning softly. "Tell me you won't make me wait."

"George."

Chiswick was sure that, at that moment, Lady Julia Chamberlayne would not have made him wait for anything.

"You know best," she whispered. "You decide."

CHAPTER 22

Isabel lingered over breakfast. Her aunt was still abed and she appreciated the solitude. She hadn't slept well, had stayed too long in bed, and her head was muzzy. Carefully, she set the cup back in its saucer and reached for another piece of cold toast.

For the first time in days, she had awakened hungry and her stomach seemed to be in an agreeable mood. Unwilling to tempt fate, she ate only coddled eggs and toast, but plenty of it. She also consumed more chocolate than she had in a fortnight.

Swirling her chocolate, Isabel contemplated the hazy sun filtering in the west breakfast room window. She was still worried about Julia. Although the girl had seemed her sunny self on the way to the Goodwright ball, the trip home had been a different story. Julia spoke very little and spent most of the ride gazing out the window of the town coach. She was not petulant as she had been earlier in the week, but she seemed preoccupied. Her responses to Isabel's questions were vague and distracted.

No doubt Julia was simply tired or she was mooning over a dance partner. Isabel had been surprised not to see Chiswick at the ball. Surprised, but relieved. She prayed Julia was not brooding over his absence. Isabel hoped her sister-in-law's uncharacteristic silence was caused by the estimable Mr. Fawley.

If only Sidney were home to deal with his sister. Isabel sighed. She wished Sidney home for more reasons than one. The house seemed dull and empty without him.

The desire to tell Sidney about the child she carried seemed to increase daily until it was an almost desperate yearning. She hoped that, when he finally arrived, she could prevent herself from flinging herself into his arms and blurting out the news the moment he set foot in the house.

"Mrs. Chamberlayne." Wharton stood at the door to the breakfast room looking as though he was ready to bolt.

"Yes?" Isabel squinted at the butler, wishing that her head felt clearer. He appeared to be in some distress.

"Er... Lady Julia's maid wishes to speak with you." Wharton stepped back to reveal Julia's abigail hovering behind him.

"Well, send her in." It was one of those days when protocol seemed to be simply an annoyance.

The tiny maid stepped around Wharton and stopped just over the threshold of the breakfast room, her hands tightly laced at her waist.

"Yes...?" Isabel desperately searched for the girl's name, but came to the conclusion that she had never heard it.

"Benson, ma'am." The girl bobbed two or three curtseys.

"Then, what is it, Benson?" Isabel knew she sounded snappish, but she was in no mood for nervous maids this morning.

"It's Lady Julia, ma'am." Benson swallowed convulsively. "She's... she's gone."

Isabel sprang up from her seat, her fingertips rigid against the tabletop. "What?"

The woman trembled so Isabel feared she might faint. "Wharton!"

The butler was no longer within earshot. Heaving a sigh of exasperation, Isabel hastened to the maid's side and put a hand under her elbow. Isabel guided her to the table, and pulling out a chair, placed her in it. Then pulled up another to face her.

"Tell me everything," Isabel said, straining to keep her voice from betraying her own agitation.

Benson's face was devoid of color and her eyes brimmed with tears. She took a few gasping breaths before she began. When she finally spoke, her voice was barely audible.

"I went in to Lady Julia's room just a short while ago. You know, she was out late." She stopped and blinked. "Of course you know. I am so stupid."

Isabel clenched her fists to keep from shaking the girl. "Go on."

"She... she wasn't in her bed, madam. She wasn't in her room nor in her dressing room. I helped her ready herself for bed last night, but I left before she retired. And... and it looked as though her bed had not even been slept in."

The girl took a deep shuddering breath. The tears she had been holding back seeped out and ran down her cheeks.

Isabel bit back an impatient question and waited for the maid to regain her composure. Once Benson had wiped away her tears, Isabel leaned toward her. "Is that all?" she asked.

"All, madam?" The maid looked confused.

"Come with me." Isabel's composure snapped. She was out of her seat and at the door before the maid had left her chair. "Now."

Julia's bed was, indeed, in its original pristine state. It had not been used. The same could not be said for the rest of the room. Clothing was flung on chairs, drawers hung open and the door to the clothes press was ajar. For a moment, Isabel wondered if there had been foul play.

"What's missing?" she asked the maid.

Benson went immediately to the chest against the

wall and began opening cases and pulling out drawers. When she was done there, she examined the clothes press, made a neat pile of the strewn garments and then looked around the room.

"Well?"

"My lady's small trunk," the maid said. "It's gone."

So, Julia had run away. Isabel was not terribly surprised at this turn of events. And she thought she could guess with whom she had gone and where. Damn! Where was Sidney when she needed him?

Was there a note? Starting with the mantel, Isabel combed every surface for something Julia might have left to say where she was going. When she found herself shaking out the pillows, she conceded that there was no note. But she didn't need a note to deduce what had happened.

"Go calm yourself," she said to Benson, "and then come back here and straighten this room. Bring me a detailed list of what is missing. Can you write?"

The maid nodded and moved toward the door.

"Wait." The girl stopped dead at Isabel's peremptory command.

"Do you have any idea of where Lady Julia has gone?" Isabel had abandoned any attempt to calm the girl. She wanted as many answers as she could find.

The maid bit her lips and looked at her feet.

"You do," Isabel said with certainty. "What do you know?"

"I... I know nothing, ma'am," the girl hesitated. "I never gossip about my lady," she said, in a mortified whisper.

"It will be to your lady's benefit if I know everything there is to know about her possible whereabouts." Isabel paced the floor as she spoke. "You must tell me."

The maid still hesitated and Isabel lost patience. "Has she eloped with George Chiswick?"

"I don't know, ma'am, but I think she might have done. She talked about him to me, she did. And there were notes." The girl looked abashed. "I know I shouldn't have helped, but she is my lady."

Isabel rolled her eyes. "Of course she is. There is nothing you could have done. Now go straighten yourself out and then the room. Bring me the list as soon as possible. And," she added as the girl scurried away, "any letters you might find in your cleaning."

* * *

What could that girl be doing? Isabel wandered impatiently around the library, kicking at the carpets, running her fingers over the furniture, staring out the back windows. It seemed like hours since she'd discovered Julia's disappearance.

Isabel had long since ordered a bag packed and the traveling carriage readied. She was going after Julia regardless of what the maid turned up.

"What is going on?" The library door swung open and Lady Louisa trotted in, clad in a gauzy morning dress and looking rather more rumpled than usual.

"Aunt." Isabel spoke on a sigh of relief and walked across the room to embrace Lady Louisa.

Louisa took Isabel's hands and peered up into her face. "Julia has bolted?"

"Oh, Lord." Isabel pulled away and walked back to the window.

Louisa followed. "So, it's true."

"Servants' gossip usually is." Isabel stared, unseeing, out the window, pleating the draperies with nervous fingers.

Isabel dropped the curtain. "I am going after her."

"Certainly not. That's an appalling idea." Lady Louisa looked suitably appalled.

"It's the only thing to be done." Isabel resumed her

pacing, her hands fisted at her sides in knots of tension.

"Send for Haddon," Louisa suggested.

"I will not." Isabel whirled around to face her aunt, her eyes flashing, her chin jutting at a stubborn angle.

"He is her brother." Louisa's tone was soft and reasonable.

Isabel gritted her teeth in annoyance. "I am her sister. And I've been entrusted with her care."

"Then do the prudent thing." Louisa assumed a militant stance in the center of the floor and placed her hands on her hips.

Isabel sighed. "Of course you are correct."

A scratch on the door preceded Julia's maid. She dropped a clumsy curtsey and approached Isabel holding out a smudged list.

Isabel gingerly plucked the paper out of the girl's trembling fingers and glanced down at the list. Although poorly spelled, it was quite detailed. "Are you sure this is all that's missing?" she asked.

Benson nodded.

"And you found no other paper?"

"No ma'am." The girl still looked like she might faint and Isabel wondered if that was simply her natural attitude.

"Thank you, Benson. You may go." The girl, who was already backing toward the door, turned and fled.

Isabel glanced back at the list. "She seems to have taken enough clothes for a week."

Lady Louisa said nothing, but her expression spoke volumes.

Isabel rolled her eyes. "Very well, I'll write to Haddon."

The Earl of Haddon was nowhere to be found. The footman who had been sent with Isabel's note reported that the Earl had left town and was not expected back for two or three days.

There was no time to waste. Isabel's staff made ready for her pursuit of Julia at an astonishing speed. Willington had packed Isabel's valise and clothes for herself and was sitting in the front hall with the bags at her feet. The carriage waited in front of the house..

Lady Louisa stood in Isabel's bedchamber wringing her hands as Isabel pulled a light cloak from the closet and hung it over her arm.

"Please stop, Aunt. I am nervous enough as it is." Isabel's heart was pounding so hard she could hear the blood rushing through her veins.

"This is so foolish." Louisa shook her head in a gesture of despair.

"What would you have me do? Leave Julia to her fate with that... that ... fortune hunter?"

"Are you sure it's Chiswick she's gone off with?" Lady Louisa laid a gentle hand on Isabel's arm.

Isabel patted the wrinkled hand. "As sure as I can be without seeing it myself." Gently, she removed her aunt's hand from her arm. "I must go."

"Let me go with you." Lady Louisa grasped Isabel's hands.

"No. Someone must be here if Julia returns." Isabel squeezed her aunt's hands and kissed her cheek.

*   *   *

George Chiswick spared the horses. He did not have the money to change teams at each stop and was reluctant to ask Lady Julia for blunt before they were properly wed. He knew that both Julia's brothers were out of town and felt fairly sanguine that no one would follow them for a day or two at least.

"You did not leave a message?" he asked for perhaps the third time.

"No, dearest. You told me not to and, I assure you, I will be a most biddable wife." Julia patted his arm.

Assuming a fond smile, Chiswick winked at his companion. Biddable or not, she had her value.

Julia giggled and squeezed his arm. "Is this not exciting? How far will we travel today?"

Chiswick consulted his watch. They'd left London before the sun had risen and were nearing Biggleswade. He guessed they could be in Northampton by nightfall. If the horse made it that far, they would have to spend the night or change horses. He glanced over at Julia. A night at an inn would not be a hardship and would serve to bind her more closely to him.

"We'll stop in the next town for refreshment and to rest the horses. Then we'll go on and spend tonight in Northampton. Will that suit you?" He peered ahead, looking for signs of the River Ivel, a sure sign they would be able to stop soon.

"Northampton?" Julia asked, her face clouded. "We will spend the night there?"

"My dear." Chiswick transferred the ribbons to his right hand and placed his left on Julia's. "You didn't think we could travel all the way to Scotland in one day?"

Julia emitted a tiny laugh. "No, of course not. How foolish of me not to think of it, though. I should have brought my maid."

Chiswick tightened his fingers around Julia's hand. "Bring your maid to an elopement? Where is your romance, my girl? Where is your sense of adventure?"

Julia leaned her head against his shoulder and Chiswick experienced a momentary twinge of conscience. She was so young and so trusting, Lady Julia Chamberlayne. Although he had spent the better part of the past decade looking for a young woman of fortune, he had never expected to elope. And certainly never with a girl in the first flush of adulthood.

Lady Julia Chamberlayne. That was the key, wasn't it? And Chiswick had no alternative. His poor choice of confederates, his unfortunate need for ready cash, his decision to abet treason. If he could recall it all and continue hunting heiresses, he fancied he might. But it was all too late for that. Now, his only option sat beside him in a borrowed curricle, nestled against him as if he were the answer to her prayers. He only hoped she was the answer to his.

CHAPTER 23

If the Carlisle Road was the most direct road to Gretna Green, Isabel was sure it must also be the most uneven. She and Willington had been jostled for almost four hours when the carriage stopped to change horses. It was a welcome relief to step onto solid ground and seek a restorative cup of tea.

Recognizing quality, the innkeeper's wife showed Isabel to a private parlor and brought in the tea and cakes herself. She set the tray down on the table by the window and turned to leave, but Isabel stopped her.

"Have you had much custom, today?" Isabel picked up the tea cup and examined it.

"Not many, ma'am." The woman eyed Isabel's examination of the crockery. "Can I get you ought else?"

Satisfied that the cup was clean and undamaged, Isabel poured herself some tea. "Nothing else," she said, "but I am seeking my... friends. A young woman and her husband. Perhaps they stopped here today."

"Aye. Might have." The woman closed the door and leaned against the frame. "Might have seen them."

Isabel opened her reticule and placed some coins on the table. "It is important that I find her. She's about eighteen years of age. Dark hair. A lady."

"Dark-haired girl and yellow-haired gent." The innkeeper's wife kept her eyes on the money. "Stopped here this morning. Off to Gretna, I figured, by the looks of them, and in a hurry."

"How long ago?" Isabel pushed the money toward

the woman, who scooped it up and slid it into her pocket.

"Three hours or more," the woman said, moving back toward the door. At Isabel's stricken look, she added, "Headed north, for sure. I don't collect they'll get farther than Northampton tonight. Might have heard 'em say so, in fact." The woman bobbed her head and slipped out of the little parlor.

Three hours. Although she longed to sit quietly for a few more minutes, Isabel knew that time was critical to finding Julia and Chiswick before irreparable damage was done. Setting down her cup, she sent to the kitchen where Willington was just finishing her own tea.

*   *   *

It was after midnight when Isabel's coach arrived at the Angel in Northampton. Isabel didn't leave the carriage, but sent the footman to inquire about anyone who had arrived that day. The negative answer sent them next to the George.

By the time they pulled up in front of the Rose and Crown, Isabel had begun to lose heart. When the footman returned to report that a Mr. Chesterton and his sister had taken rooms for the night, Isabel breathed a sigh of relief and sent him back to tell the landlord she wanted to speak with him.

Willington was wide awake and wide-eyed in her corner of the carriage. Isabel could tell she was perishing to talk about Julia's flight and their pursuit. But Isabel didn't broach that or any subject. This was between her and Julia. She only thanked God that Chiswick and Julia were in separate rooms. And she suspected she knew whose money had paid for that extravagance.

Isabel leaned her head back against the soft leather of the seat and let her eyes fall shut. It had been a long and grueling trip. She was exhausted and slightly ill. Her head swam with fatigue and she'd had an annoying stitch in her side for the past two hours. She longed only to stretch out on a clean bed and sleep.

The footman roused her with news the landlord awaited her. Accepting the footman's help descending from the carriage, Isabel sent Willington to see if she could find some refreshment and directed her coachman to take care of the horses.

The innkeeper stood, bleary-eyed and hastily dressed, in the narrow entry hall. He was irritable at having been awakened and in no mood to be helpful.

"Gentleman paid for the room. Paid for his privacy. I'm not letting you barge in there and disturb his sleep." The innkeeper leaned against a rough plastered wall and scratched his arm.

Isabel shuddered. She hoped whatever was making him itch was confined to his own quarters.

"This is very important. I have… important news for Mr. Chesterton that he will be very glad to hear." Isabel stretched her neck trying to ease the tension in her shoulders.

The man looked unconvinced. "He's a paying guest."

Isabel cast about for a persuasive argument. She lowered her eyes and was confronted by the sight of the innkeeper's bare feet. Distracted, she lost her train of thought.

"I've got to get back to my bed." The innkeeper was obviously growing impatient.

"Oh." Isabel's hand moved to her back. The carriage ride had played havoc with her body. Everything was cramped and tense.

"Ma'am?"

Isabel waved a hand. "It's nothing. You were saying?"

"I were saying that the man's a *paying* customer."

The fog cleared and Isabel finally grasped what the innkeeper was trying to tell her. "Of course. Foolish of me." She opened her reticule and placed some money on the man's extended palm.

"Will that be sufficient?"

The innkeeper closed his fist around the coins. "Number seven. Top of the stairs." He turned and stalked toward the back of the inn.

The stairwell was dark and the first floor hallway was darker still. Isabel could see light from a room at the end of the corridor and hoped it was Willington, lighting the way to a cup of tea when she was done with the odious business on which she was bound.

Number seven was, indeed, right at the top of the stairs. Isabel tried the latch. The door was locked. Of course. Only a fool would leave the door to a room such as this unlocked. Chiswick might be a rogue, but he was not a complete fool. Isabel lifted her hand and knocked. No response. She knocked again. Dead silence.

Gathering her courage, Isabel pounded on the door until she heard a muffled sound from within and then Chiswick's voice. "What is it?"

"Open the door this minute, or I shall have it broken down." Isabel kept her voice low, but its steely resolve seemed to penetrate the wood. She heard the latch snick and the door cracked open.

"Let me in." She put her foot against the door and pushed.

"Isabel?" Chiswick stepped back. He looked as though he had pulled on his trousers under his nightshirt, but Isabel could not be sure. The room was lit only by the sliver of moon still visible in the sky.

She shut the door. "Give me some light."

Chiswick fumbled on the table and finally struck a light to a lopsided branch of candles sitting by the low bed.

"What are you doing here?" he asked.

"What in the name of all that's holy do you think I'm doing here, you lackwit?" Isabel marched into the room and glared at Chiswick. Despite his unshaven face and unkempt hair, he was still a handsome man. Isabel could understand Julia's infatuation.

Sense seemed to finally penetrate Chiswick's sleep-addled brain. "Julia."

Isabel scowled. "Julia," she said, her voice hard, her jaw set.

Chiswick ran his hands through his hair and walked toward the portmanteau sitting open on a straight-backed chair near the window. "Let me make myself presentable."

"Stay where you are. You don't need to be presentable for this discussion."

Chiswick stopped dead and turned back to Isabel. "Very well, I have run off with the earl's sister. We've been here all night. It's too late."

"It's not too late. I will take her out of here and no one will know."

Chiswick's sensual lips twisted into a sneer. "Oh, someone will know. I will know."

"What do you want?" Isabel knew that the answer was money. But she did not know how much it would cost to buy off this cad.

"You know what I want, Isabel. The only thing that has changed is the woman."

"She is but a girl, George. Let me take her home." Isabel felt drained, but she would fight for Julia if she must.

"Relinquish an earl's sister? For how much?"

"Five hundred pounds." Isabel pulled a figure out of the air.

Chiswick laughed. "Lady Julia Chamberlayne is worth a deal more than that.

"Do not fence with me. Name your terms." Isabel pushed the portmanteau off the chair and slumped onto the seat.

"Ten thousand." Chiswick's expression dared Isabel to say she would not pay that for Julia.

"Ten thousand, then, as soon as we return to London."

"How great a fool do you think me?" Chiswick moved closer to where Isabel sat until he was towering over her.

Isabel stood, forcing Chiswick to step back. "I did not bring ten thousand pounds with me. How great a fool do you think me?"

"Bring it then, and I'll give you the girl."

A potent mix of anger and panic spiked through Isabel. She dug her fingernails into her palms, searching within herself for calm. Hasty action would only make this horrible business worse.

She closed her eyes, fatigue and despair overtaking anger. "Keep me with you, then. I will send for the money. Eloping with Julia will bring you nothing but trouble. Haddon will never give her a dowry if she's married a fortune hunter over the anvil."

Chiswick didn't speak, but Isabel knew that he was considering her suggestion.

"It is your best option," she said holding out her hand palm up, making the offer tangible.

Chiswick nodded once. "I suppose it is, if what you say is true."

"I'll just go wake Julia, and send her home in my coach." Isabel stepped back toward the door.

"No." In a single stride, Chiswick was beside her, his hand firmly against the door.

"But..." What did the man want now?

"I will fetch Lady Julia. There will be no private communication between you." He wrenched open the door and was through it before Isabel could speak.

Isabel pursued Chiswick into the darkened hallway. Ignoring the nagging pain in her back, she grabbed his arm before he could reach for the latch on the door he was facing. "You don't intend to enter without knocking?"

"Naturally not." Chiswick frowned and raised his

hand to rap on the door. He waited several seconds and knocked harder.

Isabel heard the sounds of movement in the room and stepped closer to call through the door. "Julia. It's Isabel."

After some scraping and shuffling, the door cracked open and Julia appeared, fully clothed and holding a candle. "Isabel?"

"Let me in." Isabel pushed against the door and Julia stepped back.

Before Isabel crossed the threshold, Chiswick shoved past her and strode to the middle of the room. Isabel followed, then closed the door and glanced around. Although hardly elegant, the room was tidy and at least smelled clean. And the bed had not been disturbed. She breathed a small sigh of relief. Chiswick had not seduced the girl at least.

Julia stood in the middle of the room looking perturbed as Isabel lit another candle. "What is going on?"

"Er..." Chiswick shrugged and glanced toward Isabel.

"You are going home," Isabel said, moving toward the bed and pulling out the valise that stood open at its foot.

"I am not." Julia crossed the room and yanked the valise out of Isabel's hand, pushing it behind her.

A wave of nausea passed over Isabel and she dropped to the bed, sitting for a moment with her head in her hands. Inhaling deeply, she looked up at the girl standing before her, hands on her hips, long brown hair cascading over her shoulders in deep waves. She looked so young and innocent. If only Isabel could prevent her from making a dreadful mistake.

"You must," she said, finally. "You must return to London before anyone knows you've gone. Please, please trust me."

"Do as she says." Chiswick's insinuating voice sounded from the far corner of the room.

"What?" Julia spun around to face Chiswick.

"Go home. You are not wanted here."

From where she sat, Isabel could sense Julia's confusion deepen. She didn't move, waiting to let Chiswick's words find their mark.

Julia stood motionless for seconds, simply staring at Chiswick.

Isabel pushed herself up off the bed. Approaching Julia, she put her arm around her shoulders and drew her back. "It is for the best," she whispered, turning the girl toward her valise. "Pack your things. My coach is outside."

Her eyes brimming, Julia shook her head. "You cannot force me to leave George. I love him."

"But I do not love you, my dear. Mrs. Chamberlayne is much more my style." Chiswick's voice issued from the corner where he still stood, arms crossed over his chest.

Color drained from Julia's face as she turned to stare at Isabel. "You?" she whispered, her voice registering the betrayal.

"Go home." Isabel said nothing more. What more was there to be said? The only thing she could do now was get Julia out of here and, if possible, have a moment alone with Willington or her coachman before they all departed for London.

Chiswick seated himself on the only comfortable chair in the room and crossed one leg over the other as he watched the ladies re-pack Julia's bag. Isabel was conscious of his avid gaze, but more aware of the tears now coursing down Julia's cheeks.

Her hand brushed Julia's as they both reached into the valise. Isabel let fall the chemise she was holding and grasped the young girl's hand. "Please trust me," she said softly.

Julia yanked her hand away.

"What's that you're saying?" Chiswick asked, leaving his chair to stand by the two women.

"I must fetch Willington to accompany Julia back to London." Isabel dropped the silver-backed hairbrush she had just picked up into the bag and moved toward the door.

"I think not." Chiswick intercepted her. "Where is she?"

"I—I'm not sure." Isabel was certain that if she were not ill and exhausted from the carriage ride, she would have been able to think of a way to speak to Willington without Chiswick overhearing. Now, all she could do was stand stupidly with her hand on the latch.

Chiswick knocked her hand away and replaced it with his own. "I will find her, then. Come with me."

Isabel didn't move. "I will stay with Julia."

"Oh no, you won't. Julia will wait while we go together to fetch this elusive maid." Chiswick took Isabel by the wrist and released the latch.

There had been no need for the foolish argument. When Chiswick finally threw open the door, they found Willington hovering in the hallway.

"Is this your maid?"

When Isabel nodded, he dropped her wrist and gestured to the woman to enter the room.

Events were spinning away from her. Willington's arrival marked one less opportunity to get a message to Sidney. Isabel's heart pounded as she contemplated the possible outcome of her situation. Quietly, she reached out and took Julia's hands

Julia pulled away from her. "Don't touch me. You have ruined all my hopes of happiness."

Isabel glanced toward Chiswick. He was listening to every word. She would not be able to say anything to purpose. She shifted her attention back to her young sister-in-law. "I only hope you will understand one day soon."

Julia shrugged. "I understand now. Sidney will hear all about this... this betrayal. You will never be able to show your face in London again."

"Oh—." Isabel's hand flew to her side and she sat heavily on the bed.

Julia looked straight ahead, her gaze fixed on the closed door. "Indeed. How could you deceive both me and my brother in this way? It is infamous."

Argument was impossible and hope was steadily dwindling. Isabel kept her eyes on her maid, willing her to grasp what was happening, to comprehend that the rescue of Julia had created a new problem, to have the presence of mind to tell someone who would act.

Willington had been viewing the activity in the room with an air of distress. "What am I to do, Mrs. Chamberlayne?"

"Accompany Lady Julia to Bruton Place and explain everything to my aunt."

"But Madam…"

"No more talk." Chiswick gestured toward the main.

"Do it." Isabel prayed Willington would know what it was she should do.

Julia took her valise and stalked to the door, her face set in a mask of misery.

Isabel started to rise from the bed, but was forestalled by a gesture from Chiswick.

He shook his head. "No. I'll see them off. You stay here."

Isabel stayed, too tired and too sick to do anything else. As Chiswick ushered Julia and Willington from the room, Isabel prayed that her maid had understood or that Julia would tell Sidney exactly what she had seen. She prayed that Sidney would trust her and she prayed that she would survive this foolhardy rescue. Wrapping her arms around herself, she collapsed back on the bed.

CHAPTER 24

The Dover road had seen its share of traffic in this season of victory. And much of it was far more illustrious than Sidney Chamberlayne, former major in the Light Dragoons. But none of it was more worried.

The sun was out, but the air was cool, promising the onset of autumn. A good day to ride. Sidney put his head down and urged Chiron to greater effort. They had stopped one night on the road, to allow the great chestnut time to regain his stamina, but Sidney was determined to reach London before another night passed. The more he thought about it, the more likely it seemed that George Chiswick was the man he sought. There were so many tiny clues that he had overlooked in the social and emotional maelstrom that had followed his marriage.

Isabel had made it clear that Chiswick was a fortune hunter and had done so on more than one occasion. Why had it only just occurred to Sidney that a man in tightened circumstances might be seeking a fortune through other, less acceptable, avenues? He cursed softly. His mind had been so full of Isabel and his perceived duty, that all he could see of Chiswick was that he had once been Isabel's suitor. Sidney wondered if perhaps he was not cut out to be anything but a soldier after all.

London loomed in the distance and Sidney could feel Chiron's stride lengthen. They both longed to reach home. When he left Dover, Sidney had thought he would go immediately to Whitehall on arrival. But the closer they got to the city, the stronger the pull toward Bruton Place, toward Isabel. If she had not captured his heart, she had quite firmly lodged herself in his imagination.

Sidney rounded the corner from Berkley Square into the midst of a commotion. Isabel's carriage, covered with mud, stood at the front door as servants streamed from the house, opening the doors, assisting the coachman from his box, and all speaking at once. He could hardly credit that Isabel would countenance such unseemly behavior.

The carriage door hung open as if someone had just left it and Isabel's maid stepped out. She looked as though she had been dragged behind the carriage for several miles. Her gown was soiled and wrinkled and her eyes were heavily shadowed. She peered around in a disoriented fashion and finally hurried up the granite steps into the house.

What had happened? Where was Isabel? Sidney signaled a groom who was part of the group milling around the carriage with no real purpose.

"What is going on here?" Sidney dismounted and stood beside his sweating horse, gently rubbing the beast's nose.

"Don't know, sir." The boy pulled his forelock, keeping his head bent low.

Sidney's impatience flared. "Take my horse and see that he is well cared for. He has had a hard ride. Now go."

The boy bobbed his head and led the big chestnut off, leaving Sidney to contemplate the rest of the crowd clustering near the carriage.

"Take these horses and the carriage to the mews and take yourselves to your occupations." Sidney's steely voice overrode the muttering of the servants. It was the voice he used in command and it had the desired effect.

Turning his back on the dispersing crowd, Sidney

took the steps two at a time and entered the house, slamming the door behind him. In the entry way, he found yet more chaos.

It seemed as though all the servants who were not out on the street were gathered in the front hall. Most of them hung back against the walls, but two of the maids fluttered around Isabel's maid who was looking even paler than she had when she left the carriage. Several were hauling in trunks that had been unloaded from the coach and one, whom he thought worked at Haddon House, was trying to hand a vinaigrette to his sister.

"Julia!" His voice brought sudden quiet to the previously noisy crowd.

Julia looked up at him, her eyes red and puffy and her expression distraught. Sidney looked around at the rest of the group. Where was Isabel? Where was Lady Louisa?

"Get out, all of you," he said in a tone so deadly calm that the hallway cleared immediately.

"Oh, Sidney." Julia gulped as tears sprang to her eyes.

"Not in the hallway." Sidney put an arm around his sister and led her to the family drawing room. He sat her on a settee, pulled out his handkerchief and returned to the door.

"Find Mrs. Chamberlayne," he said to the first footman he encountered.

The footman all but saluted. "Mrs. Chamberlayne is not at home, sir. Shall I fetch Lady Louisa?"

"Yes, I suppose you had better do that. And quickly." Sidney closed the door in the man's face and returned to his sister.

"You... you won't find Isabel." Julia sniffed into the handkerchief Sidney had given her. "You'll never see her again."

Sidney's heart plummeted. He took Julia by the shoulders and gave her a shake. "What? What do you mean I'll never see Isabel again? What has happened to her? Is she... is she hurt?"

Julia shook her head and blew her nose loudly. "No. She's not hurt. Not that conniving, faithless, horrible..."

"You are speaking about my wife and your sister." Sidney's firm voice stopped Julia in mid-sentence.

"Your wife has run off with Mr. Chiswick," Julia said and then burst into a fresh storm of tears.

The back of Sidney's neck turned to ice. Every muscle became rigid and his vision narrowed. Julia winced and Sidney very carefully released the iron grip he still had on her arms.

"What are you talking about?"

Julia sniffled and rubbed at her arms. "Isabel has run off with Chiswick," she said again, her face locked in a stubborn frown.

"Ridiculous." Sidney took a deep breath and stood up. He paced to the fireplace and back without looking at Julia. The idea was preposterous. Isabel may have had a lively past, but she would not run off with a fortune hunter.

"It is not," Julia said, drawing his attention back to her. "I saw them."

At that moment the door opened and Lady Louisa came bustling in trailed by Isabel's maid. "Sidney."

Sidney walked over to her and kissed her cheek. "My sister insists Isabel has run away with George Chiswick," he said, trying to keep his tone light.

Lady Louisa nodded.

"Surely you don't believe this?"

Louisa ignored him and turned toward Julia, reaching out a wrinkled hand to push stray hairs off the girl's forehead. Only at that moment did Sidney recognize how disheveled his sister was. Her clothes, like Isabel's maid's, looked as though they had been slept in and her hair had obviously been hastily pinned up in an amateurish fashion.

Sidney watched as Lady Louisa subjected Julia to a similar examination. The older woman's face registered Julia's unkempt state and tear-stained face. She pulled out her own lace trimmed handkerchief and placed it in Julia's hand, removing the one that Sidney had given her earlier.

Lady Louisa finally turned back to Sidney. "Willington tells the same story, but she is under the impression that Isabel did not stay willingly."

"She was with him and she was willing. I told him." Julia pointed at Sidney. "No one will believe me."

"I believe you saw Isabel and Chiswick," Louisa said.

"Well, good." Julia sat back and examined Lady Louisa's handkerchief that lay crumpled in her hand.

"Willington says you left them in Northampton." Lady Louisa held Julia's gaze until the girl nodded.

"Northampton?" Sidney exploded out of his chair.

Lady Louisa patted Julia's arm and gave her a little push. "Go to your room and have Benson send for some food and a tisane."

"No. I want Sidney to know everything." Julia crossed her arms over her chest and glared at Lady Louisa.

"I promise you, he will, but first you need some rest. Go. You go too." Louisa nodded at the maid.

"What is going on?" The minute the door shut behind Julia and Willington, Sidney closed in on Lady Louisa. His temper held only by the thinnest thread, he barely prevented himself from tearing the room apart.

Before she answered, Lady Louisa crossed the room, poured a large portion of brandy into a sparkling crystal glass and handed it to Sidney.

"Don't bite my head off," she said and then proceeded to relate the full story of Julia's elopement and Isabel's pursuit, including Willington's surmise that Isabel had exchanged herself for Julia in order to get Chiswick to let the girl return.

* * *

Isabel rolled onto her side and wrapped her arms over her stomach. The pain was excruciating. She no longer believed her cramps were the result of stiffened muscles, nor, much as she wanted to, could she convince herself that she had eaten something that made her ill. The pain was about the baby.

Almost as soon as she admitted that thought, Isabel could feel the dampness between her legs. Oh God. This was not good. She was going to lose her baby, Sidney's baby. She curled herself tightly around the life that was ebbing out of her and sobbed.

Chiswick returned just as another wracking pain shot through Isabel. Lying on the bed, facing the door, she gritted her teeth to keep from screaming, but nothing could prevent the tears flooding the pillow.

"Do not be melodramatic, Isabel. As soon as I have the money, I'll see that you're returned to your soldier." Chiswick shouldered the door shut and sauntered toward the bed.

Isabel closed her eyes. She might be able to bear the pain, but she did not think she could bear the idea of losing her unborn child while George Chiswick stood watching. "Please," she whispered.

"Please? A bit too late for pleading, my dear. Now, let us get you up and be on our way." Chiswick moved nearer the bed and stopped dead.

"What is this? Have you done yourself an injury?" He stared at the blood now staining the coverlet.

Isabel opened her eyes and turned a malevolent gaze on the man in front of her. "You have done me the injury."

"I never laid a hand on you. Now tell me what you've done." Isabel saw, with some satisfaction, that Chiswick was frightened. But, something must be done. She knew now it was too late to save her baby, but she

235

needed to assure that she lived. She desperately needed to see Sidney again.

"I have lost my baby." Saying the words drove home the truth and she choked on another sob. Gathering every bit of strength she had against another contraction, she tried to sit up.

"You fool. What have you done to me?" Chiswick's face was chalk white.

"Done to you? By all that's holy, George, please find me a physician." Isabel collapsed back onto the bed and watched as Chiswick's face was replaced with blackness.

* * *

Consciousness returned slowly. Isabel woke to find herself in a clean bed, dressed in a plain cotton shift. She tentatively tested how her body felt. The pain had subsided and she seemed to have stopped bleeding, but she felt ill... and empty. She knew with a dreadful certainty that her baby was no more.

An old woman sat beside the bed, wringing out a rag in a basin of water.

"Who are you?" Isabel asked.

"Mrs. Maynard. People here call me Mother." The woman finished wringing out the cloth and wiped Isabel's face. Only then did Isabel realize how hot she was.

"But..." Isabel couldn't seem to get any more words out.

The old woman moved to the edge of the bed and, lifting Isabel's head, held a cup to her lips. Isabel gratefully let the cool water slide down her throat.

"I'm the midwife." Mother Maynard answered the unasked question. "Your gentleman friend sent for me."

It all flooded back, every moment until she had fainted. "Not my friend," Isabel said, shaking her head.

"Dare say not, seeing as he took himself off the minute I arrived. Leastways, he did send for me and here I am. But you've lost the little one." Mrs. Maynard moved back to her chair and dipped the rag into the basin.

Isabel's eyes filled with tears and her hand went to her belly. "My baby."

"Probably not your last one. You're a good strong girl, Mrs...?"

"Chamberlayne," Isabel said, her thoughts flying to Sidney. He had not even known she carried his child and now she had lost it in a foolish, foolish undertaking. Would he ever forgive her? Would she ever forgive herself?

The old woman leaned toward her with the damp cloth, but Isabel stilled her hand. "Will I die?" she asked. Would she die without telling Sidney she loved him? Might he never know?

"Likely not if we can get your fever down. Now be a good girl and lie still. Try to sleep. I'll be here."

Isabel let her hand drop to the bed as Mrs. Maynard put the cloth on her forehead.

"Must send for my husband." Isabel was not sure if she had actually spoken the words.

"I told you, the gentleman left as soon as I got here." Mrs. Maynard's voice dripped with disgust.

Isabel managed a small smile. "He was not my husband. Sidney Chamberlayne... London... Please find him."

"London's a big place, Mrs. Chamberlayne."

"Bruton Place." Isabel's heart sank. Her head lolled back on the pillow and she stared at the ceiling. Sidney was in Dover. How long before a messenger could reach him? She closed her eyes and inhaled a deep, determined sigh. Whenever he got here, she would be waiting for him.

CHAPTER 25

Sidney pulled his horse to a halt and waited until the approaching rider caught up to him. He had delayed leaving London for what seemed an interminable length of time. Impatient to find Isabel, Sidney had left before the man he had requested from Whitehall arrived.

Captain Sneed must not have been far behind him. The captain's horse came to rest beside Sidney's. He relaxed the reins and looked out over the landscape.

"Glad you could make it." Sidney scanned the hills around Stevenage. The afternoon sun shone low over the barrows that lay beyond the little market town. Beside him, Captain Sneed nodded in agreement. Sidney was glad to see him. He had been in Sidney's regiment and it was critical to have someone he could count on.

"How much farther do you think?" Sneed shaded his eyes and peered toward the barrows.

Sidney shook his head. "Not farther than Northampton, I hope." But that was just a prayer. He thought it more likely that Chiswick had packed Isabel up and continued his flight. But where would they go? It was obvious that Chiswick had been headed to Gretna Green with Julia. That made sense. What had Isabel offered the man in exchange for Julia and where would Chiswick take her to collect it? The very thought that Chiswick's price might extend beyond money made Sidney's skin crawl and his muscles tense. It was imperative he find Isabel before another day passed.

"What's that?" Sneed nodded up the road where a curricle was rounding a bend.

Sidney squinted. It was not possible. Would Chiswick be foolish enough to bring Isabel back to London? In a curricle? "Over here," he said, turning his horse into a stand of beeches by the side of the road.

Sneed followed and the two sat silently peering at the road through the leafy barrier. Within minutes, the dusty curricle approached their stand.

Sidney twisted in his saddle to get a good look at the driver. Although the sun was low on the horizon, the blond hair and classic features were unmistakable—Chiswick. But he was alone.

No Isabel. Sidney ruthlessly tamped down the panic coursing through his veins. He had not led his men safely back from battle by succumbing to emotion. First he would deal with the blackguard and then he would find his wife.

Sidney nodded to his companion. They circled the trees back in the direction they had come and edged out from the cover of the branches directly in front of the curricle.

Chiswick's horse shied and the light vehicle slewed to the right. Rising to scrabble for the reins, Chiswick lost his balance, and toppled onto the center of the road, while the curricle wobbled toward the verge. Sidney was out of his saddle and on the ground at the same moment. The difference was that Sidney was on his feet.

As Chiswick scrambled in the dirt, Sidney approached him. Out of the corner of his eye, he could see Sneed dismount and gather the reins of the curricle, leading the horse and equipage to the road's edge. Then Sidney turned his full attention to the man in the road.

In one swift motion, Sidney reached down, grasped Chiswick's jacket and pulled him to his feet. He grabbed Chiswick's lapels in both hands and all but lifted him off the ground.

"Where is she?" Sidney's voice was like cold steel and Chiswick gave him the satisfaction of cringing. Sidney shook him.

"Where is she?" he repeated.

Chiswick stared at him. Sidney could tell that he was considering what his next move would be. If he had any sense, he would realize that there was no use in dissembling. Sidney shook him again.

"I don't know what you mean. What is this all about?" Peering down at Sidney's hands, Chiswick struggled to look nonchalant.

"Tell me now, or I will make you tell me."

Chiswick's eyes widened.

"Yes, I mean it," Sidney said harshly, his gaze never leaving his opponent.

Chiswick hesitated for one more moment before speaking. "Your wife, you mean?"

Sidney's voice was grim. "My wife. If she is hurt, I promise you will rue the day you first drew breath."

Chiswick paled.

Oh God. Something had happened to Isabel. Sidney could feel the blood rushing to his head and fought not to choke the man he held between his hands.

"Where is she?"

"She owes me money."

Good Lord. The man was totally without sense. Did he not understand that Sidney would happily cut him down where he stood if he could be sure it would not endanger Isabel?

"I will owe you something infinitely more painful if you do not tell me where she is." Sidney clenched his hands in the fabric of Chiswick's jacket and raised him off the ground.

"Northampton." The word came out on a gasp and Sidney lowered him. "I swear. I did nothing to her."

Sidney chose not to address the latter statement. "Where in Northampton?"

Chiswick blinked and Sidney gave him another shake.

"Rose and Crown." Chiswick spat out the name.

"Thank you." Sidney unwound his right hand from Chiswick's jacket, drew back his arm and punched the man in the jaw. He released the lapel he still held and Chiswick dropped like a stone.

"What are you doing?" Sneed had abandoned the curricle and was looking down at the recumbent figure of their prime suspect.

"My hand slipped." Sidney rubbed his left hand across the knuckles of his right.

"Did he confess to carrying the money?" Sneed asked, shaking his head in disbelief.

"I didn't think to ask him. I think we should bind him, don't you?" Sidney reached out a toe and poked at Chiswick.

"Yes. Probably. Although he doesn't look as though he's going anywhere at the moment. What do you mean you didn't think to ask him?" Sneed went back to his horse and returned with a length of rope.

Sidney let out a long breath. "Left that to you, my friend. Let's tie him up and you can take him back to London and do what must be done."

"And where are you going?" Sneed knelt and began wrapping the rope around Chiswick's wrists.

"God willing, to fetch my wife."

* * *

Isabel sat up against the pillows and drank from the cup Mother Maynard handed her. She made a face at the bitter taste.

"Willow bark," the old woman said. "Best thing I know for the fever."

Isabel tended to believe her. Sometime in the night, the relentless cycle of heat and chills had broken and, for the first time, she thought she might see another day.

She drained the cup and handed it back to the midwife. Resting her head against the pillow, she closed her eyes and, for a moment, allowed her grief to take her. She had awakened several times during her fever to the cries of a child. Fever dreams. Her child that was not to be.

Tears leaked out from under Isabel's closed eyelids and the old woman leaned forward and took her hand. "I know, dearie. I've lost them, too. It will get better, I promise."

Isabel's tears erupted into a loud sob and the old woman slid onto the side of the bed and took her in her arms, rocking her and crooning.

"Isabel." Was this another fever dream? Isabel raised her head. Her husband, her Sidney, stood in the doorway, dusty, disheveled and altogether wonderful.

The old woman slipped off the bed and left the room as Isabel reached out toward her husband. "Sidney."

In a heartbeat, Sidney crossed the room, sat on the bed, and took her in his arms. He was so warm, so solid, so reassuring. Isabel burrowed into him, snaking her arms under his open jacket and wrapping them tightly around his back. "Sidney."

As if sensing exactly what she needed, Sidney did not speak, but enfolded her, sharing his warmth and strength, creating a shield against anything that might threaten her. She had never told him she loved him and he had never said those words to her, but at this moment, his arms told her everything she needed to know. She buried her face against his shoulder and let the tears come.

She could feel Sidney lower his head and his lips brush the top of her hair. Eventually he leaned back against the wall and tilted her chin up so that he was looking into her eyes.

"What happened, Isabel?"

His voice was so gentle that Isabel thought she might not be able to keep the tears away long enough to tell him. She bit down on the sob forming in her throat and looked into the fathomless brown eyes that had become so dear to her.

"I... I came after Julia," she said.

Sidney put a hand to her cheek, wiping away a tear with the pad of his thumb. "I know that, dearest. Julia returned to London at the same time I did and I had it all from her and Louisa. Tell me what happened after you sent her home." Carefully, as if she might break, he dropped a soft kiss on her lips.

Isabel put her hand to her mouth, savoring the kiss, trying to keep it in place. Her gaze wandered over the hard planes of Sidney's face. Would their baby have looked like him?

"Our baby... Oh Sidney." The tears began again.

"Our baby?"

"The carriage ride... It was too much... too hard. I lost our baby." Isabel watched his face, willing him not to hate her for what she had done.

"You never said." Sidney's voice conveyed no emotion and, for the first time since he arrived, Isabel was frightened.

"It was so early. And then you were gone. I wanted to be sure. And..." She drew a gasping breath, willing herself to stop crying. "And I wanted to tell you first that I love you."

Slowly, Sidney closed his eyes. The image of Isabel's lovely face and huge amber eyes, the tears streaking her unnaturally pale cheeks, the curtain of gold hair waving over her shoulders, was a vivid as it had been with his eyes open. Her face, Sidney realized, had been with him since before he left for Dover. She had been a part of him for longer than that.

Opening his eyes, he shifted his legs onto the bed. Carefully, he lifted Isabel and sat her across his lap.

Carefully, he raised her head and placed another chaste kiss on her beautiful mouth.

"Are *you* well?" He could barely breathe as he waited for the answer.

"Mrs. Maynard says I am. But, oh Sidney, our baby."

Sidney pressed her head to his shoulder and kissed her brow. His heart ached for her and the child neither would ever know. "I am so sorry, Isabel. I am sorry about our baby and I am sorry I wasn't here when you needed me."

"I was so afraid I would die before I could tell you I loved you." Isabel's voice was barely a whisper.

"But you have told me." Sidney was stunned by the joy of that telling.

"Yes." Isabel snuggled into him, murmuring in what sounded like contentment.

"But Isabel…"

She looked up and Sidney could see the pain and trepidation still lurking in her eyes.

"I have something to tell you, as well." He pulled her a little closer.

"I know," she said, nodding.

Sidney smiled down at Isabel, warmly nestled against his chest. His wife was a wonderful puzzle. "You know? How?"

"Your arms told me."

"Let me take you home, my love, and tell you again and again for the rest of our lives."

Their lips met and clung.

And when they broke the kiss, Sidney spoke. "I love you, Isabel."

EPILOGUE

Hampshire, September 1815

Isabel leaned back against her husband and gazed out onto the sprawling park in back of their country estate. The garden glowed with autumnal warmth in the setting sun. She sighed in deep contentment. Sidney's vital presence and his surprising aptitude for estate management had revitalized the estate and banished the last remnant of Isabel's former existence.

It seemed as though life could not be any better. Napoleon was aboard the Northumberland, bound for St. Helena, this time to be kept under heavy guard, and England was at peace. After extracting information from Chiswick that eventually led to his associates and directing the operation that had brought them all to trial, Sidney had resigned Whitehall for the life of a gentleman farmer. Isabel had gladly relinquished her life in London, not sorry to see the last of any of the gentlemen who had once sought her attention.

Isabel sighed again and felt Sidney's arms tighten around her. She leaned her head back against his shoulder. His season of farming had made him broader and harder, if such a thing were possible. She wondered that she had ever thought happiness required a title. Her husband's arms were all she required to be happy and fulfilled. That and the little secret she had harbored for the last month.

Turning her head to nuzzle Sidney's chest, she slid his hands from her waist over her still-flat abdomen. "I have something to tell you," she whispered. Then she turned around in his arms and looked up into his beloved brown eyes.

Life had turned so many corners since that night in the darkened Caenby library. To try to entrap the earl had been so foolish. And yet, that foolish plan had given her the gift of Sidney Chamberlaye, the gift of love.

Incredibly, it had also given her a new family: a devoted mother-in-law who would be delighted when she was presented with her first grandchild; a brother-in-law who had finally realized that she was what his brother wanted and needed (and also had—amazingly—apologized for his initial behavior). And Julia, whose brush with ruin had created an unbreakable bond that had made them closer than sisters.

She still mourned her lost child but she was here to share her wonderful secret with her husband.

* * *

Sidney's gut tightened as he examined his wife's shining countenance. Her golden hair shone in the setting sun and her amber eyes glowed with an inner light. He knew immediately what she meant.

He raised his hands and cupped her face, brushing a gentle kiss across her full lips. "When?"

"Before the next harvest." Isabel's hand slid from his chest and came to rest on her stomach. Sidney moved his hand to cover it.

"Harvest." Sidney chuckled and slid his arms around his wife. "Who would have predicted that a half-pay soldier, who thought he might spend the rest of his life living in tents and traveling from battle to battle, would end up a contented farmer." Indeed, he would never have done so.

"I owe much to the Earl of Caenby... And to your plan to marry a title. You gave me purpose, made me a better man."

"We've made each other better," Isabel said. "And we've made something more."

"Isabel." Sidney did not know what else to say. Each day with Isabel was a delight and the prospect of their child overwhelmed him. He leaned down and said everything with his kiss.

"It is the second best gift, I have ever received," Isabel said when the kiss finally ended.

"Only the second best?" This was a puzzling statement.

"Yes. The first best is your love."

The kiss resumed.

ABOUT THE AUTHOR

Myretta has lived in Regency England since she was old enough to read Jane Austen. Unfortunately, as she never could get vouchers for Almacks, she was forced to make her way by going into trade. She spent more years than she cares to count working in the field of computer technology. It was rewarding in its own way but she never abandoned her first love. In 1997, she found an interesting way to insinuate the 19th century into the world of technology when she joined a friend in creating a Jane Austen web site. She still manages The Republic of Pemberley and invites you to come visit if your obsession runs to Jane Austen.

In 2005, Kensington Publishing published *Once Upon a Sofa* and *Just Say Yes,* which was a finalist for RWA's RITA award and which won the Holt Medallion. She has a short story inspired by Jane Austen in Ballantine Books' anthology, *Jane Austen Made Me Do It* and A novella in *Dressed to Kiss,* an anthology with Madeline Hunter, Caroline Linden, and Megan Frampton.

You can visit her at myrettarobens.com or on Facebook at https://www.facebook.com/myretta.robens. She is on Twitter @myretta but hardly ever goes there.